Lost and found

Grannie · Grandpa
Mum · Dad
   Betsey · Desmond

      with lots of love

   Love, Richard
      Sam, Luke · Mark

Other titles by the author

A Marriage of Mixed Motives

The Apparent Heir

Fickle Friends

Lost and Found

JANEY WATSON

Bosworth Books Ltd

For Sara

First published in 2009 by Bosworth Books Ltd.

Cataloguing in Publication Data is available from the British Library.

ISBN 978 0 9553289 4 7

Bosworth Books Ltd, Whiteway Court,
Cirencester, Glos., GL7 7BA

Design and typesetting by Liz Rudderham
Printed by Information Press, Eynsham, Oxford.
www.informationpress.com

Having read many historical romances where dogs were an intergral part of the scene, I often wondered why the labrador was never mentioned. It was only when I read Richard Smith's piece on the St. John's Water dogs in the Country Landowners and Rural Business magazine that I realised why. My thanks to him for inadvertantly adding to the storyline. Thanks also go to my son Mark for his insight into learning to lip read.

As always I am very grateful to Anne Rickard and Liz Rudderham and to Pippa, Val and Bill for all their hard work and encouragement.

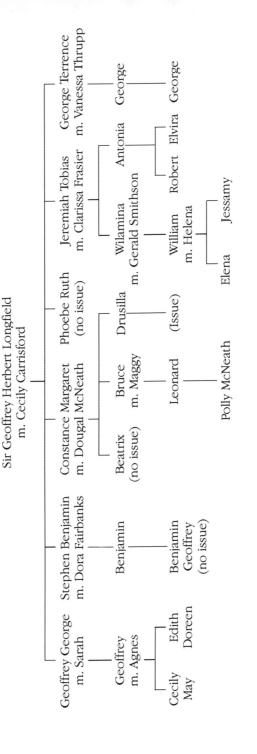

Sir Geoffrey Herbert Longfield
m. Cecily Carrisford

Geoffrey George
m. Sarah

Stephen Benjamin
m. Dora Fairbanks

Constance Margaret
m. Dougal McNeath

Phoebe Ruth
(no issue)

Jeremiah Tobias
m. Clarissa Frasier

George Terrence
m. Vanessa Thrupp

Geoffrey
m. Agnes

Benjamin

Beatrix
(no issue)

Bruce
m. Maggy

Drusilla

Wilamina
m. Gerald Smithson

Antonia

George

Cecily
May

Edith
Doreen

Benjamin
Geoffrey
(no issue)

Leonard

(Issue)

William
m. Helena

Robert Elvira George

Polly McNeath

Elena

Jessamy

1

'So, it is indeed true.' There was a hollow, almost despairing note in the voice of the pallid young lady who had uttered these words.

Miss Elena Smithson, who had been sitting primly on a very upright chair, raised her dark head from the contemplation of her hands to look at the speaker.

'I came,' she said almost apologetically, 'as soon as I had confirmation of it. I would have you know its certainty as soon as I did.' She continued earnestly: 'Have we not wondered and marvelled at the possibility for weeks now?' She cast her eyes around the room at her four friends for corroboration of her words.

There was a general assent in lacklustre terms and a silence ensued while the young ladies digested Elena's news.

Suddenly, a tall girl, who had been sitting in the window recess of the elegant room, sprang to her feet. 'Oh this will not do,' she exclaimed. 'We should be congratulating Miss Smithson on her fortune, not bemoaning our fate in losing her company. Come, Caroline, Maria, Dorothea, show a brighter aspect, I beg of you, or Miss Smithson will take home a very uncomfortable view of our friendship.'

'Oh no, never that,' Elena hurried to demur, but her utterance was lost as Lady Dorothea Delrymple, the youngest of the sisters, came up to her and, drawing her to her feet, embraced her.

'My dear Miss Smithson, of course we are delighted for you and for your admirable father but you must know what a solace you have been to us during our years of ill health. You have been our energy, our entertainment, nay even our enthusiasm. We have drawn on your strength at every opportunity; we will be bereft at your going.'

'Oh no, please do not say so,' begged Elena, her tender heart suffering for them and her eyes welling up at the thought of the sisters missing her company. Of herself she thought not a whit.

At this juncture, Lady Iona, who had already once tried to alter the trend of her sisters' thoughts, made a further attempt.

'But your father, Miss Smithson. He must surely be most delighted with his change of fortune.'

Elena, who had disentangled herself from Lady Dorothea and sat down again, sighed. 'My father is as bemused as I am that our circumstances should have undergone such a material alteration. He had very little knowledge of his grandfather's family and certainly no knowledge that his mother might have any expectations at all.'

'Do tell us again how it came about.' Lady Iona, who when she had the energy could be relied upon to keep a conversation going, demanded Elena's attention.

Elena looked about her at her friends and saw that each one of them was eager for her to obey the request. Elena suppressed another sigh; she still did not fully comprehend the vagaries of the hereditary system, which had propelled her father, the bailiff for some ten years now to the estate of the young ladies' father, into the position of recognised owner of a very large estate to the east of the town of Haywards Heath in Sussex.

'I can only explain it to the best of my knowledge,' she said ruefully, 'but I believe that our claim to the estate goes back to my great-great-grandfather. He had six children of which my great-grandfather was the fifth.'

'The fifth child's line to inherit!' exclaimed Lady Maria, whose expressive brown eyes looked abnormally large in her gaunt face. 'There, Dorothea.' She turned her gaze on her youngest sister. 'There is hope for you yet!'

Lady Iona made a tut-tutting noise at her sister's irreverence but she did not admonish her, for it was a pleasure to see the frailest of her sisters appearing so animated.

Elena, unsure whether she should continue, waited for a prompt. It came as a chorus.

'Pray continue, Miss Smithson.'

'Yes, please go on. Why should the fifth child inherit?'

Elena straightened her back and clasped her gloved hands together in her lap. 'My great-great-grandfather Sir Geoffrey Herbert-Longfield on his death passed the estate on to his eldest son named after his father but called George, George passed it on to his son Geoffrey but Geoffrey was unable to pass it on to his daughters because they did not outlive him. Neither lived beyond their fortieth year.' Elena paused, conscious that she had said something infelicitous.

There was an uncomfortable silence as the girls surreptitiously exchanged glances. Given their collective state of health, none of them anticipated getting to such an age; it would be a triumph if all of them gained thirty years of age.

Lady Caroline was the first to cast aside such melancholy thoughts. 'So we have dispensed with the line of the firstborn son; on whom was the inheritance settled after that, pray?'

Elena smiled at her gratefully. 'Sir Geoffrey's second child was also a son and his son had a son but he lost his life in the army.'

There was a general shifting of position in their seats. The young ladies were rather daunted by such a catalogue of misfortune.

Elena pressed on. 'Both Sir Geoffrey's third and fourth children were daughters; so, although they have family my great-grandfather has taken precedence and through the eldest of his two daughters it has been settled on my father.'

Lady Maria looked nonplussed. 'So your father has inherited it through his mother's line?'

'Yes,' acknowledged Elena.

'How can that be so?'

Here Elena was on shaky ground as so far no explanation her father had given her had quite clarified it for her. 'The estate is not entailed to a male heir,' she said, hoping that her uncertainty was not revealed. 'It is merely that the male progeny in each generation take precedence. Like royalty.' She finished with a flourish with the response that her father from time to time gave her when questions became too penetrating.

'So,' said Lady Caroline, showing herself to be the most intelligent of the Delrymple girls, 'the sons in a family take precedence but if there are only daughters they are permitted to inherit?'

'Yes, that's it,' agreed Elena eagerly.

'And the baronetcy, does your father become Sir William Smithson?' Maria asked.

Elena shook her head. 'No, that goes down the male line.'

'So someone is the beneficiary of the title without the country seat and lands to go with it,' marvelled Lady Dorothea. 'How poorly they must think of this arrangement! Do you know who it is?'

Elena shook her head. 'I had not thought to consider it,' she reflected. 'My father merely mentioned that it would not come to him.'

The young ladies nodded approvingly and Lady Iona turned the subject, rightly judging that Miss Smithson had disclosed as much as she was able and any more questions would be intrusive.

Some twenty-five minutes later, Elena could be seen donning a little bonnet and taking leave of her friends to set out down the lime-tree-bordered drive to reach her own home. The grandeur of the vast house behind her as she walked away left her unmoved. It was as familiar to her as the modest cottage in which she and her father and young brother currently resided.

The Delrymple family had taken Miss Elena Smithson to its heart when at the age of eleven she had been left motherless at the birth of her brother Jessamy. The young ladies, at the time ranging between the ages of thirteen and twenty, had been allowed by their father to include her in their circle. The reason for this was twofold: Miss Elena enjoyed excellent health; few could recall a time when she was ill – even the chickenpox had only affected her with three small spots. The Delrymple girls, however, had been blighted by a family weakness, which left them prey to every infectious disease. Necessarily the company they kept was limited and their sorties out into the wider world very rare. Elena, living as she did in close proximity to the village, could bring them accounts of others' doings. She would also regale them with what the ladies of the gentry were doing or wearing as everyone had a kindness for young Elena Smithson and would often say more to her than they would have divulged to anyone else.

Mixing so easily and frequently with these young ladies of the upper ten thousand allowed Elena to learn the ways of society. Her manners were refined by the friendship and her speech more cultured than might have been expected from someone who by necessity had remained at the village school. Paying for a nurse for his infant son had meant Mr Smithson had been forced to curtail his expenditure on his daughter's education. For Mr William Smithson had inherited only a small amount of capital from his father's side and his mother had but £2,000 settled on her at her marriage. His late wife had been dowerless. All the financial knowledge and considerable agricultural expertise he possessed had been gleaned from handling his employers' affairs.

Some elements of her history were running through Elena's mind as she hurried home. She had tarried too long with her friends and was aware that darkness was falling. She was a little apprehensive of the walk up to their cottage in the dark as the lane leading to it was narrow and flanked by dense woodland.

Her way took her past the church and as she came in sight of the churchyard, she saw a tall male figure walking purposively towards the lychgate from within the churchyard. Elena did not know whether to stop and wait for him to join her or to carry on, seemingly oblivious to his presence. She chose the latter and, determinedly forking in the other direction away from the church, she walked as fast as she could past the little covered gateway. She had gone perhaps ten yards beyond it when her name was called.

'Miss Smithson, Elena, please wait.'

Elena halted perforce.

The man hurried up to where she stood.

More than a foot shorter than him, Elena braved a fleeting look up into his face, and then averted her gaze to study the Michaelmas daisies that were bursting forth in the graveyard.

'I have been with your father,' the curate said without preamble. 'He has done me the honour of explaining the alteration in your circumstances.' He paused.

Elena knew not how to respond; her heart was fluttering with trepidation, and she wished she had been brave enough to make her feelings known to her father. All she could do was give a look of enquiry.

The curate took his hat off his straight black hair and began to turn it in his hands.

'He has refused me permission to pay my addresses to you.'

Elena could not suppress a gasp. He could choose to read it as one of dismay but she knew it to be one of relief. There had been an unstated understanding between her and Mr Sawyer the curate for the three years since Elena had turned sixteen. Expectation in the village had been running high over the last few months as Mr Sawyer's attentions had become more marked. Elena wished she could be sure that this had not coincided with the first whisperings of her change in fortune. She had meant to hint to her father that she was not ready to enter into an engagement but she had never found the words. She felt a surge of gratitude towards him for having anticipated her wishes. Elena became conscious that Mr Sawyer was still speaking.

'He will not even permit an exchange of letters once you are removed to Sussex. Miss Smithson, what can have prompted such a harsh decree? Our attachment has been of long standing. With the uncertainty of your future, all the unknowns of house, servants and neighbourhood, I was sure he would be minded to acquiesce to my request.' His words were spilling out chaotically and his breathing was becoming more rapid as he nourished his grievance.

Elena felt it behoved her to respond.

'My dear Sir, it must surely be that very uncertainty that has guided my father's decision. We know not what this inheritance will mean for us. Everything will be unfamiliar and I have so little experience of society.'

'Ha! That is the nub of the matter …' Mr Sawyer's feelings overcame his good manners as he leaped into speech and interrupted her. 'Both for you and your father. While you were penniless and prospectless, I was good enough for you but now, now that you have expectations the curate of Fossewold Parva should no longer aspire to your hand. I have it now!'

His anger alarmed her and she laid a gloved hand on his arm. 'Please, Mr Sawyer, please do not agitate yourself or take affront. You must see that what my father says is rational and reasonable. You are in no position to support a wife. Indeed are unlikely to be able to do so for some years to come.' She saw that she had s t ruck home and continued quickly to build on her theme. 'Nor do you have anywhere suitable to live, situated as you are in the rooms above the Rectory Coach House. I ask you plainly; could you really counsel a dutiful father to encourage such a match when there is no certainty of it being able to take place.

'You have betrayed me,' he said in a strangled voice.

'How so, Sir? This is none of my doing,' she was grateful to be able to say with honesty. 'And how can a man of your calling encourage me to go against the expressed wishes of my father?' She stopped; she had no taste for exchanges such as this. Her pretty face softened. 'Come, Mr Sawyer. Please say that you will stand my friend, for I shall surely stand yours and there is no saying that three, even five years hence our paths might cross and we find that all the obstacles in our way now are insufficient to prevent our union.'

He was not proof against the beseeching brown eyes, which were fixed so earnestly on his face. He covered her hand and managed the ghost of a smile.

'Very well. Have it as you will. I cannot like it, but as you say, I cannot in all conscience require your disobedience to your father's wishes. I will stand aside and hope you find no better man to take my place.'

2

*M*ore than a hundred miles south of Fossewold Parva
lived a man who, had circumstances treated him less
harshly, would very easily have supplanted Mr Sawyer as a suitable candidate for Miss Elena Smithson's hand. Instead he now
lay in a vast, oak bed, fighting for his life with his stepmother,
his doctor, the chaplain and his valet all in attendance.

The Squire of Holm Manor was young Edmund Leighterton,
lately returned from the Battle of Waterloo. He had been only
dimly aware of that return, having lain wounded on the battle-
field, unable to help himself. A blast from the nearby guns had
felled him to the ground, damaging his ears with their monstrous roar. Combining this with the wet and dirt, he had succumbed to an infection and had remained insensible to his
parlous state until some two days later. He had regained consciousness in a field hospital surrounded by other casualties.
He was lucky enough to have had a cousin in the same platoon,
who, as a walking wounded, had arranged his repatriation and
had him delivered into the grateful arms of his stepmother. The
journey first by sea over rolling waves followed by a jolting,
rocking coach ride had been a species of nightmare. His fever
mounting, Edmund had drifted in and out of delirium and even
now, safely in his own bed, was unable to grasp reality long
enough to establish where he was.

Mrs Clarissa Leighterton, the second wife of Edmund's late
father, was an admirable woman who had done her best to

bring up her energetic and sometimes rather wayward and resentful stepson to meet the obligation thrust on him as a result of his father's early demise from a carriage accident during a trip to London. Now approaching her half-century, she had hoped to take a lesser role in the management of his estate and to enjoy trips to Brighton or Worthing on a more regular basis than she had been allowed to become accustomed. She had reckoned without her stepson, who on hearing of a just cause, had purchased a commission in the army and set off to France to do battle against the mighty Napoleon.

Looking down now at his grey, perspiring face, his bright eyes reduced to sunken orbs in dark sockets and his sandy locks shaved in patches to give better sight of his ears, Mrs Leighterton wished she had been firmer with him in years gone by, instead of hoping to engender some affection in him by deferring her wishes to his.

Initially the doctor had taken a very grim view of the chances of Edmund's survival and she berated herself that the pain of a little discipline earlier in his young life might have spared her this anguish now. She stood up from her chair rather abruptly as if to escape her painful thoughts. The doctor gave her a dis-approving look, then, taking pity on her, he indicated to her with a flick of his head that he and she might move into the dressing room for conversation.

Once there, Mrs Leighterton waited in some trepidation to hear what the doctor had to say.

'I have detected a slight strengthening of his pulse, Ma'am,' he said carefully while looking at his timepiece as if expecting confirmation from it. 'And his temperature is not elevated to such a peak as it was this time yesterday.'

'Then you think he is on the mend,' demanded the lady eagerly.

'I can make you no promises, my dear Ma'am. Indeed have you ever known me to?'

This was an oblique reference to other occasions when there had been illness in the house and Mrs Leighterton had wanted the earliest information on the likely outcome. The good Dr Osborne, in his dark frock coat and old-fashioned wig of neat grey curls, was never to be hastened into a judgement.

'No, more's the pity, for if you were ever wrong it might dispel your self-satisfied air,' snapped Mrs Leighterton, for she was tired of revisiting this subject every time the doctor attended one of their number. 'I have need of some guidance, some reassurance about the future of my stepson. Surely you must see that anything, be it proved wrong later or no, is better than this infernal waiting.'

Dr Osborne was used to Mrs Leighterton's outbursts and saw no reason to take umbrage. He merely smiled condescendingly, took her hand and patted it. He composed his thoughts for speech. 'I can give you no certainty but one uncertainty I must impart to you,' he said gravely. 'I am afraid, dear Mrs Leighterton, that you must prepare yourself for the strong possibility that the outcome of this grievous affliction will be that your stepson will be deaf.'

Mrs Leighterton's eyes widened in alarm. 'Deaf! You mean he will be able to hear nothing?'

'In all possibility there will be considerable impairment of his hearing. He may be able to hear nothing at all.'

'No!' the lady cried out as the full implications of his words began to sink in. 'This cannot be. Surely you can do something that can prevent it.'

Dr Osborne shook his head.

'And will the damage be permanent?'

'That assumption must be made,' replied the doctor firmly.

'But, but, this deafness may not be present?'

'A faint hope only, Ma'am. I would not have disclosed my fears to you if I had not been close to certain that he will be deaf.'

Mrs Leighterton turned with a sweep of her skirts and covered her face with her hands.

'This cannot be true,' she murmured through her fingers. 'It just cannot be true.'

Dr Osborne saw no reason to reiterate his assertion. He knew Mrs Leighterton had taken his words to heart. She would not dismiss them and would make any provision she could for when Edmund regained his senses.

So it was nearly a week later, when the fever finally lifted and Edmund Leighterton found himself thinking consecutive and coherent thoughts, that he woke to a room that appeared to contain only his stepmother.

He was not immediately aware that he could not hear the sounds around him because his ears rang with a cacophony of noise. A dull ache still clung to his left ear.

'Mother,' he spoke out to her and felt himself saying the word rather than hearing it. She rose from the chair and came towards the bed. He thought it curious but not alarming that she was carrying a slate and a chalk. As she reached the bedside, he saw first the tears in her eyes and then her lips move.

'You will have to speak up,' he said testily, 'for I cannot hear you above the din in my head.'

She must have spoken again for he saw her lips move but he heard nothing. Then he saw the sadness in her tired face as she paused to write on the slate. She held it up to him. He read the words.

'It cannot be true,' he cried, struggling up and fighting off the bedclothes. 'It is not true. I won't let it be true.' In his agitation he tried to get out of bed. From nowhere, he was suddenly confronted by his valet and the footman, pressing him once again against the pillows.

'Leave me alone, curse you,' he bawled. 'I am no imbecile to be restrained.'

The men stood back and Mrs Leighterton came again to his bed. She had cleared her slate and written something afresh.

'You must try and calm yourself, my dear; save your strength for your recovery.'

It was not a big slate and she had been obliged to write quite small to complete her sentence. Edmund peered at it, forcing his bleary eyes to focus. Then as he completed his reading he lashed out an arm and knocked the slate to the ground, breaking it.

'What is there to recover for?' he growled. 'If I cannot hear the words you say, I do not want to be some piteous cripple who has to be spoon-fed words. I would rather die.' He caught sight of that pity on his attendants' faces.

'Get out,' he yelled. 'Get out all of you.'

They left him then, including his stepmother, not knowing what else they could do. Mrs Leighterton descended the great open stairs with a heavy heart. Any hope that the doctor might have been taking too dim a view of the outcome of Edmund's illness had now been dashed. Her stepson could not hear a word she was saying and she was powerless to alter that.

Alone in the bedroom above stairs, Edmund Leighterton lay once more against the pillows, grappling with the enormity of what had happened to him. It came to him that he knew not how long he had been ill or what date it was now. He thought to look out of the window to judge the season but when he struggled to a sitting position, his head swam alarmingly and he had to return it to the pillows. Panic erupted all of a sudden within him; he stretched out a hand to the bell rope, wanting his stepmother's company in a complete revolution of feeling, but he routed the almost overwhelming desire. After all only minutes before he had summarily dismissed her. He chased his hectic thoughts around his head and tried to establish some mastery over them. It became important to know more, to understand more fully his situation. He dimly recalled the weeks of fever without any handle on how many there had been. He looked once more to the window and hazarded that it might be autumn; the quality of light was not strong enough to indicate high summer. He knew his only starting point was a wet day in June, then nothing but a blur, a mirage, a mosaic of memories and sensations. He wished he could say noise but he could not arrive at a moment during his illness when everything changed, when he could no longer hear sounds around him. He saw with great clarity what he had lost: the ribald comments of his friends, the spontaneous discussions on all subjects from politics to patriotism, singing, musicals, the theatre, even bird-song, all things he had sometimes cursed in the past for their intrusiveness. He said a little prayer; if he could hear the song of the infernal thrush that had woken him at four o'clock every morning last summer, he would be so glad of it now, even welcome it as the price paid for the glorious benefits of what was now lost.

Edmund thought of the hasty, determined way he had taken on the commission; he recognised now his own arrogance in believing that he would come through the grievous war unscathed. He had never given a moment's thought to what he might forfeit as a result of his impetuosity. He cursed himself now as a fool and irrationally felt a swell of anger against his stepmother. Why had she not stopped him? Why had she not counselled him more strongly so that he heeded her warnings? Not even the whispering of the tiny voice of his conscience, telling him that he had made the decision long before he had even told her of his plans, stopped him from flinging the accusation at her as she returned to the room carrying a tray of chicken broth and rough slices of bread.

Mrs Leighterton, knowing that she could not present a defence he was capable of absorbing, stood there at the foot of the bed still holding the tray. She let him vent the bitterness, which was acute and raw, accepting that this was only the beginning. She had, after all, had nearly a week for the information to settle on her like a shroud. She had spent days carrying out her daily functions, trying to imagine what it would be like to be unable to hear what was going on around her. Her angry and weakened stepson had had but an hour in only one environment to absorb the enormity of what he now faced.

As he came to the end of his tirade, she moved to set the tray down beside the bed. She had with her another slate.

'You must eat,' she had written. It seemed so very mundane a line to write when he was berating her for all that he believed himself to have lost, and by her hand. She paused, unsure whether to confront him with it or turn and leave him to his misery once more. Her hands were shaking from the vitriol in his onslaught and, being a proud woman, she would have preferred not to let him see. She shunned the selfish thought; this was her stepson, for whom she had cared since he was but six years old. He was suffering and she must help him, however that suffering took him. She held up the board.

There was a cessation of his rant; he seemed oblivious to her movements, but, as exhaustion overtook him, his voice trailed off and he peered at the slate. He gave a huge sigh of exasperation and desperation.

'How can you possibly imagine that I could swallow a mouthful at this time? Have you no sense, no feeling for the agony of mind I am experiencing. I cannot eat. I will not eat. Don't imagine you can make me.'

Mrs Leighterton took a long look at her stepson's writhing face and then, as emotion threatened to overcome her, she turned on her heel and quitted the room. Almost tripping over the hem of her dress, she hurried down the stairs to one of the smaller parlours. There was a brisk fire burning in the grate as the September evenings were drawing in and she liked to use this room when she was on her own.

Clarissa Leighterton stood with hands clasped staring into the jumping flames. Not for many years had she felt so keenly the need for companionship. After her husband died, she had been too busy running the estate and cherishing his son to seek out either a companion or a second husband, but now faced with the overwhelming task of ameliorating her stepson's difficulties, she wished there was someone she could talk to. Even as the thought flitted across her mind there was a knock at the door.

'I do beg your pardon, Madam,' said Cleverley, the butler, a benevolent man with his face showing all the sympathy that was warranted at such a time. 'I have Golding, Mr Edmund's groom in the vestibule. He will not be persuaded to return to his quarters. He is distraught, having heard some rumour about Mr Edmund and is determined to see you.'

'This rumour says what, Cleverley?' she asked wearily.

Cleverley looked at her from beneath his heavily furrowed brows, taking in the emotion and the strain on her face. 'That he is deaf, Madam,' he said without preamble.

'I'm afraid that it is true.' She walked to the window of the small room and looked out at the formal gardens now being enveloped by the gloom of dusk. 'It is true. I will speak to the servants in the morning. They must be told the full sum of it.'

'If I may say, Madam, I am most dreadfully sorry.'

She waved away his sympathy. 'Be so good as to send Golding to me. I will tell him now. He has after all been with us longer even than you, Cleverley.'

Golding, a short spare man in his early fifties, dashed into the room as soon as he was given leave by Cleverley. The news appeared to have knocked all the stuffing out of him.

'I 'ave waited and waited, fearful for 'is life,' he blurted out hurriedly, 'but never thought of this, Ma'am. What can I do? I beg you give me some task that I can do for 'im.'

'I'm afraid there is nothing any of us can do,' Mrs Leighterton told him sadly.

'But there must be sommat I can do to 'elp. Please say there is sommat.'

'My only suggestion is that you learn to read and write!'

So, from then on, as each evening drew to a close, Golding would climb his tallet steps armed with as many bits of candle as he could glean and then sit at an improvised desk, laboriously copying out words in the vain hope that one day they would have some meaning for him.

3

*A*lthough William Smithson was determined to have his way in the matter of the young curate and his daughter, he had nevertheless awaited her return from the Delrymples with some trepidation. His daughter was of primary concern to him for he had seen her, on many occasions, subjugate her interests to those of her brother or her father. It seemed wrong then to the latter that he should deliberately prevent her from having something he thought she wanted. He expected her to be angry with him but it would not be an explosive anger. Elena rarely pitted her will against his but she would let him know that he had erred. She was no moral coward. When he heard muffled voices outside the cottage door, he knew the curate had walked Elena home. He was grateful for the service of escorting her up the lonely lane, although he was in no doubt that Mr Sawyer would have expressed to Elena the feelings he had felt constrained from uttering to her father. Mr Smithson took up his place in the dim corridor by the stairs, which was all the hallway the cottage boasted. The door latch lifted and with a call of thank you over her shoulder Elena entered the house. There in the half-light of the hall she did not at first perceive her father.

'Good heavens, Papa, you gave me a fright,' she exclaimed as she turned from hanging her pelisse on the coat stand. 'Why have you not lit the lamps? Jessamy could fall down the stairs in this gloom!'

'But it wants more than an hour before darkness falls, my dear, it would be wasteful to light them now.'

Elena looked at him balefully and they both laughed. William Smithson opened his arms and his daughter walked into them. 'It will take some time to accustom ourselves to this change in fortune,' he said by way of apology. 'We have skimped and scraped for so long; it will remain second nature for some time to come.'

'Just because we have come into some wealth, Papa, we have no need to be profligate, but employ a little common sense, I beg you,' Elena entreated.

He looked shamefaced and would not meet her eye. Detaching herself from his embrace, Elena moved to the little hall table where a lantern stood and she made to light it. She sensed that he was uneasy about something and she wanted to be able to study his expression more closely.

'What has occurred to put you out, Papa?' she asked once she had cast the full force of the light in his direction. She saw the wariness in his eyes under the bushy eyebrows.

'Need you ask me that question, Elena?' he countered.

'Ah.' Realisation dawned on her face but he could not read it as she was behind the light. 'It is your conversation with Mr Sawyer that has unsettled you,' she stated blandly with no inflection in her voice.

'Indeed it is,' he conceded. 'I have convinced myself that I would have incurred your ire. But you do not seem to be displeased.'

Elena set down the lamp and moved out of the hallway into the small, cramped front parlour. Her father followed dutifully. Elena sat down on one of the worn chairs and looked up into his dear worried face.

'In truth, Papa, you have done me a great service,' she pronounced.

William Smithson let out a huge sigh.

'You had no wish to be engaged to him,' he guessed.

Elena nodded. 'I cannot tell you from whence the feeling has come, but latterly' – she paused – 'after this inheritance became widely known, I have considered his affections overstated,' she explained carefully. There was a frown on her pretty face. 'Papa, I do believe that he was more enamoured of my prospects than of me. Is that not a dreadful thing for me to think?'

Mr Smithson found that their positions had been inexplicably reversed. Now it was Elena who was ashamed of her own thoughts, and he the sage counsellor. Fleetingly he marvelled at his daughter's happy touch of putting her companion, whoever it might be, at their ease. He took the chair beside her and patted her hand.

'It is inevitable that we should be wary, Elena,' he said sympathetically. 'He is an estimable young man but there is no denying his ambition. A wealthy wife would enhance his prospects beyond anything he could hope for now. He has no sponsor, no benefactor.'

Elena cast a quick look in her father's direction. 'You do not propose to become such a one, do you Papa?' she said hastily.

'Not if you do not want me to,' he reassured her.

'It seems so mean-spirited, so small-minded of me,' she said, jumping to her feet and almost knocking him backward in her impetuosity. 'But you have brought me a clean slate and I have every reason to believe that with your kind heart it cost you dear. I would so much prefer to move to Sussex without any attachment, Papa.'

William Smithson smiled, his prominent eyebrows flattening out across his wide forehead to give his face a benign look. Elena knew that expression, knew that they were in complete accord.

'Papa, you are too good to me,' she said.

'And you to me, my dear,' he responded automatically, for it was a verbal exchange they had used often.

'But there is something more!' Elena looked at him keenly. 'I know you, Papa; you are holding something back from me.'

There was a silence, and then Mr Smithson put his hand into his breast pocket and brought out a letter.

'This,' he said, 'is from Messrs Banbury and Southrup who act for the late Sir Benjamin Geoffrey Herbert-Longfield. He has requested that I travel once again to Sussex to sign the final papers and he makes the suggestion that you should accompany me to acquaint yourself with the domestic arrangements.'

Elena's eyes widened in surprise. 'He knows of me?'

'He does indeed; he has investigated the whole family very closely to ensure that he hands on the property to the right person.'

'So he knows of Jessamy?'

'Again, yes, and he has already released sufficient funds for Jessamy to go to school next term.'

'You are not going to send Jessamy away, Papa? Please say you are not!'

'No, not yet, I promise you. Perhaps not for three years or more but, when he is thirteen I must, my dear. For the time being there is a good school at Haywards Heath to which he can go daily but I have great hopes that he can take up a place at Eton. My kind employer has promised me an introduction when necessary.'

Elena pursed her lips, not ready to sanction any sort of parting from her little brother but willing to accept that there were many more pressing concerns to deal with before she need worry about boarding school for him. 'Will he come with us this time?' she asked.

Her father shook his head. 'Good Mrs Peabody has agreed to have him for the time we are away. He will enjoy staying with Walter and Hubert. He is always clamouring for the treat, so I doubt he will miss us.'

So four days later saw Elena and her father set out in a post-chaise and four supplied by courtesy of Mr Banbury of Banbury and Southrup.

Elena was in a bubble of excitement, as she had never ridden in such a grand carriage with two postilions mounted on the horses before. Her father tried to appear unmoved by this illustration of their elevation. He pointedly refused to meet Elena's eye as she waved to one of their village friends as the vehicle bowled along the main street.

Mr Smithson's heart was pounding heavily in his chest. He had made this journey once before to meet Mr Banbury although on that occasion it had behoved him to make his own way by the mail. The contrast this time in his mode of travel brought home to him, as nothing else so far had, that he was no longer someone else's bailiff but very likely to become his own master and that of many others.

Once away from their own familiar surroundings Elena sat in silence for some time, contemplating what they would find at their journey's end. They had chosen to pass through London rather than try and skirt it as all roads seemed to lead to it. However there was a long way to travel and they only made Watford by the end of their first day.

Unused to travelling such distances, Elena was tired when she sat down to supper in the private parlour Mr Banbury had bespoken for them.

'It is a very long way from our home, is it not, Papa?' Her voice quavered before she attempted the thick vegetable broth that had been set before her. 'We will be so very far from all our kind friends.'

Mr Smithson, himself daunted by what was before them, struggled to lift his spirits enough to answer with energy. He was about to speak when she continued: 'Can we not turn this down, Papa? Ask for it to be handed on to someone more suited to this Herculean task.'

'Do not think I have not considered it, my darling child,' Mr Smithson replied seriously. 'In the middle of the night, at the darkest hour before dawn, I have lain awake wrestling with the question. There is no clear answer. I have studied the family as set out in the documents sent to me by Mr Banbury and I can find no member of its many branches who would comfortably take the role. If I decline it, it would pass to your Great-Aunt Antonia and she at eight and sixty would certainly not relish the challenge, widowed as she is. Her eldest son, my cousin Robert, lives in the Indies and has his own estate there, while his sister, Elvira, is unmarried. I cannot in all conscience burden them with this inheritance.'

Elena lifted her eyes from contemplation of the mushy liquid in her bowl and looked deeply into her father's weather-beaten face. In the candlelight she saw the fears and the anxiety there and she felt a surge of admiration for him for she knew that he planned to shoulder this huge responsibility and give it his all.

'Very well, Papa,' she said, raising a smile to the brown eyes that were so like her own, 'you and I will meet this challenge together. United there is nothing we cannot achieve.'

Much moved, William Smithson stretched out his hand across the solid oak table and covered one of her dainty ones. He gave it a grateful squeeze. 'Thank you, my angel,' he said. 'I knew you would stand with me.'

While he found he could brazen it out in front of her, Mr Smithson discovered that sitting alone in the parlour with his thoughts after Elena had retired to her bedchamber was most uncomfortable.

Part of Mr Banbury's letter he had not divulged to Elena. Indeed he was not sure that he had read it aright so it would have been foolish to have revealed its contents with only his interpretation of what it said. Mr Banbury had written in such veiled terms that his meaning was obscured.

William Smithson believed that it purported to say that the majority of the servants at Holm Oak Reach had declined to enter the service of the new incumbents. The butler would retire on the generous annuity bequeathed to him by his late employer. The housekeeper had it in her head that the Smithson family would not be to her taste and the valet had decided there would be little need for his services if the heir were a country bailiff. William Smithson could see how difficult it had been for Mr Banbury to illustrate this tactfully in a letter and he felt for him. It did not, however, lessen its impact. To be a new master to new servants in an unknown house in an unfamiliar area could not be contemplated with a light heart. Moreover Mr Banbury had recommended that he find a lady of good character to be chaperone for Elena. Mr Smithson doubted his daughter would take well to this suggestion if it was only to further her social standing.

Two days later and they were passing through an impressive pair of stone pillars, each surmounted by a carved wide-winged eagle flanked by a gatehouse on each side. There was no sign of the occupants of the gatehouses but clearly, before the demise of the owner, money had been spent on their upkeep. The estate cottages looked well maintained. The driveway was long and traversed an open park punctuated by specimen oaks. Elena gazed around her trying to get an early sighting of the house. She had as yet given no thought to its size or age. The carriageway passed between two thick lines of trees and climbed slightly up a rise. As the post-chaise topped the hillock, leaning out of the carriage window Elena gasped. Through the flickering ears of the moving horses, she was confronted by the façade of a great mansion.

'Why, Papa, it is monstrous!' she blurted out. 'It is vast, huge. How can we possibly make such a place as this our home? You should have forewarned me what to expect.'

Mr Smithson was similarly flustered by what he saw.

'I had no notion, my dear Elena.' He hastened to disabuse her of any belief that he had hidden the enormity of their task from her. 'I have met Mr Banbury but once before and then we met in London for he had come up from his offices in Bristol. When I enquired of the house, he told me that our forebears had borrowed much from Petworth House when conceiving its design but, as I have not seen that either, I had no notion what it meant.' He finished in a rush, desperate to exonerate himself.

Elena was unimpressed. 'Had you said even that, Papa, I could have visited the circulating library, asked my friends, oh, all manner of possibilities to get some idea of what to expect. This, this …' Words failed her. She waved her arms in the direction of the approaching house and then fell silent, trying to absorb its detail.

By virtue of its size, the house was more imposing than beautiful. Great tiers of windows stretched out before them, identical on each floor. The only relief from the uniformity of the façade was that the middle section, some five windows wide, was set forward slightly from the pale bulk of the house. There was no portico to protect travellers as they arrived at the main door and the chimneys were short and virtually obscured by the curve of the roof. Elena found herself hoping that they drew properly. She had a distaste of sitting in a smoke-filled room.

The post-chaise drew up before the house after what Elena felt was an overindulgently circuitous route. They had now seen the façade from every angle as the carriageway swept in a great arc one way and then the other. There were no formal gardens in front of the house, just a wide gravelled area for carriages to turn and an expanse of lawn to a ha-ha from whence the park could be viewed.

Elena had wanted to like this house, determined to make the best of her new life. She wondered as she alighted from the chaise with the help of her father's hand whether first impressions could be overcome and, once familiar with it, she could learn to love it. It felt like a huge undertaking.

The great door was opened after a short delay by a rigidly upright butler. By virtue of there being a large step up into the hall, he gave the impression that he was looking down his aquiline nose at them. The Smithsons shifted closer to each other for moral support.

They entered the hall, which Elena guessed measured some fifty feet in each direction. The floor was a mosaic of black and white marble squares, each measuring some two feet across and the theme was taken up by a multitude of ebony doors set in almost porcelain-white walls. Up from this space swept a wide pale stone staircase, which divided at a half-landing and continued on to the left and right. The balustrades were stone too and must have been extraordinarily difficult to fashion. On the half-landing set back in an alcove was an exquisitely carved statue of some Greek goddess, the marble cut so that she was elegantly swathed in material to preserve her modesty. Beneath her, distributed around the hallway were her companions in similar states of glorious déshabillé.

Elena could only blink at these undoubted works of art. From one of the black doors, a middle-aged gentleman dressed completely in black except for the whiteness of his cravat came hurrying forth.

'Mr Smithson, welcome, welcome. Miss Smithson, how do you do? How delighted I am to make your acquaintance. A good journey I trust. Long, I know, but comfortable I hope?'

In the face of this jovial loquaciousness, Elena and her father could only murmur their agreement and thanks.

'I have ordered refreshments for you and me, Mr Smithson, in the estate room where we must discuss some details. Boring work, Miss Smithson, so I shall not trouble you to accompany us. I have arranged that the housekeeper should conduct you around some of the principal rooms and that we should meet again for a light luncheon in the west dining room.'

'Thank you,' Elena managed, wishing with all her heart that she could accompany her father. For no sooner had Mr Banbury uttered these words than he was ushering her father away. Standing in the centre of the great unfamiliar place with only the echo of her father's footsteps receding into the distance, Elena felt she had been abandoned.

4

Whatever the arrangements Mr Banbury had seen fit to make, they were destined to remain unfulfilled. The butler had withdrawn and there was no sign of the housekeeper. After a little while of standing waiting, Elena forfeited her position in the middle of the hall and walked over to a stone bench, which had been set against the wall. The whiteness of the stone suggested it would be a cold seat but some farsighted person had topped it with a black cushion. Elena settled herself down and tried to while away the time studying the great portraits that hung on the walls. Many were of dark brooding men with haughty faces, seemingly dissatisfied either with their lot or with the presence of such an unworthy successor.

Time dragged for Elena while the matching ebony grandfather clock, which ticked loudly in the near corner to the main door, taunted her with the slowness of a revolution around its face. Elena could not but suspect that the housekeeper was deliberately ignoring her.

It lacked ten minutes to one o'clock when the housekeeper finally arrived in all her austere glory. Her grey hair was scraped back harshly and hidden firmly under a severe cap. Her dress was black and rather fuller than the mode and beady black eyes took in Elena's presence and dowdy appearance.

'Goodness me, girl, what do you think you are doing out here? Interviews for the post of parlourmaid are taking place in the servants' quarters. You should have arrived at the service entrance. What can Mr Box be thinking of?'

Elena rose to her feet, her heart pounding with indignation but outwardly she retained her poise.

'I beg your pardon,' she said in as calm a voice as she could muster after such an assault, 'but I am not here for the position of parlourmaid. I attend Mr Banbury and my father, Mr William Smithson. I was given to understand that I should wait here while they transact some business and during that time you, if you are the housekeeper, would conduct me around the house.'

The woman's pinched features took on an affronted look and she was about to utter a disclaimer when the butler arrived to interrupt her.

'Mr Banbury requests Miss Smithson's company in the west dining room, if you please, Mrs Silchester,' he announced pompously.

Mrs Silchester gave him a glowering look.

'I will hand her over to you then, Mr Box,' she replied.

'No, I believe Mr Banbury requested that you should accompany her,' he replied quickly.

Elena was astute enough to know there was some deep game being played out in front of her but she was not sufficiently well versed in the tricks of servants to know what it was. She clutched her reticule tightly and waited to see who would be the victor of this strange duel. She suspected that whichever one eventually conducted her to the dining room would be the loser. It then occurred to her that it might be some kind of test for her. She cleared her throat audibly and was gratified to see the combatants cease their constrained bickering.

'I am sure we should not be keeping Mr Banbury waiting,' she said clearly. 'And if neither of you are minded to escort me perhaps you would be kind enough to direct me to the dining room and I will venture to find it alone.'

A look of distaste crossed Mr Box's refined features. 'If you would follow me, Miss,' he said, barely disguising a sneer.

Elena sallied forth in the direction he indicated and found herself being conducted through one of the ebony doors into the longest gallery she had ever seen. To her left were long windows looking out to the front of the house, while on the right-hand wall were yet more pictures of grandees of the family. Elena could not help but marvel that no worthier successors could be found amongst the descendants of these august personages than she and her father. She felt a tinge of sympathy for the foolish servants who so clearly decried the situation.

She had walked perhaps twenty steps when she realised that Mrs Silchester was accompanying her too. This outcome was so unexpected and ridiculous that Elena had to suppress a smile. She straightened her back and firmed up her step. She was prepared to interpret this as her victory.

The west dining room was aptly named. All its windows faced west so at the moment there was little natural light but it was a well-proportioned room with a gleaming mahogany table in the centre. At its full length it could clearly seat more than twenty people, if the number of chairs arranged around the wall were anything to go by, but now it was at its most reduced and covers were set for three people.

'There you are, my dear.' Mr Banbury greeted her enthusiastically. He surged towards her. 'Come, come and sit down. I hope you have enjoyed your tour of the house.' He cast a look of interrogation in the direction of Mrs Silchester's rigid form.

'I'm afraid I have not yet seen the house,' Elena announced in her clear voice.

'Good heavens, why not?' exclaimed their host.

'I can only assume that there was some sort of misunderstanding,' said Elena, her eyes looking fixedly at Mrs Silchester. The word 'deliberate', though unsaid, hung in the air.

'There was no misunderstanding,' Mrs Silchester declared. 'Mr Box did not apprise me of the young Miss's presence or I would of course have been happy to oblige.'

Mr Box did not deem this attempt to shift blame on to him worthy of a disclaimer.

'Will that be all, Sir?' he asked pointedly of Mr Banbury. 'Shall you wish for luncheon to be served immediately?'

'Yes, yes, of course.' Mr Banbury waved both the butler and the housekeeper away, knowing full well that any further delving into the circumstances of what had happened would only cause him embarrassment and the Smithsons discomfort.

The meal was simple plain fare but delicious. Mr Banbury was quick to boast the excellence of the produce provided by the estate. The ham was well cured and the apple tartlets sweet tasting. Mr Banbury apologised for the omission of nectarine and strawberries but even the most well-managed succession houses struggled to keep these fruits going deep into autumn.

'Although I believe the apple store from the orchards provides apples all the way through to May,' he assured them.

It was a safe topic and soon Mr Smithson, who had been looking rather overwhelmed prior to this point, began to take part in the conversation. Elena was able to withdraw from the discussion and let her mind wander away from the talk of kitchen gardens and home farms. She found herself thinking that if the behaviour of Mrs Silchester and Mr Box was a taste of things to come and a reflection of how the whole household was going to behave, then it was going to be a very lonely existence. Just maybe, she should have retained at least the right to exchange letters with Mr Sawyer.

She was conscious of a shift in the topic of conversation. Mr Banbury was counselling her father.

'I would advise you, Sir, to employ a companion for Miss Smithson. There will be a deal of talk about you as a family under the circumstances and it might raise adverse comment if the young lady is without a female escort. Being without a chaperone might preclude her being invited to a ball or some such. A scion of some noble family would help to gain her entrée hereabouts.'

Mr Smithson looked warily into his daughter's face as he sat opposite her, the Smithsons having been placed either side of Mr Banbury. He had not yet braved putting the suggestion to his daughter himself. Elena had not had a live-in female other than the parlourmaid since her mother had died; he did not know how she would take to the suggestion. Mr Banbury had no such worries.

'If I might make so bold I would like to suggest that you invite Miss Polly McNeath to live with you. She is a deserving young woman of four and twenty who is nearly related to you. She is in the same way related to your benefactor as you are as she is also a descendant of Sir Geoffrey Herbert-Longfield but through his daughter Constance Margaret McNeath.'

'One of my grandfather's sisters?' Mr Smithson was keen to clarify.

Mr Banbury nodded. 'And she has fallen on hard times.' He paused significantly. 'Very hard times. She is currently employed as a nursery maid at the home of one Marmaduke Yardley.'

Both Elena and her father looked at him blankly; the name was clearly meant to inform them in some way. They remained in ignorance.

'Surely you know the name Yardley?' Mr Banbury was astonished. He looked from one to the other. 'He is known in polite circles for his huge fortune and parsimonious ways, while his spouse is a hard-nosed harridan who treats her servants with disdain. I visited her not three months ago in my quest to ensure that I had researched the family tree with comprehensive thoroughness and Mrs Yardley was most obstructive. She was determined to put every obstacle in my way to prevent me having speech with Miss McNeath.'

'Did you achieve your purpose? Did you meet with her?' Elena asked anxiously, concerned as ever for the well-being of others.

'Not immediately. In fact Mrs Yardley had me kicking my

heels in the local hostelry at Little Dyreham for four days before I was allowed to meet Miss McNeath on her half-day.' Mr Banbury stood up from the dining table and paced to the window. 'I was appalled at what I discovered,' he said soberly. 'Miss McNeath was painfully thin and her complexion was very pale. Her movements were languid, whether from ill-health or malnourishment I could not tell but I fear for her future. I appeal to your good nature to rescue her from the clutches of this woman.'

There was a glint of a tear in Elena's eyes. 'And, but for the fact that her great-grandparent was a woman rather than a man, she could be seated here in place of me?' she asked, still trying to clarify the relationship in her mind.

Mr Banbury came back to the table to stand at its head and, clasping his hands behind his back, he rose briefly on to his toes. 'Indeed that is correct, young lady.'

'So where are her other relatives? How can she be so reduced?' Mr Smithson could not reconcile her situation with her lineage.

'Her father was a ne'er-do-well,' replied Mr Banbury. Moving from his position behind the chair, he parted his tails and sat down at the table once more. 'He lived beyond his income and having never trained for any profession he had no means of supporting himself. His wife took in sewing and needlework but the close work impaired her eyesight. Miss McNeath's father died in the debtors' prison and she and her mother, who was by now infirm, were left to live on the parish. As soon as Miss McNeath attained her sixteenth birthday she was sent into service.'

There was a silence from his audience as Elena and her father digested the details of this sad story. Elena was just about to open her mouth to demand that they rescued Miss Polly McNeath from her sorry life when Mr Smithson spoke with some severity.

'Reconcile for me please, Mr Banbury, the placing of this

young woman as my daughter's companion and your earlier advice that I surround her with people who can add to her consequence.' He had been periodically helping himself to a bowl of blackberries and he now mopped his mouth with a linen napkin, careless of the possible stain before reiterating his point. 'You have said that my previous lowly occupation makes establishing ourselves somewhat difficult; that engendering respect in the servants will be almost impossible. Indeed I believe we have had an example of it before luncheon when my daughter's presence was ignored. Surely we would further compound our problems if we imported a young relative out of service.'

'Papa!' cried Elena, horrified by such cynical words being uttered by her normally soft-hearted father.

He raised his hand to stop her blurting out anything infelicitous and grappling with herself Elena managed not to say any more. She directed her wide-eyed innocence at the embarrassed face of Mr Banbury.

'I confess, Mr Smithson, you have punctured my Achilles heel. I most certainly adhere to my previous advice. You must, I beg of you, take seriously my concerns but one look at that poor girl's face was enough to crumble the hardest of hearts. To leave her where she is would most surely result in her early demise.'

It was Mr Smithson's turn to stand up from the table. He went to a dark wooden inlaid sideboard which complemented the table and ran his finger across its smooth shining surface. He had approved Mr Banbury's earlier advice because it would have meant that there would have been wise counsel available to him whenever he needed it, but even when Mr Banbury had originally voiced it, William Smithson had failed to see how it was achievable. Who could he possibly have persuaded to visit them to lend them consequence? The only people whom they knew who moved in society circles were the Delrymple girls and none of them were fit enough to come for a visit of friendship. They were more likely to be in the market for a companion for themselves than to be one for someone else. This great house would be a lonely place for his daughter and giving Miss Polly McNeath a home would not preclude them from finding someone else to act as a chaperone.

'Very well,' he said heavily. 'We will invite Miss McNeath for an extended stay. You must advise us, Mr Banbury, on how this can be achieved.'

Mr Banbury rose again from his chair, rubbing his hands. 'You will not regret it, Mr Smithson, I can assure you, you will not,' he affirmed as he moved to shake the man's hand. William Smithson looked over the solicitor's shoulder and hoped Mr Banbury was right because he did not want the radiant look now adorning his daughter's face to be in vain.

5

Once the decision had been made, Mr Smithson and his daughter remained only one night at their future home before being escorted by Mr Banbury to London where they were to interview a number of prospective employees for the positions of butler, valet and housekeeper at Holm Oak Reach. There would also be the need for a lady's maid for Elena but this was felt to be a task too far given the pressures of time.

Mr Banbury had undertaken to make some preliminary choices amongst the ranks of the hopeful applicants; there were in fact only four he had considered suitable for the post of butler. Mr Smithson discounted the first whom he thought was too young and who had a permanent drip from his nose. Elena, who had only been allowed to observe the proceedings, gave her father a speaking look from her corner of the panelled room. Mr Smithson put a definite line through the man's name on his list, his nib spluttering as he did so. The next candidate was smartly dressed with gleaming shoes and oily greasy hair. He appeared personable enough but there was something shifty behind his eyes, which gave Elena the shivers.

When the third prospective butler left, she challenged Mr Banbury. 'They must all have given dissatisfaction previously, Sir, if they are now looking for a position. How can we be persuaded to place our future well-being in their hands?'

Mr Smithson coughed meaningfully, trying to curtail his daughter's forthrightness. However Elena was not to be silenced. 'This is of such great import to us, Mr Banbury. Surely you must see this. We, ignorant as we are, are at the mercy of these upper servants. They will be in charge of our household and thus far I have seen nothing to recommend any of them.'

'Calm yourself, Miss Smithson, I beg of you.' Mr Banbury came from around the heavy desk behind which he and Mr Smithson had been sitting. 'If you like none of them, then we employ none of them. We will continue searching until we find someone suitable.' He went on to confirm what she had said. 'Nothing could be more prejudicial to your entrance into society than if you do not have the trust and goodwill of your servants. Servants talk; they tittle-tattle with staff from other houses. We will find someone with integrity who will consider your interests paramount.'

There was a slight delay before the final candidate put in an appearance. He arrived a little flustered but it did not detract from his overall good first impression. His clothes were dark and, though immaculately turned out, from her perch in the corner Elena could detect a careful darn here and a stitch to save a seam there. Elena liked that; it told her he was not careless with money. His manner while not being effusive was friendly and he did not poker up and look down his nose at Mr Smithson as the circumstances were explained to him. As he had entered the room, he had cast a quick look in Elena's direction and he had bowed his head slightly in acknowledgement of her presence. She liked that too.

As he answered Mr Banbury's questions, she studied his profile, which was now her view of him, and decided that she could learn to trust him. His responses were straightforward and steady; he was not constantly looking about him. He maintained his poise even when Mr Smithson, mindful of Elena's expressed concerns, asked him directly why he was looking for a new position.

She saw a shadow cross his face as for the first time since his entrance he directed his eyes at her. He took out his handker-chief and held it as if anticipating some strong emotion.

'I had hoped, Sir, to grow old in the service of my late master as he was a young man, but sadly it was not to be. While he could not have been a kinder or fairer employer, he was assailed by one weakness. He was addicted to gaming and although there were periods of extreme wealth, I regret to have to inform you that there were also very difficult times. Latterly those times outnumbered his winning phases and in the end he lost everything. The distress was too much for him and he put period to his own existence.' Here the man mopped his brow with the ready handkerchief. 'I blame the fact that he came into his inheritance much too young,' he said with admirable restraint.

Seeing how moved he was, Elena rose from her chair and came to him and, with a fleeting nod to her father, who responded in kind, she said, 'I can assure you, Mr Timery, that there will be no such vicissitudes in our employ and I beg of you to agree to take on the role of our mentor. I know you will advise us well and will maintain a watch over us, steering us through the pitfalls of society. And in return, my father will undertake to husband the finances so that your future is secure.'

'Bravo, well said, Miss Smithson,' cried Mr Banbury, pleased that a decision had been reached so quickly.

Hubert Timery found himself blinking in surprise at the sudden improvement in his fortunes. He had, besides a wife, an ageing mother, whom he had supported all his working life and the loss of gainful employ had been putting a severe strain on his finances.

He was emboldened to offer his wife as housekeeper to the establishment and suggested to his audience that it might be best if they took up their posts before a valet was employed, so that he would ascertain what manner of man would suit Mr Smithson.

After that the proceedings were concluded very quickly. Mr Banbury arranged with Mr Timery that he and his wife would replace the current incumbents, who would be paid off the following week. Elena and Mr Smithson would make the journey home, await the appointment of the new bailiff to the Delrymples and then have all their belongings despatched by carrier to Holm Oak Reach while they travelled to collect Polly McNeath.

It was not however until the New Year that the Smithsons took up residence in their new home. Their relocation had been delayed by an unforeseen circumstance. Lord Delrymple while out game shooting in Scotland had caught a chill and succumbed to inflammation of the lungs. For some time there had been concern for his survival and then a protracted convalescence, which kept him north of the border until well into November. It was not in William Smithson's nature to abandon his employer to the devices of the new bailiff under such circumstances and he felt it behoved him to remain in Leicestershire to ensure that all was well. This turn of events made for an uncomfortable time for Elena as it meant she remained under the resentful eye of the spurned curate and it took all her resolution to meet him with equanimity as he made no secret of the fact that he felt he had a grievance.

Once Lord Delrymple had returned triumphantly to the bosom of his family, a date was set but another delay ensued. This time there was an early fall of heavy snow, which prevented them from making the journey. Eventually the third week in January was settled upon and Mr Smithson wrote a firm letter to Mrs Yardley that he would be calling to collect his cousin, Miss McNeath, on the Thursday of that week.

He received a prompt and curt reply from the matriarch, stating that Miss McNeath would not be available. She was bonded to the Yardley family as part of the terms under which they had received her from the parish and Mrs Yardley was not minded to release her.

Mr Smithson was not deterred. He replied by return express, explaining that he was happy to pay to release her and that his intentions remained unaltered. To this he got no reply but, mindful of how Mr Banbury had been treated, Mr Smithson did not change his plans.

Their welcome at the Yardley mansion was chilling indeed. The house, a dark-stoned, gloomy building was forbidding enough but on entry gained through the offices of a downtrodden butler, they found the ill-lit hall to be unheated. Given that there had been a hard frost that morning, William Smithson would not have been surprised to see his own breath.

They explained their business and were told to wait, which they did as patiently as possible when they had to stamp their feet and wave their arms across their bodies to keep themselves warm. Mrs Yardley eventually sent for them and they were escorted into a small parlour at the back of the house where even the moribund fire in the grate seemed to have given up the fight. Elena, already concerned for her cousin, realised now that there was little chance of survival in this house if one were weak or infirm. She contrasted it unfavourably with the Delrymples' house where every effort was made to ensure the comfort and well-being of all its occupants.

Mrs Yardley was a grotesque creature with unforgiving eyes and a mouth that habitually turned down so that there were deep grooves in the woman's face. Her hair was iron grey under a severe cap and her clothes were dark and sombre. This, combined with the gloom of the house, convinced Elena that she could find nothing to recommend the place. She waited to see how her father would handle this harridan.

'So good of you to see us, Mrs Yardley,' he said with creditable bonhomie.

'It is not my intention to grant your request to take Miss McNeath,' she said forcefully and without preamble. 'You have wasted your time in visiting me. If it had not been for the circumstance that I had not replied to your last express, I would not have seen you.' She continued as if it was necessary to explain away such weakness.

'My dear Madam, I do hope that you will reconsider. My cousin can be no more valuable to you than the next nursery maid. She could very easily be replaced.'

Mrs Yardley pursed her lips and Elena received the distinct impression that perhaps it was more difficult to obtain staff than Mrs Yardley would like to admit.

'Miss McNeath is devoted to the children and would not wish to be separated from them.'

'If that were the case, Madam, I would wish to hear it from Miss McNeath herself,' said William Smithson, determined not to be put off.

'Confound you, man,' exploded Mrs Yardley. 'Are you doubting my word?'

At this all held their breath.

'Hardly that, Mrs Yardley, but I must ascertain the true wishes of my cousin and I cannot do that without seeing her.'

'You cannot see her. It is her afternoon off.'

'Surely a more convenient time could not be found. Indeed, I understand from Mr Banbury that you required him to wait until Miss McNeath's day off before he could attend her. I chose this day on that account.'

Mrs Yardley was clearly worsted and it was not an experience to which she was accustomed. There was a pause, which lengthened until the tension was acute. Elena saw a flicker in the woman's eyes and then she capitulated. 'Very well.' Mrs Yardley rose majestically from her seat and pulled the bell rope. 'I will have her sent for.'

The servant came promptly and disappeared again with great alacrity, obviously relieved that the errand was simple and it was not he who had caused the look of repressed but no less deadly anger in his employer's eye. Fleetingly, he spared a thought for Polly McNeath but relief of his own escape vanquished it.

Ten minutes later Miss Polly McNeath arrived in the room.

Elena was aghast. Miss McNeath seemed scarcely able to support her own weight. She was painfully thin and her face was alabaster white with eyes like dark pools of misery and dejection. Elena could only admire her father's aplomb in the face of such a shocking sight as he surged forward and took Polly's hands.

'Miss McNeath,' he began, pre-empting any attempt by Mrs Yardley to exercise control over the situation – Elena began to suspect that he had been well briefed by Mr Banbury – 'How delighted I am to make your acquaintance at last. I have heard so much to recommend you to me from Mr Banbury, who I believe visited you not more than four months previously.' Not releasing her hands he turned sideways to encourage Elena to them, further excluding Mrs Yardley. 'Let me introduce you to your cousin, my daughter Elena Smithson.'

Miss McNeath blinked, her eyes now blank as she had failed to grasp what was happening around her.

Elena bobbed her a little curtsey and took the girl's right hand from her father's and enfolded it in hers.

'I am so very pleased finally to make your acquaintance,' Elena managed breathlessly. 'Ever since the occasion of hearing of your plight I have been anxious to bring you to our home.' Her father coughed at the rather unhappy choice of words but he did not interrupt her further. 'Please say you will accompany us and make one of our number at Holm Oak Reach.'

Here Mrs Yardley saw fit to reassert herself. 'I have said that such occurrence is impossible. I forbid it,' she declared. 'She is bonded to me.'

'And I have already said, Madam, that I will make good any loss on your part, if Miss McNeath decides to come to us.'

'Please say you'll come,' cried Elena, 'please, cousin Polly, I want you to come with us.'

The mists of languor, which malnutrition and fatigue had engendered, parted slightly for Polly. She saw the eagerness in the face of the kindly man who appeared to be championing her and the warmth in the eyes of the impetuous young girl and although she did not understand the circumstance in the round as to why they wished her to accompany them, she knew she would do anything to escape the drudgery of Mrs Yardley's domain.

She cleared her throat and then, in little more than a whisper, she gave her acquiescence.

At once Mrs Yardley found that she was no longer being attended to. She manifested her fury, her chins wobbling like a turkey stag's but Mr Smithson was a match for her. He bustled about, demanding a servant to be called to collect Miss McNeath's possessions, such as they were. He had no intention of giving up possession of Miss McNeath now that he had her. While they waited for the pitiful collection of sparse garments and a tattered Bible to be brought to them, Mr Smithson produced a draft from his bank as payment for the release of Miss McNeath. Mr Banbury had drawn up a suitable document for Mrs Yardley to sign and while Mr Smithson would have liked to transact the business out of the presence of his daughter and cousin, he was determined not to let them out of his sight in this malevolent place. Mrs Yardley attempted an ill-natured remonstration, and before conceding began to tear Miss McNeath's good character to ribbons. However Mr Smithson was quick to point out that this was in stark variance to what the lady had said at the commencement of their interview. Finally the harridan capitulated and indeed when she had sight of the very generous sum Mr Smithson was offering for the release of his cousin, her protestations began to assume a hollow ring.

Triumphant, the Smithsons bundled Miss McNeath into their carriage and commanded the coachman to have them away from the place at all speed despite the fact that the sun had set some little while before.

6

*T*he Smithsons did not travel far that evening, determined not to exhaust Miss McNeath. Not more than an hour after their departure from the Yardleys' abode, the carriage drew up at a large hostelry well used to catering for the needs of the gentry. Wrapping Miss McNeath in her own cloak so that the paucity of her clothes would not be detected by the innkeeper, Elena led the other girl into the building, her arm comfortingly around her bony shoulders.

Mr Smithson commanded the use of two bedchambers and a private parlour and because of the season, these were readily available. He knew it behoved him to explain more clearly to Miss McNeath the circumstances that had resulted in their virtual abduction of her, but so far it had not been possible. At the house of Mrs Yardley she had undoubtedly been too scared of her mistress to take in much and in the carriage she had succumbed to the most fearful bout of shaking which he could only put down to shock. Thus he had made no attempt at an explanation and had left it to his daughter to soothe and comfort as best she was able. Also Jessamy's fidgeting presence had made it inadvisable. The boy had been obliged to wait in the carriage during the prolonged interview at the Yardleys and was now bored and cold from inactivity.

In the warm bedchamber they were to share, Elena sat Miss McNeath down on the bed and, slipping solicitously to the floor at her feet, took up her previous occupation of chaffing her hands. Miss McNeath looked down at her with uncomprehending eyes. The shakes had been banished but despite the heat in the room, she shivered. After a while she shifted her position slightly and withdrawing her hands from Elena's she drew the cloak around her more closely.

'Why?' she managed eventually. 'Why me, pray?'

Elena rose from her lowly position and sat beside her cousin. Gently and choosing her words carefully, she tried to explain what had prompted them to invite her to share in their good fortune. Seldom had Polly McNeath met with kindness in her sorry life and when she did experience had inclined her to mistrust it. She tried to rationalise what was being said to her but she could not understand it.

'I'm sorry,' she said in a hoarse whisper, 'I fear I am very stupid; I cannot get all these relations clear in my head.'

'Then we will not trouble ourselves with it now,' decided Elena. 'We will find something suitable from my trunk and we will join my father for supper. He has a magnificent scroll which describes it all.'

Miss McNeath was reluctant to wear anything of Elena's but her will was not equal to the other girl's and soon she was arrayed in a warm rose-coloured silk, which did not look too ill against her pale complexion. Her figure was much slighter than Elena's but she was taller, so the dress did not sit too well upon her. Elena twitched at the hem and drew in the sash in an attempt to improve its appearance. Her efforts, though, did not satisfy her and in the end she cast a huge paisley shawl around the young woman's shoulders to disguise its shortcomings.

In the parlour, Jessamy was already tucking into game pie and mashed swede.

His father made the boy's excuses to their guest.

'He has had a tiring day, unused to travelling as he is,' explained the indulgent father. 'And I thought it advisable for him to go early to bed. I trust you will forgive me giving him permission to eat.'

Miss McNeath looked at Mr Smithson through a fog of bafflement. No one had ever felt it necessary to make their excuses to her before. She grasped that he needed a response and waved her hand in a gesture of assurance. She could not find the words.

Sitting Miss McNeath to his right hand and Elena to his left, Mr Smithson called upon the servant to serve their meal. The pumpkin soup, which arrived promptly, was hot and delicious. Miss McNeath could not prevent herself from falling on the food and devouring it in a manner showing her fearful that it might be wrested from her. When she feverishly grasped one of the crusty buns that accompanied the soup and fairly stuffed it in her mouth, Mr Smithson was moved to put up his hand and draw hers away from her face.

'Gently my dear,' he said as though speaking to a child. 'There is no hurry. And I would advise you to pace yourself. If you are not used to quantities of food, then you must take it slowly or you will most surely regret it later.'

Polly blushed rosily, finding in the depths of her memory a chord struck by his words. She put down the bread and tried to sup her soup more becomingly.

To distract her father, Elena began to question him on the nature of the rest of their journey. The consuming of the remainder of the soup was completed without further embarrassment and the game pie set out before them was served.

By now Jessamy had completed his repast and was sitting watching Miss McNeath with his dark brown eyes so similar to his sister's. From the fullness of his eyebrows at such a young age it was clear that he was bidding fair to have a strong resemblance to his father when he reached adulthood.

'Are you coming to live with us?' he asked Miss McNeath in a clear voice which carried a slight trace of a Leicestershire accent.

Polly looked first at Elena, then at Mr Smithson, both of whom nodded in assent. 'I believe so,' Polly braved. 'Am I to look after you?' she asked of the boy, finding it easier to direct questions to him than towards her adult well-wishers.

'No, I hope not,' cried the boy with a touch of defiance. 'I don't need anyone to look after me. I plan to explore our new home and make new friends.' He was silenced by his father who demanded that he beg Miss McNeath's pardon and then sent him off to bed to sleep on the truckle bed, which had been made up for him in his father's bedchamber.

'Father, would you show Miss McNeath the scroll which describes our family. I fear I have described the connection very ill and would have you explain it better,' Elena urged, keen to divert her father from her little brother's shortcomings.

Now that she was fed, Miss McNeath seemed more able to concentrate and applied herself to understanding where she sat in relation to the Smithsons on the family tree.

'It is an adventure for all of us, Polly,' Elena assured her brightly as they finally exhausted the information to be gathered from the scroll. 'I am so glad you are here to enjoy it with us.'

The Smithsons let Polly sleep late the next morning. Mr Smithson and his son went for a brisk walk across the frosted landscape to while away the time but Elena was afraid to leave her cousin unattended in case she should wake and wonder where she was. This had already happened once in the early hours when Polly's habitual waking time of five-thirty was reached. Fumbling to release herself from her covers, she had tried to get up. Her distress and laboured breathing had woken Elena who had scrambled from her own bed to soothe and calm her cousin. It had taken a little while but Elena was at last able to convince her that there was no pressing need for her to rouse herself before sun-up.

When they set out some four hours later, Polly McNeath looked about with eyes that feasted on the sights and sounds so new to her who had been confined to the Yardleys' home for so many years. The comfort of the well-sprung coach, the warmth and thickness of the rugs across her knees and the unexacting nature of her companions all combined to amaze and astound her. She could not convince herself she was not in some beauteous dream.

Their arrival at Holm Oak Reach some two days later stretched her scarcely attained equanimity almost to breaking point. Her first view of the house transfixed her, and then rattled her confidence in what she was only just being able to understand as her change in circumstance.

'This place, this vast place is to be my home?' she demanded, her voice quavering with emotion.

'Is it not astounding?' agreed Elena, whose own belief was still shaky. 'And inside, you must reserve your astonishment for the grandeur of its black and white hallway, lined with marble statues. I tell you it is a house more suited to royalty than a bailiff and his dependants.'

Polly stared out of the carriage window as the horses gained the rise. 'All this has become yours?' she said, needing yet further confirmation.

'Yes,' replied Elena and her father in unison.

Jessamy, who had reached the stage of demanding how soon before they reached their destination every ten minutes, was silenced by the enormity of the edifice before him. His mouth had dropped open and he had leaned across his sister to get a better view of it as they had been sitting with their backs to their progress for most of the journey.

Soon the sound of the horses' hooves altered to the crunch of gravel and they drew up outside the front door.

So different was this arrival to their last visit. Timery had the great door open even before the horses had halted. Those servants he had so far acquired filed out to line their entrance and a footman made himself available to help the ladies down the carriage steps, which the postilion had prepared for them.

'Welcome to your new home, Sir, let me introduce you to your household.' Timery, in the months since he had met Elena and her father in London, had worked tirelessly to find any number of housemaids and footmen. Mrs Timery had located a chef in whose hands they were prepared to commit the feeding of their new master; the only staff as yet lacking were a valet and a lady's maid. Timery did not make the mistake of thinking Miss Polly McNeath would be filling the latter role. He was well versed in her story and knew she came to make up the family numbers. He hoped not too many of his subordinates would be looking closely at her roughened hands and meagre belongings.

Jessamy, now released from the confines of the carriage, ran amongst the line of servants, looking for some indication of who would be sympathetic to the needs of a growing boy. No sooner had he alighted on the comfortable form of Mrs Timery than he settled on her as his surrogate mother. Luckily this was a role Mrs Timery was pleased to accept and very quickly she had the young boy away from the formalities of the arrival and into the parlour for some much needed refreshments of oat-cakes and hot chocolate.

Vast bedchambers had been readied for the young women, divided from each other by two dressing rooms. Polly was inclined to dissemble, wanting to be as close as possible to Elena on whom was all her dependence.

'You will soon be reconciled to this arrangement, I am sure of it,' Elena tried to reassure her.

Polly shook her head. 'This house is perhaps five times the size of Mrs Yardley's. How can we possibly find our bearings after dark? It is not yet February; there are so many hours of darkness. What shall we do?'

'But there will be candles lining the corridors, look.' Elena grabbed her cousin's hand and took her out on to the landing. 'Look here and here, and here, candles can be placed in all these holders. We will have light. Never you fear.'

Polly looked about and then shook her head in a dazed way. 'At Mrs Yardley's we were only allowed a tallow candle to light our way. Sometimes I would lose my route and be overtaken by the clawing darkness. Sometimes a draught stronger than the others would extinguish my candle. The fear, nay the terror, of being engulfed by the darkness was too terrible, just too terrible.' It was the longest speech Elena had heard from her.

'Oh Polly,' she cried, once again comforting her cousin, her arms around the stiff shoulders. 'That will never happen here. We will banish all draughts, we will not only have candles but lanterns also. You will never again need to be the victim of such fears,' she declared, putting aside the memory that she had only recently had to persuade her father to use more light.

Polly slumped back against the wall, releasing herself from Elena's embrace. 'I can never merit the kindness you have visited on me, dear cousin,' she said. 'I do not know how I can be worthy of your or your father's generosity or how I can ever repay you.'

'You have no need to be concerned about such things as we are as much hostage to fortune as you. We did nothing to warrant this inheritance, we had no expectation of it. Therefore we are happy to visit some of it on you. Our situations are comparable; you need feel no gratitude or be in any particular debt to us. Come, put aside such considerations and enjoy as I intend to our new life.'

7

*M*rs Leighterton moved towards the fire and spread her hands out in front of it as though to benefit from its warmth. In fact she had no need of it, her hands were not cold, she was just giving herself the excuse in order that she need not face the man who was now speaking to her. She knew herself to be incapable of masking her feelings from him and she had no desire to expose herself to his pity any more than had already been expressed.

'Madam, it grieves me deeply to have to say this but I can no longer remain in my post as Mr Leighterton's valet. The force of his anger at his recent infirmity is directed constantly at my person.'

'And at me, Mr Johnson, you are not alone in this,' Mrs Leighterton interjected hastily.

'Yes indeed, Madam, and I am very sorry for it but knowing that Mr Leighterton is universal in demonstrating his resentment makes it no easier for me to help him to dress or to arrange his clothes. I am most nearly affected when he hurls a boot or lashes out to break the slate. I have once even been pushed to the ground by a misplaced blow.'

'He does not know what he does, Johnson. He cannot hear what goes on behind him, he would not have known that you cried out or that you hit the floor with a thud.' Her resolution wavered and she turned to confront the man to lend power to her earnest entreaty. 'You said yourself that it is a recent affliction; he is not yet used to the limitations it places upon him. I beg you to have a care, give him some little more time.'

Johnson stiffened at her appeal; he knew this interview would be difficult but he had steeled himself to have it. The day before he had suffered from a tirade of abuse from his employer, which had culminated in him having to dodge a glass paperweight. He was not prepared to expose himself further to behaviour that was becoming increasingly dangerous.

'I will not remain with him any longer, Madam. You request more time for him to become accustomed but tomorrow is the last day of February and he has been convalescing since September. I believe I have given him long enough, if not to come to terms with his loss of hearing, at least to moderate his behaviour in favour of others. I am nearing the end of my years in service and I have not spent the better part of forty years looking after gentlemen to become the butt of a young man's displeasure at the course his life has taken.'

Mrs Leighterton knew at last that the valet was determined. 'Have you told him?' she asked, resignation creeping into her voice.

'Madam, if he had once read the words I had written on the slate, if he had once acknowledged a nod or shake of the head, I would not be standing in front of you now, but Mr Leighterton remains shut away in a world of his own, determined not to aid discourse between any of us and himself in any way.'

'So what arrangements have you made? When do you intend to leave us? Where do you plan to go?'

Mr Johnson heaved a sigh. 'I have found a young man from the village of my birth, who knowing the full sum of the situation is prepared to stand as valet to Mr Leighterton. He is a young man of conscience and dedication; he has a widowed mother and four siblings to support and has been looking to come into service since he finished his studies. He is perhaps more lettered than many of my ilk but under the circumstances I thought it no bad thing. He will arrive tomorrow and I will be taking him through the household's routine then.'

'But where will you go, Mr Johnson? As yet you have asked for no references. Few men would leave with no certainty of a position to go to.'

Mr Johnson, who thus far had looked her squarely in the face, now could not meet her eye.

'You may have heard that there is a position of valet being advertised at Holm Oak Reach', he said with a rush. 'I have had some correspondence with the butler, a Mr Timery, who is currently in charge.'

'You would leave here to become the bailiff's valet?' cried Mrs Leighterton, outraged and astonished.

'I understand that Mr Smithson is more gentlemanly than his previous employment might imply. Mr Timery has recommended him to me with some force and was good enough to suggest that I might be just the person they were seeking.'

Mrs Leighterton collapsed into a chair and shook her head first in disbelief and then in dismay. She wanted to remonstrate but Johnson's mind was clearly made up. She accepted that he would not have taken this step lightly and she was mortified that her stepson's behaviour should have made him choose to embrace an employer of such uncertain social standing rather than continue in his present post. For a moment, with her head bowed, she struggled to maintain her outward composure.

'Very well,' she said at last. 'I accept that you have been provoked into this action but I cannot like it. Nor can I think very highly of a man who is prepared to poach his neighbour's manservant. It does not augur well for him.'

'I can assure you, Madam' – Johnson rushed to counteract any unfavourable impression his actions might give of his new master – 'that Mr Smithson knows not that I come from here.'

'Then he is being ill served by his butler,' replied Mrs Leighterton tartly. 'For it will most certainly get about and cause ill feeling.'

'I am sorry for it, Madam,' said Johnson sadly 'but I will not change my course of action and only beg you to allow me to go with your blessing.'

Mrs Leighterton swivelled around in her chair so that he could barely see her profile.

'Go,' she said, waving him away with her hand, 'and send Cleverley to me.'

'Very well, Madam,' said Johnson, withdrawing in no good order. The interview had shaken him but left him no less determined to quit what had now become a very unhappy household.

While she waited for Cleverley to respond to her summons, Mrs Leighterton could not but wonder whether he too would like to escape the bounds of this blighted house. She stood up and walked to her desk, which was littered with letters and invitation cards. The local society were fascinated by her son's behaviour and repeatedly tried by fair means or foul to get sight or sound of him, so that they could marvel or disapprove depending on their inclination. So often the house would be inundated with morning callers, ever hopeful that Mr Edmund would come amongst them and give a show of his ill temper. With an agitated hand, Mrs Leighterton swept all the cards into the basket on the floor by the desk just as Cleverley entered the room. He had most certainly seen her pettish action but made no comment, only turning to the footman and requesting that he bring the mistress some refreshment.

Mrs Leighterton moved once more to the fire as Cleverley came back into the room.

'So at what point were you a party to Johnson's going?' she demanded acidly, at once appalled at her own antagonistic behaviour when she needed all the support she could master from those who remained behind.

'I was only told of it this morning after breakfast, Madam,' said Cleverley soothingly. 'I believe Mr Johnson had the whole turn of events worked out before he broached the subject.'

'And this boy he plans to have take his place? What do you think of that?'

'I think we have no choice, Madam, no choice at all. Any valet who moves in polite circles will know the score and is unlikely to accept the post.'

Mrs Leighterton's eyes flashed. 'Are you trying to imply that my stepson is the talk of the town?'

'I am afraid so, Madam,' said Cleverley apologetically. 'Need I remind you that when his friends from his Company visited him, he spurned their overtures of friendship, making them feel most unwelcome? All three were from noble families. There is very little chance of the story not getting about, I'll be bound.'

Mrs Leighterton's spurt of temper died and all that remained was a dull ache in her heart.

'Forgive me,' she said. 'I am so sickened by this desertion yet I cannot blame Johnson. Although I wish him well with his new employer, he may not find it as conducive as he hopes. I have heard much talk of the local gentry's plans to shun the new incumbent at Holm Oak Reach.'

On Mrs Leighterton recovering her temper, Cleverley had picked up the waste paper basket and was now retrieving the correspondence, which he laid back on the desk in neat piles.

'It is all words, Madam,' he said sagely. 'Where a man owns a large estate there is always going to be contact with neighbours. Most surely the hunt will want to retain the use of the land. The shooting fraternity will still want to enjoy the best coverts around and curiosity will get the better of them. I do not see Mr Smithson outcast for long.'

Mrs Leighterton gave an unladylike snort of laughter. 'You know I was worried you too would leave me, Cleverley,' she said conversationally, 'but I had forgotten in my distress how you have seen me through dark times before. Thank you for your wise counsel and moderate opinions.'

'You are most welcome, Madam, as always. And now can I press you to some tea and toast?'

Determinedly unaware of the changes that were about to take place around him, Edmund Leighterton snarled his way through the day. He had lately taken up riding again and now had further victims on whom he could vent his spleen. Such was the depth of his inner despair; he neither recognised nor understood how his unhappiness affected others. He had not seen the hours his devoted groom had pored over his letters, in order to be better able to communicate with him, so he knew nothing of the devastation caused in that man's heart when he knocked the slate he was holding containing his carefully drawn words of welcome to the ground. To Edmund nothing compared to his own misery and loss, and self-pity now cocooned him so that nothing and no-one could reach him. He shunned all company and he ignored any attempts to communicate with him. He therefore made no reference to a young man appearing in his bedroom alongside Johnson the next morning. He suffered himself to be ministered to without curbing any of his usual bad temper. He no longer changed for dinner, so did not summon his valet before the evening meal, and having sullenly ignored his stepmother throughout the duration of its eating, he then went and, as had already become another of his customs, drank himself senseless in one of the back parlours by the light of a couple of candles. He was therefore not acquainted with who it was that had carried him to bed and was completely oblivious to Johnson's departure early the next morning.

His head aching and his mouth dry, Edmund Leighterton woke around nine o'clock the next morning and tugged viciously on the bell rope. Young Albert Purvis arrived quickly, glad that he had laid out suitable attire for his volatile master the night before.

'Who the devil are you?' demanded Edmund as soon as he realised that someone other than Johnson was holding up his cravat for him.

'Purvis, Sir,' the young man replied, knowing full well that he would not be heard and that the piece of paper on which he had inscribed his name would be ripped to shreds as soon as he presented it to his new employer.

Edmund cast but a fleeting glance at the paper and turned his back on the hand extending it. 'Get me Johnson,' he snarled, 'I will have no other.'

Purvis stood his ground until Edmund whirled around, his arms raised. 'Get out and get me Johnson,' he yelled. Seeing the intent in the man's eyes, Purvis withdrew hastily as he had been advised to do by Johnson. Edmund was left to make what he would of the non-appearance of his valet. It was only after he had waited some twenty minutes that he accepted that Johnson was not coming to him. Be the man dead or ill he did not know but his absence lit a spark of alarm within him. He struggled into his clothes and strode down the corridor to the landing where he bellowed for his parent.

'Mother, Mother,' he yelled at the top of his voice.

Mrs Leighterton, thankfully close at hand, came out into the hall and looked up into his angry face as he hung over the banisters.

'Where is Johnson?' He hurled the question at her.

Mrs Leighterton took up a slate, which was lying on the ornamental table by the wall and began to write an explanation. Taking one glance at what she was doing Edmund flung himself away from the banisters and ran down the stairs, grabbing a heavy coat from the stand by the front door. He tugged the door open and plunged through it and hurried away to the stables. Mrs Leighterton, her face a study of distress, turned on her heel and went back into the morning room, where she could indulge her misery in peace, away from the fascinated eyes of the servants.

8

*S*lowly, slowly as spring came nearer, Elena and Polly familiarised themselves with their new home and position in life. There had been very few visitors thus far. Most held the winter weather to be their excuse although many of those who voiced this had no difficulty in wending their way to the Leightertons, ever hopeful of seeing one of the outbursts from Edmund which had in no way abated with the passage of time.

Polly continued frail, and though eating quite well did not seem to be gaining much weight. Elena feared it was the state of her nerves that worried it away, for Polly still could not grasp that her good fortune was permanent and would not be whisked away from her by a throw of the dice or a twist of fate. Mr Smithson had been unable to settle on a suitable companion for the young ladies although he had interviewed more than half a dozen. They seemed to fall into one of only two moulds, either dragon-like, expecting the girls to conform to a strict code of conduct neither would have enjoyed, or too meek to lend the social gravitas the girls needed. He had been luckier in finding them lady's maids, who cheerfully fulfilled their dressing needs, and he and Johnson had quickly established a rapport. And if Johnson sometimes felt a twinge of guilt that he had left young Purvis a poisoned chalice, such was the comfort he now found himself in that he regularly convinced himself it was his entitlement after so many years of looking after other people's needs.

Young Jessamy, whose school attendance had been disrupted by the delay in the family's arrival in Sussex, had swiftly found himself companions, having discovered that the tenant farmer at the home farm was blessed with two young sons of a similar age to himself. He had boldly ridden out to investigate on one of the working ponies and had introduced himself to them when he discovered them making a den in the adjoining woods. It mattered not to these three young men whether it rained or snowed, they stalked pigeons with catapults and taught the farmer's rough terriers to catch them rabbits which they skinned and ate from a spit over fires they had kindled themselves. They were watched over by an indulgent gamekeeper who was pleased to see that the new young master was well versed in country ways. Only once did he have to tell them something and they would adhere to his stipulation. They kept well away from his pheasant drives and, as spring arrived, they respected the sites of nesting birds and were careful not to disturb them. Tolputt only had good words to say about these lads. That very little book learning was achieved passed everyone by. Mr Smithson was too taken up with acquainting himself with his new property to wonder what his son did all day as, thanks to Mrs Timery's kind offices, he would arrive neat and scrubbed at the dinner table each evening. Elena, too, was too much occupied with the care of Polly to do more than ensure that her little brother had eaten a hearty breakfast before he set off in the morning. There was plenty of time, she told herself, for her brother to have book learning later on in life. So Jessamy was allowed to have his freedom and as it caused no complaints, no-one at Holm Oak Reach interfered with his activities.

As the sun became stronger, Elena persuaded Polly to take up walking. The park was blessed with so many avenues, carpeted first with snowdrops, then daffodils with the promise of bluebells to come, that they could have spent every day taking a different route and enjoying a variety of vistas, but Elena was beginning to feel a little trapped inside the park walls. She wanted to see what villages and towns lay beyond and she had to admit to needing more stimulating company. Polly was a dear but she had no wider knowledge than the situation she found herself in and Elena missed desperately the lively conversations she had enjoyed with the Delrymple girls. She wrote to them, of course, but it was without the same satisfaction of the days when she had sat amongst them and regaled them with all she had heard in the village.

After six weeks of confinement within the park's environs, Elena was sufficiently chaffed to encourage her cousin to join her in accompanying the groom to the smithy in the nearby village of Oxfold when three of the carriage horses needed re-shoeing and the estate's blacksmith was away visiting a sick relative. The groom, rather overwhelmed by the responsibility, was almost more difficult to persuade than Polly. However, eventually he agreed, bringing with him a stable boy to manage the horses while he drove the ladies.

On entering Oxfold, Elena was enchanted by the red stone houses that lined their way. There was a bustle that thrilled her and struck a chord with her previous life. She acknowledged or greeted anyone who looked her way and encouraged Polly to do the same.

At the smithy it seemed that half the district had brought their horses to be shod and whilst the Holm Oak groom had no difficulty in claiming precedence even he did not expect the blacksmith to break off midway through one horse to start on his.

Aware that a chilly wind had sprung up, Elena suggested that she and Polly might go for a little walk rather than shiver under rugs in the open trap.

Together they marvelled at the decorative tiles on the cottages and the older timbered houses with jaunty angles and wavering roofs. It was not long before they had reached the end of the street and, knowing that it would be a while yet before their horses were ready, the girls pressed on along the primrose-lined lane. The banks were high with hedges on the top so the girls could not see much beyond, but such was the prettiness of the flora that they were beguiled into walking further than perhaps they should have done. When a sudden shower of rain burst upon them from nowhere, Elena was made abundantly aware of her own rash conduct. Although dressed in a warm pelisse, Polly had begun to shiver.

Elena guided her quickly under a thick holm oak tree, hoping it would protect them from the worst of the rain, but such was the force of the shower that it penetrated the leaves and left their shoulders and bonnets soaked. Then the shower was over as quickly as it had begun and Elena hurried Polly back along the lane towards the village. They walked briskly for nearly twenty minutes but Polly was tiring and Elena found she no longer recognised the route. Somehow, in their haste, they had missed their way and were now thoroughly lost.

'Please, Elena, I can go no further,' moaned Polly, folding her arms across her front and bowing her head. 'I am so cold, please can we stop, pray.'

For a moment Elena was undecided, wanting to hurry onwards in search of the village but she knew she could not leave Polly unattended so she put her arm around the girl and led her to a tree stump in the hedgerow where she might be seated. Taking off her own pelisse, Elena placed it so that she and her cousin might sit on it and be protected from the damp of the improvised seat.

'I am sure someone will be along soon to aid us,' she said to Polly, determinedly matter of fact in the hope of convincing herself as well as her cousin that all would be well.

They sat in stoical silence for what seemed like an age before the sound of a single horse's hooves could be heard approaching along the road.

Edmund Leighterton was on one of his solitary rides. It was only on horseback that he found any solace. The thud of the horse's hooves on the ground would carry through his body and allow him to believe he could hear it. He could fool his mind into translating the crackles and whistles in his head into the birdsong he had been used to being able to hear and the sensation of the wind or the rain on his face chased away briefly the dark inner gloom that beset him. He would not normally have taken the lane, preferring to gallop across the fields, sure in the knowledge he would meet no-one. Today, however, the short, heavy burst of rain had turned the ground into a quagmire and in the interests of his own safety and that of his horse's he had pushed through the hedge and on to the carriageway.

He saw the figures up ahead of him and ground his teeth in irritation. He had no desire to acknowledge anyone else's presence or be acknowledged by them. As he drew closer, he saw that they were young ladies and that one had risen purposely from her seat to waylay him. He made to ignore her and squeezed his calves against the horse so that it picked up speed as it covered the gap between them. However when he made to go past her, studiously setting his head away from her direction, he was staggered to have the reins of his horse grasped and the animal brought to a standstill.

'Stop, Sir, please stop, I beg of you.'

He turned to look down at the agonised face below him and could see the lips moving.

'Unhand my horse, Madam,' he said angrily. 'I can be of no use to you. I cannot hear a word you say, so unless you have a slate and chalk about your person, I can do nothing for you.' The irony of his own words was not lost on the man who had thus far broken every slate before him.

He looked fleetingly across at the pale girl still sitting on the stump and saw her recoil at his words. He imagined it to be at his infirmity, not for a moment appreciating that the harshness of the tone in his voice and the undertones of violent anger in his demeanour could generate such a reaction. He brought his gaze away from her immediately and looked down into the dark eyes of the lady at his horse's head. She was looking pensive, her expressive face giving away that her mind was very busy. Suddenly she had released his horse and captured his free hand, which had been resting on his thigh. Such was the extraordinary nature of her action that Edmund did not immediately drag it free. He looked down in fascination and stupefaction as she turned it palm upwards and began to pass one finger across it. He felt the movement but could not interpret it until it came to him that he had just had an 'L' drawn across the surface of his hand. It was quickly gone and almost before he had acknowledged it another letter followed, this time a 'P'.

'A moment, Madam,' he said, finding his voice. 'If you would recommence and more slowly, I believe I might be able to follow you.'

Painstakingly the girl traced out the words. 'We are lost. Please help us. My cousin is very frail.'

Edmund had been watching the movement across his palm but as she finished the final word with a brush of her hand across his he looked again at the other girl. She was indeed looking very frail and almost ill. He released his feet from the stirrups, swinging his leg over the horse's back and slipped to the ground.

'Where do you need to be, Madam?' he asked. All the latent chivalry, which had been dormant since the previous summer, surfaced to banish any churlish thoughts he had previously been nurturing.

The determined little hand spelt out Holm Oak Reach. Edmund took a step back from her, nearly bumping into the horse. The look of appraisal he gave her should have offended her but the young lady squared up to him, in no way intimidated.

'And your name?' he asked, his curiosity now firmly engaged. The young woman whom he suspected must be very cold in the absence of her pelisse, which was now draped around her cousin who had risen to her feet, was made of stern stuff.

The girl pointed inward to herself and wrote her name for him on his outstretched palm, then indicated her cousin and wrote another name.

'Well, Miss Smithson, if you will hold my horse, I will endeavour to place Miss McNeath upon it and I will escort you home.' She faced him then and he saw her lips move but he did not need her to write it on his hand. For he had understood their movement as he had understood the look of profound gratitude and relief in her brown eyes. Inside his head it felt as if a door had been opened and a candle had been lit: there was understanding to be had from expression and movement; why had he not allowed himself to see it before? He marvelled at his own stupidity as well as at Miss Smithson's courage and determination to break into the world in which he had cocooned himself. There was no time to indulge in self-recrimination or speculation on how he might improve his lot; Miss McNeath was clearly in immediate need of succour and attention. Removing the pelisse from her bony shoulders so that Miss Smithson might wear it again, he stripped off his own overcoat and wrapped Polly in it. Then, making nothing of her weight he tossed her on to the back of his horse and held her there until the horse had settled and she had made herself as comfortable as possible with one leg encircling the pommel.

'My horse is not used to a lady rider, Miss Smithson, so I would ask you to lead it awhile; I must remain by Miss McNeath's side in case she should feel unsafe.'

His instructions were immediately adhered to but it was soon seen that the horse, tired from its long ride, was happy to amble along with its fair burden, so much lighter than its usual rider. So it was not long before Edmund allowed himself the luxury of walking beside Miss Smithson, the better to become acquainted with her. He now led the horse with one hand, deliberately leaving his left hand free for Miss Smithson to use.

'You may think me ignorant, Miss Smithson,' he said by way of a start, 'but I did not know Holm Oak Reach had new occupants. The last I heard it was empty and lawyers were searching for the heir. How long have you resided there?' His own words startled him, as he realised they were so true. He had heard this information because it had been before the battle that had robbed him of his hearing. Almost he succumbed to a burst of his previous ill temper, but even before the bile had risen it had been captured, as had his hand as Miss Smithson replied.

'January. My father, William Smithson, is the heir.'

He had to review his own words to explain the cryptic nature of her answers.

'So you and your family have been installed since January?'

She nodded.

'And how is your father related to the previous incumbent?'

'From a second cousin, via a great-grandfather.' The little hand traced out the words.

'Tenuous!'

She nodded again, a smile in her eyes.

'Well, I do congratulate you on your good fortune, Miss Smithson. So give me the details of your family.'

For Edmund, that he could hold a conversation with someone without the introduction of exasperation or pity was a revelation. Miss Smithson had a way of combining a minimum of written words with a wide spectrum of facial expressions, which illuminated her meaning. Edmund was no fool; he knew that the method she was using would be totally unacceptable in company but it allowed him to see that he must let the use of chalk and slate into his life if he wanted to further his acquaintance with this formidable young lady. Miss McNeath was all but forgotten except in that she must be cherished and he needed to be assured that she still clung to the back of the horse. He wanted the walk with Miss Smithson never to end as she toppled the barriers he had built around himself and communicated to him the story of their arrival in Sussex.

It was not too long before they had reached the outer wall of the park and not more than half an hour later that the house was reached. The sun was now low in the sky and the temperature was falling. Elena had abandoned her conversation with Edmund as she became increasingly anxious about her cousin. She could not have been more relieved when they reached the gravel and made for the front door.

'I will leave you here,' said Edmund as he lifted the slight girl down from the horse's back. 'You will not want me to intrude.'

'No,' she said forcefully and as the door opened to reveal her father, followed by an anxious entourage coming hastily towards them, she grasped Edmund's hand and pulled him with her to greet them.

9

*I*n the bustle that followed Edmund caught little of what was said. Clearly an explanation was given by the chastened groom who had returned to Holm Oak Reach post-haste when he discovered the loss of his mistress and her cousin. Miss Smithson, after taking both of Edmund's hands and mouthing her thanks had vanished to attend to Miss McNeath and apply herself to getting warm; only Mr Smithson remained but his presence had been enough to set the seal on a day of revelation for Edmund. The man's gratitude was so heartily expressed that Edmund could understand every word with its endorsements of handshake and emphatic head movements. Even when the man offered him refreshments Edmund was able to understand because it followed on so naturally in the way events unfold at times like these.

'You are too kind, Sir,' said Edmund just as if he had heard the words as clear as a bell. 'But my mother awaits me at the Manor, we keep country hours and I would not want her to have to hold dinner for me. She would only become anxious.'

'Of course, my boy, of course,' agreed Mr Smithson, slapping him on the back before holding the coat himself for the young man to put on.

Once on his horse, Edmund gave lie to the words of concern for his stepmother, which had harped back to another life. He allowed the horse to dawdle and he relived the afternoon's events, feeling again the touch of the girl's hand as she described to him her life in Leicestershire, of Mr Sawyer and his pursuit of her and of the reclaiming of Miss McNeath. His mind, which had previously been closed to all other considerations than his own miserable concerns, now revelled in these new thoughts. He watched the sun set in a glorious blaze of colour and felt a stirring of remorse as he considered his actions over the last few months. At first it was only a niggling feeling that he had isolated himself unnecessarily, but when he reached the portals of his own home he looked about with fresh eyes as if wakened from a long sleep. As he handed his damp and mis-treated coat to Cleverley he was prompted to thank him for his kind attention and, catching a look at the man's face, was mortified to see the surprise exhibited there. In deep chagrin Edmund Leighterton stood passively while a bemused Purvis helped him into his evening wear before joining his stepmother in the small dining room for dinner.

Clarissa Leighterton had managed to recover in part from the anxiety she had been experiencing as a result of Edmund's late return to the Manor. She had paced the rooms with a view of the drive, agonising over whether she should send out a search party, knowing with certainty that it would ignite Edmund's ready ire if he had not needed rescue. A wave of relief on his return had left her feeling weak and she had needed the combined efforts of her maid and the chambermaid to have her changed for dinner.

Since his illness she had given up waiting for him in the drawing room and had moved to the dining room. There had seemed no benefit in multiplying the occasions that exasperated his temper.

Now she waited nervously. It was so unprecedented for Edmund to be late returning from his ride that she had convinced herself that something must have happened to upset him. She was therefore inordinately surprised to have him arrive properly attired for the first time since his illness and in thoughtful mood. Unusually he waited for her to be seated before taking his own place at the table and though he made no attempt to converse with her, he appeared uniquely conscious of her needs and passed dishes he knew she liked when the servants had withdrawn from the room. Afraid to do anything to break this mellow mood, Mrs Leighterton sat quietly and ate her meal, hopeful that Edmund would give her an inkling of what had brought about this longed-for change.

At the end of the meal, he rose when she did, bade her good night and was seen heading towards his bedchamber at an hour long before his customary time, without repairing in solitary misery to the parlour to drink until he was oblivious to his surroundings.

Edmund shrugged off his coat and cast himself full length on to the bed in which he had spent so many bitter and fevered weeks. He lay on his back, staring at the ceiling with which he was over-familiar. He knew every crack and stain, every swirl of the plaster moulding and crenellated cornicing but tonight he was not seeing them clearly as an image of Miss Smithson's vivid and mobile face rose in their stead. He dwelt on the details he could remember: the expressive dark eyes and the wisps of brown hair escaping from her bonnet, sticking damply to her face as a result of the downpour; her trim figure revealed because she had given up her pelisse in favour of her cousin; her voice – such had been the clarity of her written words and facial expressions that he could convince himself he had heard it and that it had been clear and musical. He recalled the strength of character in sweet Miss Smithson's face, which even he could see had been engendered by the selfless care for her cousin.

Having dwelt for more time than he liked to acknowledge on Miss Smithson's charms, he found himself pondering when they might next meet and where. This was easily answered; if Mr Smithson was acquainted with the ways of society, as Edmund was sure he would be, he would bring his daughter on a morning call to thank him for his kind offices. The only question would be whether Mr Smithson would exhibit extraordinary civility and call the very next day. It occurred to Edmund that he must apprise Cleverley of the possibility, as the butler would not be aware that there had already been contact between the two houses. As his mind worked around the possibilities for the morrow, a niggle, which had been festering in the back of his mind since the ride home, now made its presence felt with a vengeance. A wave of shame assailed him, as he looked back at his conduct over the past few months. The few looks he had cast in his stepmother's direction that night at dinner had shaken him to the core. He could see without being told what a toll his illness and subsequent behaviour had taken on her. She had sat rigidly but with a certain edginess whenever he had turned towards her. She had almost appeared scared of him. Edmund sat up with a jerk; swinging his legs over the side of the bed he ran his hands through his sandy hair. Finally he had to admit that his stepmother, whom he had blamed for all that was now wrong with his life, was in no way culpable. It was he who had strode through life, determined to follow the road he had chosen without recourse to the feelings of others, and in particular his stepmother. She, despite her affectionate care of him and selfless regard for his concerns, had never been able to overcome the resentment the small boy had felt at having another woman thrust in the place of his own adored mother just a year after her demise. Edmund had never quite forgiven his father for replacing her so rapidly, being too young to realise that in his father's case it should have been seen as a compliment to his mother's memory. For he missed her so much that his only solace was to try and fill the void she had left behind. Edmund's father had insisted that Edmund call his stepmother Mother, so there was no reminder of his loss. As Edward reached adulthood he could have dropped its use but he had deliberately retained it as a barb.

He was brought to realise that he had a lot to thank his stepmother for and that she deserved that he should eliminate many of the causes of her distress. It was fortunate that he had retired early for it was many hours before the ferment in his mind subsided enough for sleep. Before drowsiness eventually overtook him, Edmund had plotted a course of renewal and reconciliation, which he hoped his stepmother would embrace.

The cold woke him early despite only a few hours' slumber. He was still dressed but he had fallen asleep on the bed and so had not benefited from the heavy covers. He raised his head and looked blearily in the direction of the fire, then raised himself to a sitting position. The fire was no more than a few glowing embers in the ash. A spurt of anger rose within him, to be captured like a bird in a net. He had been about to tug on the bell rope and let his rage that the fire had not been made fall upon the hapless servant who was brave enough to respond to his bell pull. Then he recalled his own behaviour only the week before when he had been surprised by the presence of the new valet bringing him washing water without being asked. Edmund fell back against the pillows, both nauseated and appalled that he could have exhibited such ungentlemanly conduct. He wondered fleetingly whether this would preclude this new man agreeing to help him in the way his heart-searching had persuaded him he needed.

He sat up once more and put his feet down gingerly on the bare floor. Having stood up he moved his shoulders in large circles trying to loosen the muscles, and then taking a deep breath he gave the bell rope a measured tug.

It did not take Purvis many minutes to appear. He fumbled with the door because he was carrying a steaming pitcher, then came warily into the room. He was confronted by the view of his employer leaning against the great wooden end of the bed. That he was dressed evidently surprised the valet. Edmund saw all the uncertainties and emotions cross the younger man's face as he took in the crumpled white shirt, the unbrushed hair and the general dishevelled nature of Edmund's appearance.

Edmund straightened and stood before his servant, not knowing how to commence a conversation that was weeks overdue. Edmund cleared his throat and manfully met Purvis's startled gaze.

'I'm afraid I know not your name, nor how you came to be here,' he managed. 'But I must presume you have taken Johnson's place.'

'Yes, Sir.' Purvis nodded as he spoke, not knowing how best to communicate with this changeling.

'Did he leave or is he dead?' Edmund realised too late he could not expect a reply he could understand if he gave the man alternatives. He drew a deep breath and started again.

'Did he leave?'

'Yes, Sir.' Purvis repeated his previous reply, marvelling at the exchange.

'Did he leave because of my treatment of him?' Edmund watched the valet's face; there were a few moments of confusion, and clearly the valet was deciding how best to answer.

'Yes, Sir,' he said at last, once again accompanying the words with a nod.

Edmund turned away and walked to the window, his demeanour indicative of his smouldering anger. Purvis hastily put the pitcher down by the washbowl in readiness for a strategic retreat from whatever missile might come to his employer's hand. There was a leaden silence until suddenly Edmund heaved a ragged breath and turned back to confront the valet.

'Thank you for your honesty,' he said with constraint. Then he paused, as he realised he still did not know his manservant's name.

'And you are?' he asked eventually, not at once appreciating that he had set a test for the young man's ingenuity.

Purvis did not immediately attempt to reply. His eyes scoured the room for any remnants of the slates or pieces of notepaper Mrs Leighterton had originally kept everywhere when her stepson might have wanted to communicate with someone. It was clear that the room was devoid of anything that might remind its occupant of his infirmity. Then Purvis recalled the laundry list, which he had stuffed into his pocket the night before when he had discovered it discarded on the backstairs. He withdrew it and, seeing a small piece of charcoal still in the grate, he bent down and picked it up. Negligent of the blacking of his fingers but with care not to extend the dust to the furniture or his clothes he wrote his name on the crumpled piece of paper.

Edmund's eyes widened in surprise as he watched Purvis's inventiveness. As on the day before he felt humbled by others' willingness to overcome the blockade that had seemed impenetrable to him. He read the name and was cut to the quick that Purvis saw it as necessary to put 'Sir' after it. He felt he did not deserve the deference.

'Well, Purvis,' he said, conscious that there was a constriction in his throat. 'You must know that I owe you an apology. I have behaved in a manner completely contrary to my station in life. I was born a gentleman; I should conduct myself as a gentleman. I crave your forgiveness.'

'You have it, Sir,' said Purvis, carried away by the magnitude of what he was being offered. He thought that this oversight might ignite his employer's anger but Edmund Leighterton must have understood the sentiment if not heard the words for a slight smile crinkled the edges of his lips.

'Thank you,' he said gratefully. There was another pause as Edmund searched for the words to articulate his request. Purvis waited, knowing there was something of great import to come but with no inkling of what it might be.

'I have not been used to beg favours from others, Purvis,' Edmund said eventually, 'but I have one to ask of you.'

Purvis raised his eyebrows in mute enquiry. Edmund took it as encouragement to continue.

'It was yesterday, Purvis, that for the first time I discovered that conversing with others is not wholly reliant on hearing what they say. To date I have refused to acknowledge gestures, even expressions such as yours just now. I persuaded myself that they were the spawn of pity.' A look of deep distaste crossed his handsome face. 'I will not be pitied,' he said forcefully.

Purvis kept his own face bland, masking the unflattering reflection that had flitted into his head.

Edmund's eyes met his and Purvis sustained a shock as the other man spoke again. 'You think I speak a falsehood, don't you, you think that no-one has pitied me more than I have myself? Don't you, don't you?'

Purvis gave a gesture of futility with his hand. There was no point in denying it for it was the truth, after all, and he had no way of softening it with words that could be understood by Edmund Leighterton.

'Get out,' snarled Edmund. 'Get out. There is nothing you can do for me.'

Purvis turned on his heel and made for the door but even before his hand, placed on the handle, had a chance to turn it, Edmund was calling him back.

'No, no, this is not how it was meant to be. Stay Purvis, stay please.' The appeal held so much anguish that Purvis turned without a moment's hesitation.

'Thank you,' breathed Edmund as he digested that he had not yet burned all his bridges. Once again there was silence as each man collected himself. Edmund, still so full of bitterness and frustration, paced the room, battling to get control of his emotions. 'Are you a man of letters, Purvis?' he at last enquired. Purvis nodded. 'Then I must explain. Yesterday when I watched our neighbour speak, I saw the words clearly and knew what he was saying. If there are words such as "good day" and "thank you" that can be followed by the movement of the mouth then there must be many others. If I watch as people speak, I believe I can understand what they mean. Can you help me to learn how words look as they are spoken?'

Purvis, whose unlikely education had included some study of ancient Greek with the local rector during a time when it had been hoped that he might go far in the academic world, recalled the writing of Aristotle who had thought that it was impossible to teach the deaf. In one mental leap he wiped such thinking from his mind and nodded vigorously.

'Good, then we will start tomorrow, early so that no-one will discover what we are about until I have mastered it.'

Taking this to mean that their dealings were to remain a secret, Purvis spent the next few minutes working on how best to do this in his head as he helped his master into a clean coat and supervised the tying of his cravat.

Once fully dressed Edmund descended the stairs, determined to take breakfast with his stepmother. He knew that whatever his attempts to communicate better with those around him, he could no longer sustain his previous behaviour. The appalling thought of Miss Smithson's face if she saw him demonstrate such ill will convinced him of that.

Clarissa Leighterton was still sitting at the breakfast table.

'Good morning, Mama,' said Edmund as he entered the room. She turned in her chair in surprise.

'Good morning, Edmund.' He caught the movement of her lips and knew that she had replied. Helping himself to food from the selection of dishes on the sideboard, he then moved to sit at her right hand.

Silence ensued as Mrs Leighterton cast around in her mind for what next to do or say. She longed to ask him what had brought about this extraordinary change in him. Indeed she had wasted several sleepless hours throughout the night trying to explain even the alteration in him the evening before but his behaviour in joining her so willingly this morning was unprecedented.

After a little while when he had eaten perhaps half his plateful, he turned his face to look at her.

'Are you receiving morning callers today, Mama?'

'Yes,' she replied bewildered.

Edmund did not quite catch the word shape.

'If you could nod or shake your head, I would appreciate it,' he said gently.

Her expression was so wary and startled that Edmund almost abandoned his breakfast in shame. Instead he forced himself to sit quietly waiting, hoping that she would take the risk and respond.

'Yes,' she nodded at last, 'Yes I am receiving today.'

'Thank you.' Edmund thrust his plate away from him and got to his feet. It was all too much, this awakening; it assailed him with remorse and guilt. 'If you'll excuse me.' He quitted the room, leaving Mrs Leighterton at a loss as to what to make of it. She knew not whether she had given the answer he had wanted or not. Cleverley, had he not been so surprised at his own subsequent exchange with his employer, could have enlightened her.

Edmund, remembering as he strode across the hallway his concern of the night before that Cleverley might deny the Smithsons if he was not apprised of their possible visit, knew he needed to speak to the man. Fortuitously at that moment the butler appeared from the nether regions of the house.

'Ah, Cleverley,' he said as though it was the most normal thing in the world for him to consult with his butler. 'Should Mr Smithson and his family call, I would be grateful if I could be informed of it.'

'Yes, Sir, certainly, Sir,' replied Cleverley, not able to mask his surprise any better than Mrs Leighterton had been able to.

10

*C*oming slowly down the grand staircase, Elena's thoughts were so preoccupied by concerns for her cousin that for once she did not marvel at the grandeur of the black and white hall before her.

'Ah! There you are, my dear.' Mr Smithson came bustling out of a door below her. Even before she had descended to his level he continued: 'I would that you would accompany me to pay a call on the Leightertons. Mr Leighterton's extraordinary civility in bringing you home yesterday behoves us to do so.'

'But what of my cousin Polly, Papa. I cannot leave her, surely.'

Mr Smithson looked up at her under his curly eyebrows. 'My dear Elena, you must not worry. I have it on good authority from Mrs Timery that your cousin is suffering from nothing more than a mild chill which does not even warrant the intervention of a doctor. Had I realised Polly would be the cause of you losing your customary cheerfulness, I would never have invited her to make her home with us.'

Elena had by now reached her father. She put out a beseeching hand. 'How can you say that, Papa? When she has suffered so much. How can you not want to help her?'

Mr Smithson covered his daughter's agitated hand with his own great paw. 'I did not say that I wished not to have helped her, only that her being here disturbs your peace and that I cannot like.'

He watched her mobile face as she digested his words.

'Come.' He drew her to the marble bench. 'Can you not tell me what about her causes you so much disquiet?'

Once seated Elena tried to find the words to describe the doubts and uncertainties that jostled daily in her head.

'Papa, I believe it is that I cannot convince her that she is safe and that this will not all be removed from her as quickly and as easily as it was given. And I am ashamed to admit that I fear that I cannot convince her because I cannot convince myself that it is truly ours. I have this overwhelming feeling that this is all temporary. That we are fleeting visitors and that one day someone will be found to whom it rightfully belongs and we will be left with nothing, not even the employment you were used to have with Lord Delrymple.'

William Smithson let go of her hand only so that he could pat it reassuringly. 'Do you not think that I have had all the same fears and uncertainties, that I did not put them to Mr Banbury at the time of him telling us we were the beneficiaries? I did repeatedly beg him for the sort of assurances you are looking for now. He is so strongly of the opinion that he has discovered the fate of all the possible preceding family members that he has no doubt that I am entitled to this house and this position. However.' Here his eyes took in the deepening look of concern on his daughter's face as he qualified his words. 'However, Mr Banbury who, being a family man himself, understood my fears of being cast adrift in the world if he was proved to be wrong, has used his powers as executor to make me a gift of a small lump sum and an income should someone else come along who has a rightful claim to the estate. We would be in a position to retire to a comfortable cottage and to put food on the table. I ask no more than that.'

'Neither do I,' agreed Elena, looking more cheerful. 'I will do my best to persuade Polly to let go of her fears as I shall most determinedly let go of mine.'

'Then will you accompany me to the Leightertons?'

'Most certainly I will, Papa. I would be delighted to do so.'

So, much to the astonishment of Mrs Leighterton, who was already holding court to at least three local families, a little after noon Cleverley announced to the room the arrival of Mr and Miss Smithson. Mrs Leighterton's eyes flew to Cleverley's face, for she wanted some explanation as to why these visitors had not been denied when as far as she was aware, they had had no introduction. All Cleverley could do was remain expressionless for he had not yet had a chance to inform Mrs Leighterton that her son had been expecting a call and seemingly welcomed it. Cleverley was still undecided whom to send to inform Mr Leighterton that his looked-for guests had arrived.

Faced with a room full of critical and curious faces, Elena quailed, but William Smithson had not been the silent observer of society for two decades not to know how to overcome this awkward moment. He had insisted on a description in minute detail of his hostess from Johnson and had no plans to make an error.

'My dear Mrs Leighterton,' he cried warmly, walking straight up to her. 'I came as I am sure you can imagine to express my deep obligation to your son for his kind offices to my daughter and her cousin yesterday. Miss McNeath sends her apologies for not being able to come in person to thank both him and you, but the astringencies of her ordeal have resulted in a chill and she has to remain in bed. My daughter, as you can see, is however made of sterner stuff.'

'Yes indeed, I mean …' Mrs Leighterton cast wildly around the room for help. She could think of nothing Edmund might have done that would warrant such praise. Her neighbours however were equally at a loss. They had come as ever in the to-date vain hope that Edmund would appear and exhibit some of his by now notorious bad behaviour. To have someone arrive and praise him to the hilt was unnerving and possibly even disappointing.

Outside the room Cleverley had decided that Purvis would have to search out Edmund and tell him that his guests had arrived. Cleverley sustained another shock when he discovered Purvis quite willing to carry out this service.

The young valet made haste to his master's bedchamber, knowing that Edmund had repaired there after breakfast. He opened the door to find Edmund sitting in a chair in the bay window reading a book. Purvis walked straight in and went abruptly up to him. The movement must have caught his eye for Edmund looked up from the text.

'Have they come?' he asked.

'Yes,' Purvis nodded.

Edmund put the book down carefully and then stood up. Purvis could see that he was nervous. As a distraction, he quickly reached for a clothes brush and started to brush away the invisible pieces of dust or hair on the coat.

'Thank you,' said Edmund rather weakly before pulling down his wine-red waistcoat with a decisive tug and making his way out of the room and down the stairs. Purvis followed him to the top of the stairs and wished he could have said good luck to him. If ever it was a case of Daniel entering the lions' den then this was it. There must be something very special about the Smithsons, Purvis concluded.

At the door to the withdrawing room, Cleverley made to open it for him, but Edmund stopped him with a shake of the head. Then he drew in a deep steadying breath and nodded.

Had he been able to hear, Edmund would have been greeted with an audible and collective gasp as many turned at the sound of the door and took in who was standing there.

The wall of delighted but curiously hostile faces was daunting. Poised for flight, Edmund stood momentarily in the doorway before William Smithson surged forward.

'My dear Mr Leighterton, how delighted I am to see you and be able to thank you for the service you rendered my daughter yesterday. You have my heartfelt gratitude.'

Somehow it did not matter that he could not hear what the other man was saying; Edmund knew that Mr Smithson was only reiterating what he had said the day before.

'You are very welcome, Mr Smithson,' Edmund said, accepting the outstretched hand and allowing his to be shaken vigorously. Now Mr Smithson was drawing in Mrs Leighterton.

'My daughter and her cousin had become grievously lost while out on a walk,' he explained to any one of the group around them who would listen. 'But luckily Mr Leighterton came upon them and brought them safely home. You will recall that there was a downpour yesterday. It was most fortuitous that he had them home so swiftly or Miss McNeath could have become seriously ill.'

Edmund let William Smithson run on as he could see that it was diverting attention away from him. Gradually, as his eyes scoured the occupants of the room for Miss Smithson, the sea of faces began to separate out into individuals he recognised. It came to him that he should be introducing his new friend to these neighbours if his stepmother had not already done so.

'Mr Smithson,' he said when next he saw that he had stopped speaking. 'Have you been introduced to Colonel Campden and his son, Jolyon?'

Mr Smithson indicated that he had not and soon Edmund was conducting his guest around the room. Clarissa Leighterton could only look on in amazement. Edmund had always been a good host, always finding a few key words about each person to allow a conversation to start up between previously unacquainted guests but he had made no attempt to have any contact with any of these people since his illness. She watched, her mind seething with conjecture while she chatted with her other guests, ensuring that they wanted for nothing and calling over the footmen when someone needed additional refreshment.

Miss Smithson had been further in the room than her father, having been quickly absorbed into a gaggle of chattering young ladies who had all wanted to know about her meeting with Edmund Leighterton. Elena had answered as best she could without giving anything away. She was aware that Edmund was an object of curiosity to them all. She had therefore deliberately not turned round to face the door when he came in and had tried to maintain the conversation with the Colonel's youngest daughter, Beatrice, who from the moment of Edmund's arrival made every attempt to peer over Elena's shoulder to get a view of him.

'Is he not handsome?' the girl whispered. 'Pray do have a peep, Miss Smithson; he looks so smart in that dark coat and snowy cravat. Will you not have a look? I have been wishful of meeting him this age, for I was still in the schoolroom when last our families met. Now of course, one hears such tales of his doings but looking at him today, one cannot credit it.'

Edmund had located Miss Smithson and was working his way towards her. He could tell by the slight hunch of her shoulders that she was having to listen to a conversation under sufferance. He guessed it was about him and found, in the midst of all these people and the role he was playing, that he wished desperately that he could hear what was being said about him. Then it occurred to him that it was likely to be uncomplimentary and a feeling of mortification assailed him as he thought of Miss Smithson being set against him by idle gossip.

He was behind her now and momentarily free of the guests he had set talking one to another. 'Miss Smithson.' Her name escaped his lips without him even quite realising it.

Elena turned and her face lit up at the sight of him. It took his breath away to see her shining eyes welcome him with so much goodwill after all his dark thoughts. It was all he could do to bow to the demure little curtsey she was making him. He longed to be able to talk to her unfettered by his own short-comings, yet he would not have missed their first encounter or the touch of her hand as she traced the letters for the world. He gave himself a mental shake; there were so many things he could not have now and had he not already decided that he should not ruin any further the life he did have?

'How do you do, Miss Smithson,' he said formally. 'I trust you have recovered from yesterday's ordeal.'

'Yes, thank you, Mr Leighterton,' she replied primly with an accompanying nod of the head.

'Excellent, and Miss McNeath? I do not see her here.' Elena considered for a moment, then opened her reticule and brought out a small slate which had but two words upon it: 'abed ill.'

Close by Mrs Leighterton held her breath for she feared the young lady had done the one thing that would upset her stepson. To her amazement he gave a crack of laughter and continued to exchange conversation with her as though there was nothing untoward in using the slate as a mode of communication. Mrs Leighterton felt tears prick her eyes and was not sure how she was going to sustain the small talk necessary on occasions such as these. However it seemed her guests were on the move. Perhaps disappointed by the normality of Edmund's behaviour, they had sated their desire to visit her. Mrs Leighterton divined that unless Edmund slipped back into his old ways, she would not be receiving so many morning callers in future. As she shook the hands of those departing in a near daze, she did not immediately appreciate that Mr Smithson was nearby, awaiting his turn with an expression on his face that told her he understood in no small part her feelings. When she was finally free to speak to him, she thanked him for coming with genuine warmth, almost the antithesis of her expressed sentiments before their meeting.

'As you know, I stand in your stepson's debt, Mrs Leighterton. Our cousin Polly is very fragile.'

'I believe, Sir,' she managed quietly, as her eyes looked once more towards Edmund and Elena, 'that it is more likely that we stand in yours.'

11

Next morning found Purvis, armed with a number of sheets of paper and writing slates, make his way early and unobtrusively to Edmund's bedchamber. It might be imagined that there would be no slates left in a house where they had been systematically smashed by the head of the household over an extended period but the lady of the house had insisted that a stock should be kept just in case he were ever to change his mind.

Mr Cleverley had caught Purvis raiding that stock and had demanded to be told what use Purvis planned to make of them. Unwilling to break his word to his employer he had to promise to replace them out of his own wages if he could not return them intact. He prayed that he could trust this new Edmund Leighterton not to let him down.

He had expected to find Edmund still on his couch but when he entered the room he found his employer dressed in shirt and breeches and moving a small table from the window embrasure to the centre of the room.

'Bring up another chair, man,' he said as Purvis deposited his burdens on the table. 'We will need to sit face to face.'

As instructed, Purvis drew up a chair across the table from his master and followed his lead by sitting down. Edmund looked into the eyes of the young, lean man and hoped that his demonstrable eagerness to help would continue beyond a few days. He heaved a sigh.

'Let us begin then,' he said. 'Where shall we start?'

To Edmund's surprise, Purvis had planned a lesson and had listed many of the common social phrases that Edmund had already begun to grasp. It made the lesson go quickly as much progress was made because it was built on that foundation. Neither man had any illusions that it would continue to be so easy.

To maintain the secrecy, the lesson finished in time for Edmund to complete his toilette and join his stepmother for breakfast. Today she had braved bringing a slate. If Miss Smithson had got away with it then she was prepared to try again.

One look at his furrowed brow made her think she had chosen ill and should perhaps have waited for further proof of his acceptance of the tool. She tried surreptitiously to slide the slate from the table into the folds of her skirt but his hand caught hers and stopped it. He said nothing, so she replaced the slate beside her plate and in expectation of an outburst she bowed her head.

Edmund had turned away to fill his own plate, not realising the effect of his action on his stepmother. He had merely wanted to reassure her that he would now use the slate. His furrowed brow had simply been the manifestation of tiredness brought on by two hours of study.

As he sat down beside her, he cast a look in her direction and was once more smitten by shame. She looked as though she expected to receive a blow. The enormity of what he saw there was too much, indicative as it was of a change in a woman who had always been so strong, and he could not find the words to apologise. In fact he believed there were not words sufficient enough to express his regret.

He cleared his throat. 'Mama ...'

She brought her head around slowly to face him and he saw a spark of hope in her eyes. What was she hoping for he wondered?

'Yes,' she said.

This time he saw the lip movement and understood it.

'If you wish to make a morning call to Holm Oak Reach, I will happily accompany you.'

'Thank you,' she replied faintly.

'When do you plan to go?'

Tentatively she wrote the word tomorrow on the slate.

'Good,' was all he could reply and she collapsed back into her seat with relief.

To Edmund this new path he had chosen continued to be full of barbs to his conscience. Having finished his subdued meal and knowing that there was no outing to the Smithsons that day, he changed to go riding and then made his way to the stables.

He supposed that he must have spent the last six months either wearing blinkers or looking at the ground for when he came across his groom, Golding, he saw a depth of misery in the man's face and constraint in his dealings with him that he had not recognised before. He tried to recall what he might have done to offend the man and could think of nothing other than the general manifestation of his anger.

The arena of the stable block where he stood surrounded by the interested stable lads was not a venue for private speech. In a rash moment Edmund invited Golding to accompany him on his ride, something he had done frequently in yesteryear but never since his accident. Edmund saw a look of surprise and delight suffuse the man's face and notched up another pang of guilt.

They rode in silence for a long while, the horses cantering rather than galloping, as the ground was rather hard from a series of severe frosts. At last they came to a broad meander in the river where there was actually a ford. The river however was in spate and it would not be safe to cross. Edmund dismounted and pulled the reins over his horse's head. After a moment's hesitation, Golding followed suit and stood a little way off from his master, awaiting his next move.

'I think I owe you an apology,' Edmund said with a rush, finding the words he had not yet been able to utter to his stepmother. He went on, determined to assuage some of the guilt he felt. 'If you have suffered at my hand in any way over the last few months I must tell you that I am truly sorry.'

Golding was clearly taken aback. Whatever he had expected from his master it was not this. He had had no time to bring a slate along with him and at first knew not how to reply. A moment's pondering, however, showed him a solution and he hitched his horse's reins to a nearby bush, then selecting a solid stick from the debris around it on the ground, he took it to the water's edge where the mud was soft enough to mark.

Golding paused, stick poised, finding he had no words to write. If he wrote the words of forgiveness, they might seem antagonistic without the nuance of meaning given by speech.

Edmund came up behind the groom as he stood irresolute beside the raging water. 'If you have it in your heart to forgive me, then let me know it, I beg you,' he said. 'For everywhere I see in people's faces distrust, dislike, even fear. What kind of creature have I allowed myself to become that this is their reaction to me?'

Golding turned his sparse frame round to look at Edmund and saw that he was being sincere; there was no guile, it was no ruse to trip him up but only an expression of the man's bewilderment. He stepped back to the river and squatting down wrote: 'I forgive you, Sir,' for he had no answers to the questions.

Edmund, who had abandoned his horse to graze nearby, sat down heavily on the bank of the river. He stared hard at the unsteady words in the mud and wondered afresh at the ways people devised to reach him if he would let them.

'I have been such a fool,' he said on an out-breath. 'A blind selfish fool. What respect can I look for now in the people around me?'

'They will forget, Sir,' wrote Golding laboriously. He had to smooth the small patch of ground so that he could write some more. 'Or they will see it as part of the illness.'

Edmund watched the painstaking formation of the letters and words and read them trying to remember Golding's voice, but the words and his memories did not coincide. It struck him why.

'You have learned lettering for my sake!' he said aghast.

Golding nodded his grizzled head.

'You have learned all this for my sake!' He leaped to his feet, startling Golding's horse standing close by. 'My God, Golding, what can this have cost you in time and effort? And I have thrown it back in your face. Each fresh revelation is purgatory. How can I bear it and how can I ever be worthy of such dedication?'

Golding stood immobile while the waves of emotion crashed over his master. He had heard the rumours from the indoor staff that Mr Edmund was recovering his temper and his manners but Golding had not expected anything quite so powerful. The man's reaction was the complete opposite of the behaviour he had been demonstrating previously.

A cheeky wind picked up and sent a shiver through him. Ever the groom, whose first priority must be the horses, Golding moved to catch Edmund's bay and then collect his own horse. He touched Edmund's arm and when his master looked round, indicated that it was time to be gone. He could not have the sweating horses getting cold.

Edmund nodded and took the horse's reins.

'Thank you,' he said. 'Thank you for all the hours you must have spent learning to read and write. Thank you. What more can I say?'

Golding squeezed his arm and shook his head.

'Nothing,' he said. 'There is no need for more.'

And if Edmund did not understand each word he got the gist. Swinging himself up into the saddle, he looked down into the sympathetic face of his groom.

'Let us go home,' he said.

12

*E*lena had only entertained a slight expectation of the Leightertons calling the next day. She was fairly certain that they would allow more than a day to elapse before they returned the visit. So she did not waste much time watching the driveway. Instead she spent the hours with Polly, who remained in bed. Elena's attempts to teach her several card games were futile and Polly was not much interested in being read to. It was only when Jessamy appeared at teatime with a large-pieced wooden puzzle that she brightened up and took an interest. Elena left them to it, knowing that if she helped the puzzle would be completed too quickly. She went in search of her father and ran him to earth in the rather grandiose room he was inclined to call his study.

'May I come in, Papa?' she asked as she stood in the doorway, seeing him staring in some concentration at papers on his desk.

He looked up and smiled. 'Of course, of course, I would welcome the interruption.' He came over to her and drew her to the fire. 'What can I do for you, my dear?'

Elena gazed down into the flames of the determined little fire. 'It will be my twenty-first birthday in less than a month, Papa,' she said. 'And I know not how to celebrate it.'

'Ah,' he smiled, admitting, 'this very serious matter has been exercising my mind somewhat as well.'

'I do not want a large party, Papa,' she said hastily. 'We have not enough acquaintances here and those we met at the

Leightertons are not the sort of people I would like to associate with intimately.'

'My little Elena already becoming too nice in her ways,' he mocked gently.

Elena's eyes flew to his face. 'Do not say so, Papa,' she objected. 'I would not dream of having an elevated opinion of myself but you must agree that many were there simply in the hope of seeing some interesting spectacle, some outburst from Mr Leighterton,' she fumed gently. 'I am very glad he did not gratify them.'

Mr Smithson looked in the mirror ostensibly to straighten his cravat but in truth to take covert stock of his daughter's reaction via the reflection as he asked the question: 'You know then of his behaviour prior to your meeting with him?'

'Oh yes,' said Elena blithely. 'Johnson told Mr Timery and Mr Timery told Mrs Timery. Mrs Timery told my maid and she told me. Was it all true, Papa? Was he really so violently angry?'

'I believe,' said Mr Smithson carefully, 'that there was no intention to hurt others physically, but outbursts did include the throwing and breaking of objects.'

Elena digested this. 'His anger is at his weakness, is it not Papa?'

'I believe so.'

'I like him, Papa,' she said abruptly. 'I believe that if he would accept himself as he is now, he could be comfortable again.'

'Do I detect a rival for Mr Sawyer?' Mr Smithson and his daughter had always been close. He had no fear of asking such things.

Elena's troubled face cleared and she laughed. 'Don't tell Mr Sawyer but I'm afraid that he has most certainly been supplanted.' Then she turned the table on her father. 'And I would hazard a guess that you were quite taken with Mrs Leighterton,' she retaliated.

'You see too much, young lady, much too much. And do not go matchmaking there, for she was distinctly cool on our entry into the room.'

'Yes but she became a deal more cordial when she realised you were giving her stepson a good character,' replied Elena with vim.

'Be that as it may,' said Mr Smithson, judging it was time to bring this particular conversation to a close. 'That's two guests for your birthday celebration at the very least.'

By the time she sought her bed that night, Elena had thought of four other guests she would like to include. As the owner of Holm Oak Reach, Mr Smithson had the gift of the living at Reachfold, the large village to the east of the estate and owned in part by it. The previous incumbent had gone the way of all flesh some two years before and it had not been a priority of Mr Banbury's to fill the position.

Now that Mr Smithson was installed, he had undertaken the task of finding a rector. If Mr Smithson had stopped to review how he had spent his time over the preceding weeks and months, he would have been staggered by the hours he had spent interviewing candidates for a multiplicity of posts. Fortuitously, the task of finding a rector had been relatively easy and he and Mr Banbury had been able to agree on a candidate quickly. There had been one man who had stood out.

In his early fifties, the Reverend Ezekiel Lansdale was a full-set man with a neat beard and whiskers and a decided twinkle in his eye. Mr Smithson, despite reading the man's testimonial, which had been glowing, was expecting a stern moralist based almost entirely on an opinion generated by the man's name. The warmth of the man's personality had disarmed him immediately. Reverend Lansdale brought with him his elder widowed sister to keep house and her two daughters, Hannah, aged three and thirty and Jemima, aged one and thirty. All three ladies were plain but jolly and Mr Smithson took to them at once, as did Elena when the introductions were made.

Having ridden out that afternoon with her father to see that the family had arrived safely to take up residence in the Rectory at Reachfold, Elena was minded to include them on her birthday guest list.

With her own family to include Jessamy and Polly, she now had a party of ten but with a disproportionate number of ladies. The next morning, however, a letter from one of her Leicestershire friends, Lady Caroline Delrymple, resolved even this ticklish problem. After some lengthy preamble about the improving health of her sisters and some less than flattering gossip about Mr Sawyer's gravitation to the latest wealthy beauty to take up residence in Fossewold Parva, Lady Caroline wrote to request a favour for the son of one of her father's friends. Mr Ingram Deacon was lately back from the West Indies after a long sojourn there and was now staying with a friend in Eastbourne until he could have a reunion with his parents who would be coming down from Cumbria for the season. Lady Caroline assured Elena through the pages of her epistle that she could recommend both young men highly and that they would be most appreciative of an invitation to visit Holm Oak Reach.

Nothing loath, Elena took her friend at her word and applied to her father to include the two gentlemen at the party. She was just sitting at the writing desk in the withdrawing room forming her reply to Lady Caroline when the Leightertons were announced. Putting her pen aside, Elena rose to meet them and requested Timery to apprise her father that they had guests.

Mrs Leighterton was clearly flustered by the fact that Elena had been alone and interrupted in her task by their visit but Elena earnestly assured her that she was delighted to renew her acquaintance with them both. Mr Smithson was quick to appear and he had not been long in the room before the Colonel and his family were announced. A shadow of annoyance crossed Elena's face when she heard their names called out. She had not yet had a chance to do more than a formal curtsey to Mr Edmund Leighterton and she knew any conversation with him would be nigh impossible with the Colonel's two bumptious daughters watching his every move.

Edmund had seen the look as he was now making a special effort to watch people's expressions to gain clues as to what they were saying. With his back to the door and having been unaware of the arrival and announcement, he first interpreted it as a rejection of him, then a flurry of movement gave him pause and he turned to see who the new arrivals were. He could not prevent a slow smile spreading from his lips to his eyes. Miss Smithson's expressive face had said all he needed to know about her feelings and they so matched his own that any irritation he might have felt at not being allowed a private conversation with his hostess was chased away.

'You will have to control your features, if you do not wish to offend your honoured guests,' he murmured as she stepped past him to welcome the newcomers. The look she cast him spoke volumes and he chuckled quietly to himself, content for the time being to stand back and savour their accord. It also allowed him to study Miss Smithson, to ensure that his overactive mind had not exaggerated her charms. She was certainly pretty; her dark hair now framed her face in carefully positioned curls, her brown eyes for him a window into her thoughts. She was dressed in a simple blue dress, which was expensively but unobtrusively made. Her neck was adorned with a plain gold cross and there were no rings on her fingers. Mr Leighterton thought that she had not yet decided how much of their new-found wealth should be on show and thought it praiseworthy that she had been so restrained at the outset. She would soon see that it was acceptable to trim her dress with more beads and bows; one of the Colonel's daughters had it down to a fine art and while he would not want Miss Smithson to model her conduct on that young lady's, she could take a few lessons from her apparel. He wondered if the Smithsons planned to go to London for the season. He trusted not unless Miss Smithson had someone to advise her. He looked around the room again but saw no-one who might be deemed to be her companion. He considered the situation and wondered whether he should ask his stepmother to counsel her. It was only as his thoughts continued to meander in this direction that it struck him that as on the other occasions of his meetings with Miss Smithson, his mind had become divorced from thoughts of his own shortcomings.

He toyed with the idea of breaking with his isolation and joining Miss Smithson and her other guests. However as he watched them he saw that the young Miss Campden whose apparel he had just admired was clearly not matching it in taste with her conversation. She appeared to be speaking and possibly flattering Miss Smithson in terms that were clearly embarrassing her. Cravenly, Edmund remained where he was until he saw Mr Smithson good-naturedly attempt to prise the Campden ladies away from his daughter. He had almost succeeded in gaining their attention, giving Edmund some hope of conversing with Miss Smithson when there was another flurry of movement and Miss Polly McNeath entered the room. Edmund saw at once that she would have all Miss Smithson's attention, as she was looking overwhelmed by the company. Nobly he withdrew from the lists and went to stand beside his stepmother who was making laborious conversation with young Mr Campden. He made no attempt to understand what was being said even though good-naturedly Mr Campden tried to include him and very quickly Mrs Leighterton took the hint and started to say her goodbyes.

As they were bowling away from Holm Oak Reach, Edmund felt he should make some reference to the visit. His stepmother was exhibiting signs of having been unsettled by having to leave so abruptly when they had not been there above twenty minutes.

'I do not think the Smithsons will be offended by our leaving so soon, Mama,' he said, knowing that it had been his fault and that he ought to apologise. As before the words would not come. 'I am sure that they knew no slight was intended.'

Clarissa Leighterton turned her head to meet his eyes and he saw the disbelief there. He could not sustain the look and turned away from her to look out of the window. He hoped very much that he had not done Miss Smithson a disservice.

13

*T*hankfully the Campdens had not seen the Leightertons arrive so knew nothing of the length of their visit. It was only the Smithsons who were left to wonder and they, more in tune with Edmund's difficulties than most, were inclined to make excuses for him.

Not many days later Edmund reprieved himself by calling with a request to take Elena for a drive. As it was an open-topped carriage with the groom in attendance, Mr Smithson was minded to allow the excursion and Elena delightedly climbed aboard. For some little while they travelled comfortably enough with Edmund driving and pointing out the landmarks on their way. However it was soon borne upon him that he would be better letting Golding drive, so that he could have conversation with Miss Smithson with the help of a slate.

The exchange was duly made and the young couple demurely installed in the forward-looking seats of the landau.

'So what do you think of the Campden family?' Edmund asked as he saw Elena bring out a slate and chalk from her reticule. 'You have not met Mrs Campden yet. She enjoys ill health and is inclined to keep to her rooms or her day bed.'

'Enjoys?' Elena wrote the single word and accompanied it with a look of enquiry.

'Well it must be so,' Edmund countered, 'for she must feel the benefit of it, if it allows her the excuse to detach herself at will from her tedious family.'

Elena admonished him with her eyes but she could not suppress a rueful smile. The younger Miss Campden's conversation had really been too fulsome for comfort and she hoped that their visits would not become too regular.

Abandoning the Campdens, she began to write out a sentence on her slate but Edmund gently relieved her of the device and then put his hand out for her to write on with her fingers instead. Elena's expressive face spoke volumes as she was torn between what she wanted to do and what she knew to be wrong. If anyone saw them so intimate, she knew she could easily be stigmatised as fast. She looked at the rigid back of the groom and knew that he would not betray them but wondered whether the sides of the carriage were high enough to obscure what they were doing from the casual observer, and also would she be breaking her father's trust? These questions jostled in her head for answers.

'Please humour me in this, Miss Smithson,' Edmund pleaded, taking her small, gloved hand and writing on her palm. 'It makes conversation more of a game than a chore.' He had written the words as well as saying them and although the letters had been drawn far too quickly for her to follow them, the sensation of his touch conveyed his argument. It also endorsed the knowledge that this was more of an illicit pleasure than a justifiable means of communication. Her eyes met his and she knew she could not gainsay him.

She wrote without speaking the words: 'On one condition.'

'What's that?' he asked eagerly.

'That you promise to come to my twenty-first birthday party.' It took her some little while to spell out the lengthy request. Glancing up into his face and seeing the consternation there stirred her emotion to a degree she had never experienced when being courted by Mr Sawyer.

'I cannot come to a party,' he wrote in reply, not wanting Golding to hear him being so pudding-hearted. 'You saw how ill at ease I was when we called upon you.'

The two young people were lost to their surroundings as they struggled to convey the depth of emotion on each side. Golding heard and saw nothing but it did not mean that he did not sense that something was afoot.

'This party will not be like that.' She paused in her writing as he digested this. 'The Campdens will not be there!' she continued as a clincher.

'I cannot,' Edmund shook his head sadly, not bothering to write it. 'A whole evening. It is not possible.'

'Please,' she wrote the word slowly and deliberately. 'Please,' she wrote again.

Edmund turned away, unable to witness the appeal in her eyes. He looked out across the wooded countryside and wished profoundly that another Edmund had met this girl, an Edmund who could meet her demands, accept her challenges. For this was what he saw this invitation as: a challenge to him to rise above his affliction. She was tugging at his coat now and as he turned his head back to face her she mouthed the word 'please' again.

'Does it matter to you so much?' he asked.

'Yes,' she nodded emphatically.

'But why? Why should you want me? I might find I am incapable of sustaining the evening. I might be unable to control my temper, have to leave early, be rude to one of your other guests. In full, I am an unreliable guest, I might ruin your party.' He spoke the words in a hurried low voice, charged with emotion.

'You would more surely ruin it if you did not come,' she wrote brazenly.

'Why? How can you say that?'

'Because you were my first true friend when I moved to Sussex away from all I had ever known.' This time she had collected up the slate and had written the words at speed and in some agitation.

Edmund read them and then read them again.

'Very well,' he conceded. 'I will come.' He expected profuse thanks but she surprised him with a single word on the slate.

'Promise?'

'On my honour.'

Then she smiled a warm twinkling smile and he knew that come what may, he was committed and his heart sank for he genuinely believed that he was not equal to the ordeal of a room full of people with whom he could only communicate with difficulty for a whole evening. Fortunately he had been brought up a gentleman and could school his face not to betray his feelings. Miss Smithson was left to some measure in ignorance of the trial she had set him.

As the day approached, Edmund's fears grew inside his mind, as he retained an unwillingness to unburden himself to his stepmother. He had surprised her profoundly when he acquiesced to her mute enquiry when the formal invitation had arrived. Mrs Leighterton had expected to have to cajole him into accepting and eventually divined that he must have had previous knowledge of the event and had made his decision already. She was only conscious of the toll this decision was taking on him on the evening before it was to take place.

Edmund had come into dinner and had sat beside her but instead of the desultory conversation they now made on these occasions with the aid of a slate, he was silent. He had drunk three glasses of wine before the meal had finished being served on to his plate and she counted a further three before he had completed his repast. He then called for another bottle and was almost all the way through this before getting up from the table. He said a slightly slurred 'good night' and left her abruptly, to go and read in his room, she hoped, as this latterly had become his custom. She repaired to the withdrawing room and settled in solitary state to set some stitches in the cushion covers she was making. It was only when she came to go to bed that it occurred to her to wonder whether Edmund had indeed gone to bed or whether he had returned to his previous habit of drinking late into the night in the small back parlour. A slight noise from that room as she crossed the hallway made her heart sink. Bravely she went to the parlour door and opened it gingerly. Edmund was sitting at the table with his head in his hands and his fingers raking through his hair; there was an empty bottle on the table and the room was in semi-darkness, being lit by a single candle on the table and the last of the candles in a holder fixed to the wall. Most had already gutted.

'Oh Edmund,' she said sorrowfully. 'What has brought this on?'

He was unconscious of her presence but she knew she could not just leave him. She had a horror of him returning to his old ways. She went back to the withdrawing room and relit the ornate candelabra by which she had been working, then taking a deep breath she returned to the parlour. Edmund directed bleary eyes at her as he turned to the additional light.

'Go away, Mama,' he said thickly. 'There is nothing here for you.'

Mrs Leighterton took a moment to digest his words. While on the face of it they could be taken as a rebuff, she heard something more in the timbre of his voice and thought they were a cry for help.

She came fully into the room and placed the candelabra on the table. Then picking up a slate from a pile on the sideboard she wrote three words.

'Is it tomorrow?'

He had the courtesy to read the words and although he pushed it away, he did not dash it to the floor. Mrs Leighterton waited, standing beside him, uncertain what to do but intuitively knowing that he wanted her to stay. Then, not wishing to provoke him, she left the slate on the table and took another one from the sideboard.

'Let me help you to bed,' she wrote.

The bloodshot eyes struggled to focus on her elegant scrawl, and then he nodded.

'That would be best,' he acknowledged.

Mrs Leighterton moved forward and tried to help him to his

feet but he swayed and collapsed back on to the cherry-wood chair. Mrs Leighterton was worried that the weight of him would destroy the rush seat. She decided that she could not manage his relocation on her own. This presented her with a dilemma, as she had no plans to broadcast this untimely indiscretion to the staff. Even though Edmund's improved behaviour had lasted so far for little more than a month, his previous conduct was sliding from people's memory. They were now more inclined to see it as part of his illness from which he had recovered than as a permanent feature. It therefore behoved her to protect him from the malicious. She did not want rumours of a relapse to be spread abroad. Cleverley, she knew she could trust, but of the valet she did not have the measure. There was a moment of indecision, then she tugged on the bell rope and waited with the door only slightly open, so that she could shield Edmund from prying eyes.

Thankfully Cleverley was the one who answered her summons.

'Mr Edmund is unwell,' she said euphemistically. 'I need you to aid me in getting him to bed. I do not wish to disturb the household.' Gathering her meaning instantly, he nodded.

'I will fetch Mr Purvis,' he said, taking one peek at his master around the door. 'He will know how best to handle this.'

'Will he?' Mrs Leighterton was surprised.

'Oh yes,' said Cleverley with certainty and disappeared into the servants' wing to inform Purvis that he was needed.

It was not many minutes before the two men returned and during that time, Edmund had remained immobile on the chair almost as though he was frightened to move in case he fell to the floor.

Mrs Leighterton allowed the valet and the butler to take control. Purvis looked down at his master in some concern.

'He has given his word to a lady, you see, Madam,' he said apologetically to Mrs Leighterton, conscious that she deserved an explanation. 'He has given an undertaking that he will attend this party, yet he cannot see how he is going to endure it.' He heaved a sigh. 'I have told him and told him that it is but five hours' duration and that the Smithsons would never abandon him in his silence but I cannot convince him.'

Mrs Leighterton could not mask her surprise. This was the most she had ever heard the valet speak and he was alluding to an understanding between him and his master, of which she would never have guessed.

'Should I cry off with some indisposition so that he need not go?' she asked, willing to do anything to protect Edmund from his fears as if he was a small boy.

'I would not recommend it, Madam,' said the earnest young man. 'He might still feel honour-bound to fulfil his obligation and then he would be bereft of your supporting presence.'

Mrs Leighterton nodded, just managing to hide her surprise that Edmund might be capable of thinking of her in such a positive light. 'Then let us get him to bed and hope that daylight brings him comfort.' She turned to Cleverley. 'Is the corridor clear? Can we reach his bedchamber without detection?'

'Yes, Madam, I have sent all the servants to bed except Millie the maid, who awaits in my parlour until I summon her to clear the withdrawing room. I will make all right in here.'

'Thank you.'

It was not an easy task to help Edmund up the stairs because Purvis was a spare man only three-quarters Edmund's weight and Cleverley suffered from a certain stiffness of the joints. However, determination and a little help from Edmund himself saw him safely delivered to his bed.

'Leave him to me now, Madam,' said Purvis as he held the door for Mrs Leighterton to quit the room. 'I will see that he is recovered enough to attend the party tomorrow.'

She could only nod and thank him again but she sought her own couch in some anxiety and spent many waking minutes trying to think how she might best help him during the following evening.

Edmund woke the next morning betimes and was soon reminded that he had spent a debauched evening by the taste in his mouth and the pain behind his eyes when he looked in the direction of the window.

He cursed himself for a fool. Now he had compounded his own difficulties by giving himself physical discomfort as well as mental anguish.

He raised his head slowly and peered around the room; nothing looked different from the morning before. He could not remember much of the evening but he hoped very much that he had not regressed into the snarling animal he had previously been. He pulled the bell and watched the door. He wanted the earliest sight of Purvis so that he could gauge how much ground he had to make up. He hazily remembered Purvis's and Cleverley's presence but nothing more.

The door opened shortly after his summons and Purvis arrived carrying the ubiquitous pitcher with a determinedly cheerful face. This did not bode well, for Edmund knew as well as any that it was not the valet's role to carry the pitcher. He would know he had reclaimed his reputation when some lowlier staff member was allotted the task.

Edmund pulled himself gingerly to a sitting position.

'Out with it,' he barked. 'Tell all. How badly did I behave last night? I must know the full truth of it.'

Refusing to be pushed, Purvis put down the pitcher and turned to his master.

'Not badly. Not badly at all,' he enunciated clearly. Then he wrote on his ever-present slate. 'It was all very discreet; you need not concern yourself about it one bit.'

'Well, thank God for that,' said Edmund and flopped back on his pillows, forgetting only briefly that his head was in no condition for such treatment.

14

*M*rs Leighterton gave her stepson's hand a reassuring squeeze as the coach drew up outside the vast façade of Holm Oak Reach that evening at a few minutes past seven o'clock. He responded with a rueful smile. He did not remember her having any part in the pageant the night before but it was clear that she was aware of its cause.

'You look very fine, Mama,' he said as he tweaked a dyed ostrich feather that adorned her brindled locks. 'Very fine indeed. I meant to say so when you descended the stairs. The russet dress looks very well with the garnet set my father gave you.'

Mrs Leighterton gave an audible gasp but, as he was not looking at her, he was unaware of it. She could not recall a time when he had coupled her with his father in a complimentary way. She had to take a deep breath to steady herself but still her knees felt rather wobbly as she descended the carriage steps. She fancied later that she had clutched at Edmund's supporting hand rather wildly.

Their announcement in the vast saloon seemed rather superfluous when there were only a handful of people assembled there.

Mr Smithson surged forward to welcome them both and Edmund happened to be looking in the right direction so he caught the admiration in Mr Smithson's expression as his gaze alighted on Mrs Leighterton.

Mr Smithson was quick to make the introductions to the rector's family. Edmund made each one of them a formal bow and was grateful for the foresight which meant that he had been handed a guest list on his arrival. Reverend Lansdale's name he might have caught from the movement of Mr Smithson's lips as 'bs' and 'ds' were the sounds he found easiest to follow, but the names of Mrs Hanrahan and her daughters, Jemima and Hannah, would have been indefinable. Mr Ingram Deacon and his friend, Oswald Kelwich, had clearly not arrived yet. Edmund sipped the glass of wine he had been offered by the circulating servant and waited in some trepidation for the evening to unfold.

There was a tap on his shoulder and Edmund turned to get his first sight of Miss Elena Smithson. Tonight she looked every inch the beautiful young debutante. Her hair was laced with spring flowers and her corsage matched the arrangement in her hair. She was wearing a pure and expensive-looking pearl necklace with matching drop earrings and her soft pink dress picked up the rosebuds in her cheeks. Edmund knew in that instant that he would endure all that was sent to try him that evening so he would not be guilty of spoiling the sparkling happiness in the girl's face.

'Good evening,' she said, dropping him a curtsey.

'Good evening,' he responded with aplomb, glad that she did not resort to the slate for commonplace phrases. 'Are you well?' he asked for form's sake alone because he could see that she was blooming.

'Yes, thank you,' she replied. 'And you?' The movement of her head made it clear that she was returning the question.

'A slight malaise of no consequence,' he said, 'but otherwise in perfect health, thank you.'

He watched her face to see if she had heard of his misconduct the night before and sensed she had not. She simply smiled, making the assumption that he was ridiculing himself and referring to his hearing impairment.

'Good,' she said. Then she appeared startled and turned abruptly away. Edmund, surprised at such treatment from her, followed her with his gaze. It did not take him long to grasp what had happened. Jessamy, who had been in high spirits with the excitement of it all, had been tearing around tweaking his cousin, Polly, and then running away. On one of his sorties, he had knocked over a vast bowl of potpourri, which had been positioned on an inlaid rosewood card table little more than three feet wide. There were faded rose petals strewn across the floor, sprigs of rosemary dropping their tiny squirls of dried flowers and lavender heads just waiting to be stepped upon. Polly had somehow reasoned that she was responsible and was sobbing indelicately into a lacy handkerchief. Edmund watched as Elena rushed to administer comfort and issue orders to have the mess cleared up. He anticipated the removal of young Jessamy.

Into the melee walked two strangers who could only be Mr Ingram Deacon and Mr Oswald Kelwich. Seeing that both Mr and Miss Smithson were still much taken up, Edmund introduced himself to them and welcomed them to the party. Both men gave him a formal bow but Edmund saw dismay on Mr Kelwich's face. He was not to know that Mr Kelwich had heard the stories of Edmund's misdoings and not those of his reclamation. He had therefore not expected Edmund to be out in society and had not briefed his friend. Thus he foresaw too some terrible pitfalls ahead.

Fortunately Edmund interpreted it as concern at the scene before them and began to assure him that soon all would be well. Edmund had hardly finished speaking when Mrs Hanrahan spotted Mr Kelwich as a previous acquaintance and with a nod of her head and many waves of her arm, she indicated to him to come over to her. Mr Kelwich, feeling rather chicken-hearted, gratefully obeyed her summons. It left Edmund standing alone with Mr Deacon.

'Have you come far, Mr Deacon,' he enquired. 'I am not familiar with your name.'

Mr Deacon responded as anyone might to such a question. 'My father's estates are in Cumbria but I have been in the West Indies these last seven years.'

Edmund had watched intently as the man had spoken and thought he caught the word Cumbria and West. He realised he had a choice. He could assume that he was right and ask another question resulting in a further answer he might or might not be able to catch in any sense. Or he could admit his shortcomings and ask the man to repeat what he had said. He gave his companion an appraising look and what he saw there he liked. Mr Deacon had too square a jaw to be considered handsome but he was well-looking enough and there was a kindness in the hazel eyes which had not been extinguished by the exigencies of his trips abroad or marred by the wrinkles from many days squinting in the sun. His head must have spent many years under a hat because it was not bleached by the sun's rays but was a nut brown. His appearance gave evidence to his sojourn abroad and allowed Edmund to guess at the West Indies but it was not enough. He decided to allow this stranger into his confidence and very much hoped that his trust was not misplaced.

'I beg your indulgence, Sir,' he said, 'but I must inform you that I am profoundly deaf. I hear not a word you are saying but I have been learning to follow the movements of the speaker's lips. I believe I saw you say Cumbria and the West Indies. Am I right?'

'You are indeed, Mr Leighterton,' replied Mr Deacon, nodding and turning slightly so he was standing directly in front of Edmund. 'I am most impressed.'

Edmund held up a hand. 'Then I am delighted but I beg you to keep it our secret. I am insufficiently proficient to want my friends and family to know yet awhile. I wish to surprise them with my skill once I have a real chance in understanding more than one word in six!'

Elena, looking up anxiously from her position on the floor amongst the debris of the potpourri, was relieved to see

Edmund with Mr Deacon in attendance. She had hoped to be the one who ensured that Edmund was not left isolated on the fringes of conversation but Jessamy's antics had prevented that for the time being. Mr Deacon had his back to her, so in that brief glance she assumed he was using a slate and thought nothing more of it.

Anyone who considered that Jessamy's conduct would now bar him from the evening's entertainment was due to be disappointed. Mr Smithson certainly drew him away from the guests and in a low voice spoke to him firmly. The boy himself gave all the appearance of being contrite but there was no quitting the room in disgrace by the young man. He went unobtrusively back to his sister and cousin and apologised as his father had requested him to do. Elena was not overly put out but poor Polly was taking it very badly, accepting much of the guilt upon her own shoulders. It took Elena a little while to soothe her before she could pass her on to Hannah Hanrahan, a kind and undemanding companion.

Elena was on the point of reaching Mr Deacon and Edmund when the butler entered and announced that dinner was served.

Edmund, unaware of the announcement, was given notice of it by a flick of Mr Deacon's head in the direction of the butler.

Edmund held out his arm. 'May I be allowed to escort you to dinner on this special day, Miss Smithson?' he asked. Elena curtseyed her acceptance and, in deference to her birthday, she led the party to the dining room on Edmund's arm. They were followed by Mr Smithson and Mrs Leighterton. The rector took his sister's arm to allow the younger men to partner his nieces, which they did good-naturedly. Jessamy and Polly brought up the rear.

Much planning had gone into the seating arrangements. Mr Smithson took his seat at the far end of the magnificent oak table, which shone in the candlelight with a vibrancy that was testament to the activities of the maids earlier that day. The crystal glasses and bowls picked up the individual candle flames and made them dance on the silverware. Elena was almost overwhelmed by the beauty; the Timerys had done magnificently in ensuring that the spread would be worthy of a princess's birthday. There was a vast bowl of colourful fruit in the centre and an eclectic mix of dishes spread along the table's length. Jessamy's face was a picture as he took in the stuffed pig and succulent goose surrounded by red and purple berries. There were jellies and ices and patterned tartlets, a feast to behold.

Mrs Leighterton was to Mr Smithson's right and Mrs Hanrahan on his left. Elena seated at the other end had Edmund on her right and Mr Deacon on her left. Next to Mr Deacon sat Miss Hannah Hanrahan, who in turn had the rector and Polly between her and Mrs Leighterton. Down the other side sat Miss Jemima, Mr Oswald Kelwich and Jessamy. Elena deplored the fact that she had two ladies sitting next to each other down one side and two gentlemen, if account was taken of Jessamy, down the other but there had been no other persons she felt could be trusted with Edmund's first sortie into a formal society event. Good form had to be sacrificed.

Discreetly positioned beside the covers of those around Edmund were small slates and chalk. Forgetting that she had thought he was using one in the withdrawing room, Elena looked for an opportunity to convey to Mr Deacon the reason for their use but found that he was indeed already a party to Edmund's need for he had scribbled a few words on the slate and passed it across to him to conclude some earlier conversation.

The meal was lively with everyone determined to include Edmund where possible. Elena was thankful for it but conscious that he might think she had forewarned them. She had spent many hours choosing and devising games in which he could be included and she did not want his enjoyment soured or compromised by instances during the meal.

At last the meal was concluded and the men looked expectantly at the ladies in anticipation that they would withdraw.

'Please remain seated, ladies,' Elena said primly as she got to her feet and indicated that she wished Edmund to exchange places with her so that he was now at the head of the table looking down its line to Mr Smithson. As she handed him a scroll, she nodded at the footman who began carefully to place three shining silver coins at each diner's right hand.

There was a crescendo of murmured enquiry as the guests picked up the coins and examined them.

'What is this, Miss Smithson?' Mr Deacon was bold enough to ask directly. Elena merely smiled at him.

Edmund, who had remained standing reading the scroll now cleared his throat and, finding a gavel had been placed conveniently for his use, let go of the scroll with one hand and picked it up, banging the table to get everyone's attention.

As he stood, his gaze slipped from face to upturned face, to ensure that he carried them all with him.

'Ladles and jellyspoons, I have been entrusted,' he said, 'to inform you that I am your master of ceremonies.' To the most acute, it might have sounded as though there was an edge to his voice but when his eyes alighted on Miss Smithson's sweet anxious face, his demeanour altered subtly and he appeared to take on the mantle of the role willingly enough.

'You have before you each, three shiny new silver shillings, minted as you will see in this year of our Lord, 1816. On one side is the head of his Majesty, George III; on the other his Majesty's shield. Now it is for you to decide which you prefer.' He paused and looked around the company to determine that he still had them all with him. Even Jessamy's face was rapt. 'We take one coin at a time. Make your choice, ladies and gentlemen and place your first chosen coin in front of you.' He waited again, making his own choice randomly without looking. 'Then I call upon Mr Timery to come forward.' The butler obviously knew his role; he carried with him a low square box into which he spun a coin. Edmund peered down at the result.

'The coin displays his Majesty's head,' he announced. 'Each

participant who has chosen correctly retains their coin in front of them. Those who have not must pass their coin to the right until it reaches someone who still has their coin.' There was a wave of chatter and laughter as coins were passed around the table. 'And then we do it again,' Edmund instructed them. Very quickly everyone acquired the manner of the game and entered into it with eagerness and good humour. The first round saw only Mr Deacon and Mr Smithson as casualties, but swiftly others lost their coins until it was finally a match between the rector and his niece, Miss Jemima. Much to his relief, the rector made the wrong choice and his niece became the proud possessor of a neat stack of coins.

The next attempt at the game was swift as luck was not with their choices. Mrs Leighterton found herself the lucky winner but as with games of chance, the third game went round after round with tension mounting as four people kept guessing correctly. Finally Mr Kelwich lost lady luck's favour and the game was left between Jessamy, Polly and Edmund. In the very next round Edmund lost, and then at last Jessamy, whose eager enjoyment of the game made several fear that he would make a scene, guessed wrongly and Polly was announced the winner. Unexpectedly Jessamy took it in good part. It was clear that despite her recent good fortune, Polly had not experienced holding so many valuable coins in her hands before; she looked fearfully around the company, not knowing what to do. Mr Smithson came to her rescue.

'Bravo, my dear,' he cried fulsomely. 'A worthy winner and may I say, my son, a good loser.'

'Here, here,' came the chorus.

'Yes, indeed,' said Miss Jemima fervently, 'and may I make a present of two of my coins to the young man for such gallant behaviour.'

'And I too,' squeaked Polly, pleased to relinquish some of what she saw as undeserved riches.

While this little pantomime was playing out, Mr Kelwich

found a way to speak, behind Miss Jemima as she sorted out her coins, to Elena.

'I am most impressed, Miss Smithson,' he said, 'that you have acquired the coins so early in the year. I had read of their advent but did not expect to see them so early in circulation.'

Elena could not resist looking slightly smug. 'You are in the right of it, Sir; I had to make special applications to London. It was most exciting for I was certain that they would not arrive in time and that we would be reduced to using tokens. I was thrilled to find them at the receiving house yesterday morning.'

'You are to be congratulated, Miss Smithson, for such an ingenious form of entertainment.'

Elena could only bow her head in acknowledgement, as Miss Jemima was now sitting back in her seat and it would have been rude to continue the conversation across her.

15

*I*f the assembled company thought that the entertainment had come to an end, they were mistaken. Elena now handed Edmund a further scroll and Timery was distributing paper and quill to each guest.

Edmund unrolled the scroll and perused it.

'Now this will exercise your minds,' he said with laughter in his voice. 'Each one of you must write a four-line ditty in praise of another guest. You must then hand all efforts to me and I will read them out. It follows that you must then write the name of the person you think has composed the rhyme upon the slate and you score a point if you guess correctly. We do this for all the writings and the person who has guessed correctly the most times is declared the winner.'

There were some appalled faces at the prospect of having to conjure up a verse, but it did not take much to cajole them into making the attempt. Once again Mr Timery provided the props, which this time were manifested in the shape of an hourglass with only enough sand to last five minutes. The race was on to produce something that could be read out.

Edmund, who the night before had drowned his sorrows based on the premise that there would be nothing for him but boredom and isolation this evening, was already hearing rhymes and rhythm in his head. He took his seat and, putting down the scroll, started to scribble furiously on his paper. He was only halted when Mr Timery tapped him on the shoulder to indicate that the first five minutes were up.

'Well, Ladies and gentlemen, now pass all your labours of love to me,' he commanded.

There was considerable reluctance on the part of Miss Hanrahan and Polly to give up their blotched and untidy scribblings but Jessamy travelled around the table to twitch the paper out of Polly's fingers from behind. The rector used less physical methods but was equally successful in freeing Miss Hanrahan's efforts from her fingers.

Once in possession of all the crumpled pieces of paper, Edmund cast them into a small barrel provided by Mr Timery and shook them about. Then delving in for the first one, he made his selection.

'Let us commence,' he said, watching Elena's face with amusement. 'Ah, this one is about our birthday girl. Come, I ask you to make your choice as soon as I have finished reading.'

> *Tonight we have a birthday party*
> *At which we have partaken of a hearty*
> *Meal at Miss Smithson's behest*
> *Because she is a friend of the very best.*

Elena blushed rosily and knew not who could have written so kindly of her; she looked around her at the myriad expressions that had settled on her companions' faces. Some were puzzled, some amused while Jessamy, as only little brothers can be, was unimpressed; only the rector's face carried a benign smile. Elena scribbled his name upon the slate.

When all the slates were revealed, she was proved to be right, so only she and the rector, who had of course nominated himself, were awarded a point on Mr Timery's board.

The next paper withdrawn, Edmund guessed, was Polly's for it hardly had a complete line upon it. He made what he could of it but such were his alterations that even she did not recognise it as hers, so scored no point.

The next one drawn had Edmund laughing even before he had read the first two lines. It was a witty and rather disparaging verse, which could only have been written by Mr Deacon of his very close friend Mr Kelwich. The humour was very well received in all quarters but one. Mrs Leighterton, seeing her stepson enjoying himself so fully for the first time in nine months was moved to grateful tears. She put her handkerchief to her face to disguise her feelings, but her action did not escape the eagle-eyed attention of Mr Smithson.

'Hold hard, Madam, do,' he said quietly. 'I understand your feelings, even enter into them, but you must have courage and contain them yet awhile. Let us not disturb the moment.'

Mrs Leighterton straightened her back and with a final wipe of her handkerchief returned it to her reticule. Once her hands were again inactive in her lap, she felt Mr Smithson give one a sustaining squeeze. She found herself returning the pressure, grateful for the comfort. Only afterwards when she examined her feelings did she accept that she should have been shocked and repelled by such a gesture, rather than responding in a way that spoke volumes of her need for comfort and reassurance.

The hilarity continued as Jessamy's offering was read out. He had written an unflattering ditty about Polly's ability to play cards, from which she did not take offence so no harm was done. As they worked through the scrolls it was soon seen that Elena knew her friends for she had an unerring ability to guess who had written each one. Edmund realised that the game was made much easier if you retained the information of who had already been guessed. However it became increasingly difficult to remember who was left. His was the penultimate offering and he wondered suddenly what the others would make of it.

There stood at the end of a very long drive
A great house, empty for years more than five
Then came one day in the depths of winter
A family from far off Leicestershire

It comprised a sound man with his young son
A niece called Polly and Miss Elena Smithson
Into the house, its surrounds and its neighbours
They breathed new life with their gentle favours.

There was a silence amongst his auditors at which Edmund could only guess because he could see no lips moving, then a sudden and spontaneous burst of applause and had he but known it a chorus of 'Here, here.'

After that everyone wrote upon their slate Edmund's name as the scribe and it was left to the verse of Mr Smithson to bring the evening to a close. His offering rather conveniently wished his daughter a very happy birthday. It brought the games to a natural end with Edmund raising his glass and leading the toast to the birthday girl. Once that little formality had been concluded, the party returned en masse to the withdrawing room where Timery had set up the tea tray.

The meal and the games had taken up much time so it scarcely lacked fifteen minutes to midnight when the gathering broke up.

The party had been planned for the night of the full moon, so that guests might see their way home. Although there was a brisk wind, which forewarned the appearance of a cloud, for the time being the sky was clear.

Mrs Leighterton climbed into their carriage with the aid of her stepson's hand. She had mastered her feelings during the evening but the combination of emotion and fatigue allowed tears to come to her eyes unbidden. Edmund's solicitous care only exacerbated her vulnerability. Once settled in the darkened coach, she found she was weeping gently. She laid her head back against the squabs, ignoring the protests of her elaborate hat, and shut her eyes to feign sleep. In the dark, she hoped Edmund would not notice the tears cascading down her face.

Edmund himself was tired and he saw no point in lighting the carriage lamps for the short distance home. He could not see the tears but he sensed from the general form of his step-mother's demeanour that she was suffering from some deep emotion.

The urge to unburden himself with the apology that was so long overdue came upon him but even as he formed the words in his head, he knew that to utter them would be both unfair and futile – in the dark and without a means of communication he would not receive the absolution he so desired as Mrs Leighterton would be unable to convey her feelings to him. He settled instead on giving her shoulders a sympathetic pat and hoped that she would not embark on an attempt to respond.

Too overwhelmed with emotion Mrs Leighterton made no such attempt; instead she favoured him with a wan smile that he was only just able to make out in the gloom and then turned her head to look out of the jogging carriage's windows at the landscape bathed in moonlight. Alone then with his thoughts Edmund was at leisure to review the evening. As he went back over the events of the party, what he had enjoyed at the time became overtaken by the embarrassment of the realisation that everything had been preordained to suit his needs. His face burned with shame and he felt bile rise in his throat. Were they all laughing at him rather than with him? He was frightened by the fact that he could not now distinguish between the two possibilities.

Before he knew it, the carriage had pulled up outside the Manor and he moved to help his stepmother alight. In the full candlelight of the hall, he could see the aftermath of the weeping on her face and he bent forward to kiss her on the cheek.

'Goodnight, Mama,' he said.

'Goodnight, Edmund.' Mrs Leighterton could hear Mr Smithson's words ringing in her ears, so she determined that she must maintain a strong front and keep her emotions in check. She made quickly for the stairs and her bedchamber, where she hoped she could enjoy a release of the pent-up feelings inside her.

It might perhaps have been sensible if she had encouraged Edmund to bed as well for he was prey to his own demons. With no-one in a position to challenge his recollection of the evening, he fed his grievance and inevitably made for the parlour to drown his sorrows. Mr Cleverley watched him go with a heavy heart and deep anxiety in his eyes. Having not been present at the party, neither he, nor Mr Purvis for that matter, was in a position to reassure their master that he had indeed been amongst friends who had keenly shared his feelings as had been demonstrated by the reaction to the poem.

Entering the parlour and finding it in darkness, Edmund did not bother to call for a servant to light the candles; instead he collected a candle from the holder on the wall in the corridor and lit the few candles around the fire. He then bent down and lit the fire before returning the candle to its original site.

Edmund had not imbibed too freely at the Smithsons' for the entertainment had prevented him from being idle, a prerequisite for his drinking. The decanter glittered seductively from the ornate sideboard. He took off his jacket and loosened his cravat before helping himself to a good measure of strong brandy. He then took a large swig so that in a matter of moments the glass was empty. Picking up the decanter in the same hand as the now empty glass he went to draw back the curtains and fold back the shutters. He felt caged and shut in and hoped this action would relieve the festering anger and suffocation that dogged him. Sadly it had no such ameliorating effect. The moon had been extinguished by a large storm cloud and it gave the darkness a heavy cloying aspect.

Edmund flung himself down on to one of the hard-backed chairs and set to drink in earnest. He was on his fourth brandy when he saw the light of a lantern through the window. Not too drunk to be able to investigate but not sober enough to be rational, he immediately assumed it was burglars. Here was a good outlet for the belligerence he was feeling; a set-to with a burglar might assuage his wrathful temper. He went immediately to the back door, which led out into the courtyard where he had seen the light. He snatched up a silver candelabrum and set out in pursuit.

'Halt, who goes there?' he demanded in a loud voice, forgetting in his preoccupation that he had no hope of gaining the answer.

The light had stopped moving away from him and now remained gently swaying as its owner had clearly turned to confront Edmund. Unfortunately the light obscured the features of the man holding it and Edmund remained in ignorance of who it was.

As he stepped forward, the prevailing wind blew out his candles and pitched him into darkness. He dropped the candelabrum, careless of the fact that he might have dented or even broken its silver holders. Edmund lunged forward into a lurching run and came quickly upon the man. With flaying limbs he reached out to grab the arm holding the lantern, but such was the impairment of his balance that he missed and hit the lantern, loosening it from the man's grasp and sending it tumbling to the floor. Now both parties were cloaked in the all-enveloping blackness. No feature on either face could be distinguished. Edmund tried again to grab the man's arm but found instead hands held up to ward him off. He lunged again, this time yielding a mighty punch, which connected with the man's jaw and felled him to the ground. Throwing himself on his quarry, Edmund set about trying to pin the man down but his fevered groping uncovered a square hard item in the man's breast pocket. Even in his inebriated state Edmund knew what it was: a slate. He had tackled one of his own staff. A wave of nausea hit him and Edmund gave a shuddering groan of despair.

'My God, what have I done now, who are you?' he demanded brokenly, only then realising that forgetting his hearing impairment he had landed himself in yet another unfortunate situation. He rolled off the man, who remained alarmingly still. Edmund searched gently with his hands to discover the man's head, which he guessed had hit the cobbles hard. Indeed, when he stripped off his own shirt and rolled it up to put under the man's head, he could feel a sticky bump forming. Edmund's thoughts were incoherent and horror and mortification seared his brain. The dreamlike quality of his intoxication had turned into a nightmare; he struggled to think clearly through its fog about what to do next.

The body beside him shuddered slightly and relief washed through Edmund. The man, whoever he was, was not dead. With frenzied groping, Edmund found the damaged lantern, then he located his tinderbox in his pantaloon pocket and lit the lamp through the broken aperture with trembling fingers, heedless of any risk of cutting himself.

It was difficult to protect the candle against the fickle wind but he was eventually able to shed light on his victim.

There were no bounds to his remorse when his worst fears were confirmed and he glimpsed the ghastly pale face of his devoted groom, Golding.

'Golding, Golding, forgive me,' he begged. 'What have I done?'

Golding, who had regained consciousness, put up a weak hand to grip Edmund's shoulder. Both men were oblivious to the irony that it was Golding on the ground who was comforting his assailant.

Edmund, struggling to master his feelings, at last made a decision on what to do next.

'Come,' he said, setting the lantern down to lift the man bodily. 'I will take you into the parlour. We must attend to your wounds.'

Golding attempted a feeble shake of the head but it was too painful to be sustained.

'No, no,' he cried, knowing it was fruitless; he was left with no alternative but once more to ward off Edmund's hands.

'Oh Golding, no please let me help you. It was a mistake, a ghastly mistake. Please forgive me. I give you my word I will hurt you no further.' In his agitation Edmund was not capable of reading the signs and did not interpret Golding's movements correctly. Golding fumbled for his slate but when he drew it out of his pocket pieces fell out of its wooden surround; it was useless. It did however, serve one purpose; it drew Edmund up short and made him realise that Golding needed to communicate with him.

'Here,' he thrust his hand out to Golding, 'write on my hand.'

Struggling painfully to a sitting position with Edmund's help, Golding looked blankly at him, not understanding.

Edmund put his hand out again. 'Draw the letters on my hand, Golding. I can feel what you say. I have no need to see it.'

'The mare foaling, in trouble.' The words he used may have been disjointed and a surprise to Edmund but he grasped their meaning immediately.

'You were going to help her?' He stated the obvious. 'But you are in no fit state to go now. Let me call one of the other stable boys and help you to your bed.'

'No.' Golding's fingers were wooden from the effects of the fall, but he was determined to get the message across. 'Too nervous, too valuable.'

'Then I will help you for you cannot do it alone.'

Golding was in no position to object. He allowed Edmund to help him to his feet and then once the other man had re-donned his crumpled shirt, leaned on him heavily as they crossed the courtyard to the stable block.

Once inside there was the warm glow from flaming torches in the wall holders and Edmund was able to see what havoc he had wreaked on Golding's face and head. The cheek below his left eye was swelling and beginning to bruise and his lip was bleeding from having been bitten when he had hit the ground. The lump on his head was the size of a hen's egg. Edmund was appalled.

He went to the water trough, which luckily contained clean

well water, and soaked his thankfully pristine handkerchief in it. Before he would allow the man to go forward into the mare's stable, he washed the wounds and then rinsing out the handkerchief folded it into a damp pad, which he placed on the lump. Then while Golding held it in place, he looked around for some means of fixing it more permanently in place. A foray into the tack room resulted in him retrieving a horse's tail bandage, which he wound around Golding's head.

'Well,' he said with a crooked smile, 'you're not very pretty but it is better than nought.'

Then the two men went quietly towards the stall that held the brood mare. She was a lovely bay creature with glossy black mane and tail and a coat that normally gleamed, but tonight it was staring and there was sweat at the top of her beautifully shaped legs. She was clearly in much discomfort as she was fidgeting and swaying turn and turn about. However the appearance of Golding appeared to calm her and she let the man put up a hand to the head collar and draw her head to him. He began to whisper soothing words and her agitation grew less.

Edmund, who by choice had spent half his childhood in the stable, made an assessment of her. All the signs spoke of a foaling in trouble. As one being, the two men worked in silence to help the poor mare. There was no need for words, as each knew what had to be done. With great skill, they helped ease the stuck foal out into the world and with a final push from the mare, a rush of long spindly legs and a gush of liquid, the wonder of birth was demonstrated before them. The two men stood exhausted yet euphoric as the gentle mare began to nuzzle and tend to her offspring. Edmund leaned forward and cleared the mucus from the foal's mouth and then looking up was aghast to see Golding swaying on his feet. Edmund was just in time to catch him before he fell to the straw-covered floor.

'Enough now, Golding. It is your bed for you.' When Golding moved to protest, Edmund heaved him over his shoulder and carried him out of the stable. 'I swear to you that I will come back and ensure that the babe gets on its feet, but you must go to bed, man, or you will be dead in the morning.'

Snatching up a lantern, Edmund carried his groom across the stable yard to the tallet steps, which led up to Golding's room. Knowing he could not carry him up the uneven stone steps, Edmund set him down at their base and put an arm under his shoulder. They struggled up the steps together. By now Golding was so weary that Edmund virtually had to undress him and put him in his hard truckle bed.

'I wish I could do more for you, my friend,' he said to the grey face now lying on the rough pillow. 'I cannot forgive myself for having injured you.'

Golding was already unconscious. Edmund could do nothing but blow out the candles and make his way back to the mare.

Such had been the ordeal the foal had undergone that it was not until the first light of dawn was stealing over the horizon that Edmund, bone weary with fatigue, felt able to leave it solely to its mother's ministrations. He made his way quietly through the house and gained his room with a sigh of relief.

Catching sight of himself in the mirror, he knew he could not just flop into bed, so he took up the jug of now cold water left on the side for him and washed away the blood and the dirt from his skin. He knew not whether it was Golding's or the mare's but by now he cared not. At last he felt he had cleansed himself sufficiently and climbed gratefully between the well-aired sheets of his bed. As his head touched the pillow his last thoughts were of Miss Smithson and what she would think of what he had done, but that was for another time as Edmund decided tomorrow would have to take care of itself.

16

*T*omorrow was in fact already today as Edmund had made it to bed not an hour before the household awoke. In another place Elena awoke quite early and lay in her bed revelling in the remembered success of the evening. Her mind's eye dwelt on the image of Edmund consumed by laughter, his face cleared of the lines of bitterness that had threatened to leave an indelible mark on him. While never boastful, Elena could not help but congratulate herself on having set the games well. She never expected to be a grand hostess of huge balls or parties but to have succeeded to make all her disparate party guests comfortable had been her aim and she believed she had achieved it.

Eventually she decided it was time to get up and she rang the bell for her morning chocolate, knowing that Tillie the maid would be eager to discuss the previous night's events.

The girl arrived quickly enough, her appearance prim and smart, a testament to the success of Mrs Timery's appointment as housekeeper. The girl's cap was a brilliant white, as was her apron, and the misty blue-grey of her dress was practical without being drab. She set the chocolate down on the table beside the bed.

'Good morning, Miss.'

'Good morning, Tillie.'

'I'se hope you slept a'right after all the kerfuffle last night.'

'There was no kerfuffle,' Elena said sharply, surprised out of her normal calm. 'What can you be thinking of?'

'Oh but there was, Miss,' said Tillie dramatically. 'When 'e got 'ome, Mr Leighterton got drunk and milled down his groom. Near killed him I 'eard. Broke his skull. There's talk of calling in the Justice of Peace. Folk is tired of Mr Edmund's vicious 'abits and Mr Golding is well liked. Assault 'n 'battery they're calling it.'

'This cannot be true,' cried Elena, appalled. 'Mr Edmund would never, never do that to Mr Golding; he holds him in very high esteem.'

'I'm only telling what I 'eard, Miss,' said Tillie, drawing back at the anger and disbelief in Elena's face.

Elena did not want to hear any more; she flung back the bedclothes and grabbed the nearest wrap she could find, which turned out to be a lacy negligée she had been trimming for the summer. Mindless of the fact that her hair was still in a long plait and careless of any footwear, she wrenched open the bedroom door and raced along the corridor to the stairs.

'Papa, Papa,' she started shouting before she was even halfway down. She found him before he had a chance to respond. He was in his study just accepting some refreshments from Timery. He had breakfasted much earlier.

'Good God, what is it, Elena?' he demanded as she erupted into his presence.

'Have you heard the stories that are being put about regarding Mr Leighterton, Papa, have you heard them?'

Mr Smithson looked enquiringly at his butler. 'What stories are these, Timery? Tell me, tell me this instant.'

Timery looked uncomfortable. 'They are not really suitable for a young lady's ears, Sir,' he said by way of a delay.

'Oh dammit man, spit it out, you can see that my daughter is already a party to some lurid version of the events. Give us chapter and verse at once I pray.'

'Very well, Sir, but I must stress that I have only heard a very garbled version.' He paused, trying to decide for himself what was fact and what was fiction. 'I understand that when Mr Leighterton returned from the party, he withdrew to a parlour where it had previously been his custom to drink himself into a stupor. He had curtailed this activity over the last month but resumed it last night. In his cups he attacked the groom, who was badly beaten and unlikely to survive.'

'This cannot be true.' Elena almost stamped her foot. 'I won't let it be true. I beg you, Papa, go to the Manor, ascertain what really happened before they send a lynch mob determined to find him guilty of a crime for which there is no evidence. Please Papa, please.'

Mr Smithson looked down into his daughter's agonised and anxious face and nodded. While he suspected the story would be factual in some part, there were elements that did not ring true. Even at his worst Edmund had never sought out someone to hit. Mr Smithson wished to establish how Edmund had come into contact with the groom before he would accept him guilty of premeditated murder.

Calling for his horse, Mr Smithson rode with all good speed to the Manor. Mrs Leighterton was surprised by such an early visit and briefly wondered whether Mr Smithson was determined to pursue the intimacy he had hinted at wanting the night before. She felt a quiver of pleasure at the thought that this man could be interested in her and was mystified with disappointment when he strode in without any reference to his feelings for her.

'You must understand the seriousness of the situation, Madam,' he said briskly. 'We must get to the bottom of the matter before any mob takes it into their heads to mete out a rough justice of their own.'

Mrs Leighterton could only stare at him bewildered for a time, as she had heard nothing. No-one had dared to tell the story to her. Then the need as ever to protect her stepson, though he was a grown man, asserted itself and she tugged at the bell rope. Cleverley came in response and she demanded the presence of Purvis as well. Neither of these two men was able to give any more coherent a picture of events than the one they already had.

In exasperation, Mr Smithson said he would visit the groom, be he ever so ill. 'Take me to him,' he demanded of Purvis.

'I will accompany you,' said Mrs Leighterton at once.

'No, Madam, I think not,' said Mr Smithson, taking her right hand as if to shake it and dismiss her. 'It is no place for a lady and I give my word of honour that I will tell you of every detail I glean.'

She looked into his eyes and saw sympathy and understanding there and knew that she had to acquiesce. There was no room for further histrionics.

Purvis led Mr Smithson to the back of the house.

'Let me see this infamous parlour,' he requested the valet.

In the morning light, the parlour gave away very little but Mr Smithson noted that the brandy decanter still held some liquid and that none of the furniture had been disarranged although Edmund's beautiful coat remained draped carelessly over one of the chairs.

'And this is how it was discovered this morning?' he asked.

'Exactly, Sir, including the open shutters and curtains.' Mr Smithson went to the window and looked out at the view across the cobbled courtyard to the stables, some two hundred yards away.

'Very well,' he said. 'Now take me to Golding.'

As they repaired across the courtyard, Mr Smithson's shoes crunched unexpectedly. He looked down to see the fragments of glass from the broken lantern.

'So this is where the fight took place,' he said with no inflection in his voice.

Purvis nodded and looked at him. 'I wish you joy in your attempts to exonerate him, Sir,' he said heavily. 'For my will is broken; I have laboured so hard these last few weeks to help him and now this.'

'As you say man, a few weeks. His deafness is for a lifetime!'

Mr Smithson walked forward to the tallet steps. A chastened Purvis, floored by the man's words, could only stand and watch.

'Come on, man, don't dawdle,' adjured Mr Smithson, and made his way up the steps.

Golding was lying in bed, his face ashen where it was not bruised but his eyes open under the makeshift bandage. Mr Smithson went to him immediately.

'Begging your pardon, Mr Smithson,' said Golding in a hoarse voice. 'I should be on my feet before you but when I try I come over all dizzy like and 'ave to take to my bed again.'

'Think nothing of it. I am just glad to see that you are not as seriously injured as I have been led to believe. Has anyone brought your breakfast, tended your hurts, anything?'

'No Sir, not since Mr Edmund wound this cursed tail bandage round me 'ead. Not so much as a glass of water from one of the stable lads. Wait till I'm on my feet again. They'll be 'earing from me. They will.'

'I'll attend to it,' said Mr Purvis abruptly and went and found a lackey to go to the kitchens and bring back a laden tray.

Once Purvis had returned, Mr Smithson waited in some impatience for Golding to be raised up comfortably and for victuals to arrive before questioning him further.

'I would have from your lips the truth of what happened last night, Golding,' he said. 'There is trouble brewing for Mr Edmund and I can only combat it with the truth.'

Golding, who until this point had not considered why he was being honoured by a deputation, stopped in mid-chew of the crusty bread with which he had been supplied.

'What trouble?' he asked thickly with an edge to his voice.

'You tell me,' replied Mr Smithson unhelpfully.

Golding looked from one man to the other.

Mr Smithson urged again. 'I need to know what happened between you and Mr Edmund last night.'

'Begging your pardon, Sir, but that's between 'im and me,' barked Golding, misguidedly determined to protect his master.

'And if it stays that way, then you will do Mr Edmund no favours. I need to know what happened.'

'Tell him, Golding,' urged Mr Purvis tightly.

So Golding did. He spared them nothing: his own frantic attempts to communicate with Edmund, Edmund's overwhelming remorse at the mistake he had made, the hard work and the joy of the foal's successful birth and then Edmund's ministrations to his injuries.

As he concluded his tale, Mr Smithson blew out a long breath. He took a turn around the room, weighing up how best to play it.

'It has to be the truth, the tale we tell,' he said at last. 'Mr Edmund mistook you for a burglar in the dark, simple as that. When people see that you are not dead they will begin to disbelieve the more fanciful tales. Mr Leighterton's recovery in the eyes of his critics may suffer a small setback but not if I can help it.'

Purvis frowned. 'Is it enough to save his reputation, Sir?' he asked dubiously.

'It will have to be,' said Mr Smithson emphatically. 'Now show a more cheerful countenance and we will set about telling the true tale.'

So when Edmund woke some two hours later at nearly noon, he was not confronted with a host of angry faces pointing accusing fingers at him. Instead Purvis was there, brushing out the coat from the parlour and bundling up the shirt, which was unlikely to be worn at a party ever again.

'It is not what it looks like,' said Edmund grimly as he watched Purvis study the maltreated shirt. 'I have made a real mess of things, Purvis. I feel I have destroyed my reputation all over again.'

Purvis came up to the bed and looked Edmund straight in the face.

'It will be hard,' he said slowly, 'but you are blessed with friends who will fight your corner with you, Sir. Remember that, remember that always.'

Mutely Edmund handed him the slate so that the words could be written down for him to understand.

17

*A*s Golding refused to die and was back on his feet within a matter of days, the original version of events was soon supplanted by a semblance of the truth. It was also much aided by the Campdens suffering a genuine burglary. It did not take much to twist the tale of Edmund's exploits to make him sound brave and more the hero by his willingness to confront an intruder.

Hearing neither the good nor bad gossip, Edmund tried to put it behind him but he was reluctant to leave the Manor, knowing that he would be even more notorious in the eyes of his neighbours. His feelings about seeing Miss Smithson again were ambivalent. He longed to see her, yet dreaded it for he could not bear to think of her despising him. For whatever construction was put on the turn of events, Edmund knew his predilection for drowning his sorrows was a weakness she must abhor and decry. As the days passed and she did not accompany her father on his morning calls, he began to believe that he had transgressed beyond forgiveness. He was not to know that it was Miss Smithson's embarrassment at her own behaviour that kept her from the Manor. She believed she had exposed herself to the censure of the neighbourhood. It was inevitable that the tale would get about that she had been careless of her own reputation, running barefoot and déshabillé through the house to save his. Her feelings for him must now be as clear as day to everyone but Edmund.

While it should have been Mr Smithson's place to counsel his daughter, he had more pressing concerns of his own. His early meeting with Mrs Leighterton on the morning after the party had forced him to confront his feelings for her despite the shortness of their acquaintance. Outwardly he had been brisk and matter of fact but seeing her anxious and confused had made him want to get down on one knee and offer to protect her from that moment onwards. So on the pretext of seeing how she was faring after the event, he called daily and although he did not consciously notice that she was dressed in a selection of new gowns, he thought her even more attractive and appealing. Her character, too, was reasserting itself after the months of keeping it in check so as not to incur Edmund's wrath. Mr Smithson was in love for the first time in a dozen years and he had no plans to let the lady slip through his fingers.

To this end, he wrote to his friend Lord Delrymple asking for advice on jewellery suitable for an affianced lady. He could hardly contain his impatience for the reply and when it came it had him heading post-haste to a jeweller's in London recommended by his lordship.

Elena could only blink at him as he came to say goodbye during his preparation for departure.

'Why must you go, Papa?' she asked, concerned that it might be some adverse business that was taking him away so urgently.

'Never you mind, young lady,' he said, tapping his nose with his forefinger. Then seeing the anxiety in her brown eyes he relented a little. 'There is nothing to discomfort yourself about, Elena, my sweet. All is well, I assure you.'

And she had to be satisfied with that for he would say no more although she could see the smile lurking behind his eyes and the spring in his normally solid step. Her father was enjoying himself, she realised and she could not fault it.

Once he had gone, she was left to be entertained by just Polly's and Jessamy's unexacting company, which did little to leaven her spirits. Her only solace was the continuing regular arrival of letters from the Delrymple girls twice a week.

She was surprised to learn from Lady Caroline that Mr Ingram Deacon was to visit them in Leicestershire two weeks hence. Elena had thought him fixed in Eastbourne for another month at the very least and a visit to Leicestershire was not in keeping with his original vowed intent to await his parents' arrival in London. She had to wait until the following day to get a letter from Lady Dorothea to find out why. Lady Dorothea had a much greater predilection for gossip and was therefore much more forthcoming.

'My dearest Elena,' she wrote, her letter heavily crossed, as she explained, not because she could not get a frank from her father but because the sisters wrote so many letters, one of their few forms of entertainment, that there was a dearth of paper in the house.

> 'No doubt, you will have heard from Caroline that we eagerly anticipate a visit from Mr Ingram Deacon,' she continued in full flow. 'His plans have changed. His father broke his ribs in a fall and cannot sustain the journey to London, so his mother has decided to remain in Cumbria also. Mr Deacon has resolved to travel north to see them and Papa offered him to break his journey with us. He wrote a most appreciative letter and thanked Papa again for the introduction to your family. I understand that he and Mr Kelwich enjoyed a very convivial evening on the occasion of your birthday party. He wrote very warmly of your hospitality and of his pleasure in coming to know you. He spoke particularly kindly of Mr Leighterton and expressed the wish to pursue a further acquaintance with him when he decides to re-enter society. He has excited our curiosity, my dear Elena, you have been too reticent about Mr Edmund Leighterton in your letters.'

Elena folded the letter with a snap, blushing even though she was alone in the stately room. It seemed that the whole world was keen to couple her name with Edmund Leighterton's and she had done nothing to resist it. She feared that she could not now be in his presence without showing her deep embarrassment. What must he think of her? She wondered, not daring to hope, if a man who had so many pressing obstacles to overcome could find it in him to reciprocate her feelings.

Mr Smithson took three days to achieve his mission in London and returned clutching a diamond set of ring, earrings, necklace and tiara. He had never spent so much money before and had waited for an express from Mr Banbury to give him leave to do so. Mr Banbury's epistle had assured him that he had every right to spend his income as he saw fit, but reminded him that the bank held the family emeralds and that he might like to see this set before embarking on his purchase. Dutifully Mr Smithson had visited the bank and was led by a most obsequious gentleman to the vault to be shown the heirlooms. While the brilliant green of the emeralds would have suited Elena's strong-coloured hair and eyes, Mr Smithson felt he would be doing his beloved no favours if he pressed her to wear them. These jewels would not complement Mrs Leighterton's more muted hair and pallor. He retraced his steps to the jeweller's and bought the diamond set.

With excitement pumping through his veins he had hardly stepped out of the carriage, once home, to embrace his children before he was calling for his horse and determinedly making his way to the Manor.

Mrs Leighterton, who had also been in ignorance of the nature of his errand, had passed through disappointment to despair when he had not visited her for four days complete. She had revisited each of their recent conversations to see how she might have offended him and could find nothing to the point.

When Mr Smithson was announced a little before noon on the fifth day, she could hardly contain her eagerness to see him.

William Smithson was pleased to see that his premature

arrival before the correct time for a morning call had served him well and that she had no other guests. He wished he could command Cleverley to deny her to anyone else but he had not yet won the right to speak on her behalf so held off, hoping that he could say his piece before they were interrupted.

He came forward and took her hand, and bowing over it lightly brushed her hand with his lips. Mrs Leighterton was momentarily bereft of speech. Her pleasure at seeing him came with such force that she was rocked from her normal composure.

No sooner had Cleverley shut the door than Mr Smithson announced his intentions.

'My dear Mrs Leighterton, I can contain myself no longer. I must tell you of my admiration for you and all you have endured and I request the favour of being given permission to pay my addresses to you.'

'Mr Smithson!' she could only exclaim. She had not pursued the consequences of their mutual attraction beyond wishing that they could be more often in each other's company. She had not dared hope that he might be serious enough to suggest marriage. This huge step must be given proper consideration.

Without saying anything further, she tugged the bell rope and Cleverley reappeared. 'I believe, Cleverley,' she said rather unsteadily, 'that I am not at home to morning callers today.'

'Very well, Madam.' Cleverley looked in the direction of Mr Smithson and drew his own conclusions.

After the butler's second departure, Mrs Leighterton sat herself down on the chaise longue and indicated to Mr Smithson to sit beside her, which he quickly did.

She turned to face him. 'I am deeply conscious of the honour you do me, Sir,' she said, her voice still rather shaky. 'This is so unexpected.'

'But you must have been aware of my deep regard for you, Ma'am. I believe I have not hidden my admiration.'

'Yes, no, how can I tell? Your disappearance over the last few

147

days had left me wondering and fearful that I had inadvertently turned you against me.'

'No, never that.' Mr Smithson had possessed himself of one of her hands and held it firmly between his two great paws. 'My admiration has grown steadily from the first day I met you for many reasons: your stoicism and patience when dealing with your stepson; your courage in facing your neighbours daily – what I have not seen, I have learned from Johnson. You and I both know what it is to have been left alone without our life partners for years, let us take this chance offered to us and put aside that loneliness.

Tears were pricking under Mrs Leighterton's eyelids.

'Oh, but I wish that we could,' she said, sighing.

'But why should we not?' asked Mr Smithson, seeing no impediment.

Putting her hand over his, Mrs Leighterton patted it then stood up, so that she was above him. He made to stand too but she pressed down on his shoulder so that he had to remain seated.

'If it were just you and me to consider, dear Sir,' she said, 'I would grant you your request immediately and announce our engagement to the world, but I have given near twenty years of my life to looking after someone else's child and look how little I have been rewarded. I could marry tomorrow and were something to happen to you, I could be back in the role of stepmother to a young boy. I do not have the resilience to attempt it again even as duty dictates that I should.'

Mr Smithson saw immediately the dread in her that she would be a prisoner of her duty once more. 'You have nothing to fear, my love,' he said gently, his voice warm with reassurance. 'While I cannot guarantee that I will survive to Jessamy's maturity, you must see that he is a very different case from a youthful Edmund. He never knew his mother and has an independent soul. He would not trouble you. Further, his sister would have much to say on the matter if I were to leave anyone else as his guardian other than herself.' He slipped to the ground on bended knee and removed the packet containing the jewellery set.

'I beg you to do me the honour of becoming my affianced wife,' he said and opened the case to reveal the sparkling riches.

Mrs Leighterton looked first at the diamonds and then at him and smiled. 'What woman,' she said, choking back a laugh, 'could resist such a double: wealth' – here she drew her hand gently along the line of his chin – 'and beauty,' as she then touched the dazzling jewels. 'Yes,' she said. 'I would be delighted to accept your kind offer of marriage.'

Mr Smithson got to his feet and, casting the jewellery box on to the chaise longue, drew Mrs Leighterton into the circle of his arms and kissed her full on the lips.

18

*M*r Smithson and Mrs Leighterton, while desirous of declaring their love to the world, were circumspect in making their announcement. They resolved that Edmund deserved a few more weeks to distance himself from the consequences of the aftermath of the party before having to face the prospect of living an independent life if his stepmother removed to Holm Oak Reach. Secretly Mrs Leighterton hoped that a match could be made between Edmund and Elena so that she could put aside any guilt she might feel on deserting him. However, she was growing very fond of Elena and had no desire to sacrifice her to aid her own comfort unless the girl was willing. Mrs Leighterton dared not suggest the match to Mr Smithson because of its very convenience.

Indubitably the status quo would have been maintained for too long if circumstances had not conspired to bring Edmund and Elena together again.

Bored by and slightly suspicious of her father's defection to Mrs Leighterton, Elena had taken it upon herself to encourage Polly to ride. Polly was at first rather nervous but, surprisingly, she had a natural seat and quickly achieved a rapport with her mount which was a delight to see. Elena, who had thought that without Edmund in attendance she would be unable to explore the lanes and byways beyond their estate, was pleased to discover Polly willing to accompany her. In turn Polly was eager to include Jessamy, who, on agreeing to come, bounced along on an overweight cob, which their head groom had managed to borrow for him from a local farmer. The weather had suddenly improved and wild daffodils were beginning to show their colours along their route.

The little troupe found there was much pleasure to be had in getting their bearings. Jessamy had an unnerving sense of direction, which rarely let them down. It was then rather a surprise when cantering along the verge between two high hedgerows that Polly reined in and called out to the others to stop.

'What is it, Polly. What is amiss?' cried Elena as she dutifully trotted back to her cousin.

'I thought I heard a groan and a whimper,' replied Polly rather breathlessly. 'I think someone may be injured on the far side of the hedge.' By now, Jessamy had turned his horse by virtue of hauling its head round; the cob had a very hard mouth.

'What is it? What is it?' he demanded excitedly.

Elena put her fingers to her lips and they held the horses steady while they listened for the noise that had caught Polly's attention to repeat itself. There was a whimper and then a single yelp from a dog, which startled the horses so that they rocked on the spot. Jessamy slid to the ground and headed towards a gap in the hedge some twenty yards back. Elena and Polly followed suit and Elena gathered up the reins of the cob to tether him and her mount to a sycamore sapling. Polly made to do the same with hers.

Jessamy stepped carefully through the meagre gap. As the hedgerow was thick with may and blackthorn, he did not fancy being scratched for his trouble. The girls found passing through into the field even more difficult for, although their long skirts protected them from the thorns, they were inclined to get caught up on the stray branches.

The sight that confronted them brought them up short. Lying flat on his back was a man, his booted feet facing them so that as they stood there they could not see his face. By his side sat a sturdy black dog, the like of which none of them had ever seen before.

Jessamy made to step forward but Elena put a hand on his shoulder to prevent him. 'Pray be careful, Jessamy, the dog may be savage.'

The boy pushed her restraining hand away and stepped slowly towards the panting dog. Wary brown eyes watched him but the gentle soothing nonsense he was talking seemed to comfort the dog. It stood up stiffly, revealing it to be a bitch, very soon to whelp, which had clearly been slightly injured in whatever altercation had resulted in her master's current predicament.

Jessamy lifted the strap from his water bottle that he carried over his shoulder and undid the lid to pour some liquid into one cupped hand. He knelt down and held it out to the dog. She moved forward jerkily and lapped thirstily.

'Here, pour it into both my hands,' he demanded of Polly, who immediately responded to his instructions after he handed her the bottle.

Elena gave an exclamation of mock annoyance.

'Trust you, Jessamy, to succour the animal before the man,' she said indulgently. Then the man groaned again and she was recalled to his woes. She gave him her full attention and stepped towards him gingerly, fearful that the dog might not allow it.

'Save some for the man!' she cried as Polly let more water gush into the boy's hands.

Ruefully Polly put the lid back on the water bottle. She mumbled an apology and also trod carefully to the man's side. He was lying awkwardly amongst the rough grass close to the hedge and, despite his previous groans, he was unconscious. Momentarily Polly feared he had died in the time they had tended the dog and then she saw the rise and fall of his chest and the trickle of blood from a fresh wound on his head.

Elena came up beside her and knelt down for a closer inspection. What clothes he had on were damp and torn. His left arm looked in an alarmingly uncomfortable position. The wavy dark hair was stuck to his forehead by blood and sweat. Elena lifted off her hat and undid the scarf that adorned it; she folded it into a pad and slipped it under his head.

'He is so cold,' Polly said, taking his hand and chaffing it.

'Yes, I think he has been here all night,' agreed Elena, who was now taking off the green coat of her riding habit and covering him with it. He stirred and moaned again but did not open his eyes.

'We must get him to the doctor,' she announced decisively.

'But how can we do that?' asked Polly, wide-eyed with dismay. 'We have no means of conveying him anywhere.'

Elena looked around her. They were completely obscured from the lane by the thick hedge. The lane itself was a quiet one without much traffic, either horse drawn or pedestrian, and they had come some way without seeing even a farm worker's cottage.

'Jessamy, you must take my horse and go to the Manor for help. It is some three miles closer than the Reach.

Jessamy, who was completely absorbed with the needs of the dog, which, now that her master was no longer her responsibility, was showing all the signs of going into labour, ignored her. Elena sighed and got to her feet.

'Will you be all right here if I go?' she asked Polly uncertainly.

'Yes, yes, do not spare a thought for me, I will be fine,' said Polly, who was now wiping the man's forehead with her lace handkerchief. 'Is he not good-looking Elena, such a fine face?'

'Fine indeed, but we must get him help,' she said impatiently. A sense of urgency was overtaking her now that the shock of finding him and his dog had worn off. 'I will be as quick as I can,' she said as she strode purposively back to the gap in the hedge. She was not however sure that either her brother or her cousin were much interested. Jessamy was totally absorbed with the bitch and Polly was now gazing worshipfully down into the face of the unconscious young man.

Elena struggled to mount the horse without the aid of a groom or mounting block but eventually she lowered the stirrup enough to get sufficient purchase on it with her foot to haul herself up on to the saddle. Grimly, she gathered up the reins and pressed the horse into a lively canter, conscious as she did so that the other two horses might attempt to follow suit. Thankfully they, particularly the cob, were too interested in eating the spring grass to take too much account of what she was doing.

Hoping above hope that she could recall the way, Elena kept the horse at a good pace and was rewarded some twenty minutes later by the sight of the Manor gates. Hardly had she reached the environs of the house than she had the good fortune to be spotted by Edmund. He had been out riding and had he returned from any other direction, he would not have seen her as he could hear nothing of her horse's hooves pounding along the drive or her shouts for help. He did however grasp the urgency of the situation immediately, seeing her flying along towards him; her hair with the hat absent had freed itself from the confines of its pins and clips and was dis-arranged and streaming out behind her and her face as it came into focus was a study in anxiety and urgency.

All previous considerations and embarrassments that had kept them apart were forgotten; Edmund went forward on his horse to greet her. She reined in, her expressive face fleetingly showing relief but in her agitation she forgot momentarily that he could not hear her and launched into an animated description of what they had found.

Edmund watching her mouth keenly, caught the words 'man' and 'dog' and was tempted to pretend that he had understood the rest but the case was clearly too desperate for false pride. He took a deep breath and withdrew a slate from his breast pocket.

'My dear Miss Smithson, please.' He indicated the slate and made to hand it to her.

Elena was mortified and it showed in her face. She was appalled at herself for overlooking his impediment.

Edmund held out the slate again, adjuring her to take it. 'I will hold the reins of your horse while you write,' he said.

She took the slate, an apology expressed in the intensity of her brown eyes. 'Forgive me,' she said and made the attempt to write. Faced however with the overwhelming number of details and such difficult circumstances under which to convey it, her agitation and frustration were suddenly manifest in those windows to her soul. She turned her head away in exasperation.

Edmund felt the pain of rejection like a knife to the heart. His first instinct was to protect himself. To abandon her here and gallop away in anger, making the powerful rhythm of the horse dissipate the hurt and desperation that he felt but a greater power, one he had been cultivating with the help of his faithful servants and indeed Miss Smithson herself, overcame that urge.

'Compose yourself, Miss Smithson and take it slowly,' he said evenly. 'You wish to tell me about a man and his dog, I believe.'

Turning back, she nodded eagerly and finally found the words to write. The slate would not hold more than two sentences at a time and her writing was necessarily uneven because of the movement of the restive horse, but Edmund soon had the gist of what they had discovered and before Elena knew it he was sending one stable boy off for the doctor and had Golding prepare a farm wagon to convey the man flat.

'Have the doctor come here,' he ordered the stable lad. Elena touched his arm and shook her head.

'The Reach,' she said.

Edmund knew immediately what she was saying and was about to argue the increased distance when he remembered that his stepmother had had enough of sickrooms and Dr Osborne. He dutifully endorsed Elena's amendment to the man's instructions.

The heavy farm horses that drew the wagon would do no more than a trot and Elena had to curb her impatience to be travelling faster. She rode beside Edmund not knowing how to express the sense of her obligation to him nor the depth of her mortification at the way she had treated him.

Edmund in turn was struggling with himself. His efforts at his morning lessons with Purvis had had some success and he could now have a passable conversation with him or Cleverley, who both knew to look him full in the face and speak distinctly. He searched for the courage to confide in Elena and beg her indulgence, not withstanding the variety of emotions she had suffered when she had been reminded that she could not have an ordinary dialogue with him. Until today there had been no hint that she might not always be equal to the restrictions his impairment put upon them. It was a severe blow to Edmund's self-esteem to have sensed her impatience but he was man enough to acknowledge that she had an entitlement to be less than perfect.

'Miss Smithson,' burst from him as he launched himself down a path he might regret.

She turned soulful eyes upon him, her emotions still a maelstrom as a result of what had gone on before.

'Yes, Mr Leighterton.' She had since handed back the slate to him, so now looked to have it returned to her. Edmund's two hands remained firmly on the reins of his horse and he had now straightened his head and posture so that he looked forward between the horse's eyes and could not see her mobile face.

'If you would bear with me, I would explain something to you.'

Elena remained silent, knowing that nothing short of physical contact would reach him now so she waited and listened as he gave her an insight into his world and how he had been learning to see what people were saying. To Elena, who had not made the extension beyond the obvious social words, which could be mouthed in isolation, it was a revelation.

'So I am begging you to exercise a little patience with me and suffer me to watch your speech. And if you could speak more slowly, not carefully but clearly, I would hope to understand you. I would also ask you not to betray me yet to others. My step-mother is not ready for such a revolution in the way communication is affected between us. I have asked too much of her already, I cannot demand this courtesy also.'

Elena listened in wonder; she saw no reason why his step-mother would not be delighted to aid him in any way she could, although on careful reflection she perceived and understood his desire to be sufficiently proficient that it would not need his companions to make any special provision in their speech for him. She willed him to look her way, so that she could reassure him and start a conversation with him, but he continued to look straight ahead as though afraid to confront her reaction.

Eventually Elena could stand the suspense no longer and she drew her horse right alongside his. She laid a hand upon his arm. He turned to look at her at last.

'Yes,' she said. 'Yes, I would willingly help you. Very willingly indeed.'

His face broke into a smile of real gladness and he put his own hand on hers.

'Thank you,' he said wholeheartedly. 'Thank you.'

19

*H*appily the recovery of the young man from his ditch had been achieved without more than a few thorn splinters and bramble scratches suffered by his rescuers.

The cavalcade arrived at Holm Oak Reach just as Mr Smithson was returning from the Manor. By some mischance, he had missed Elena's arrival at the Manor and the subsequent uproar as wagons were sought and the stable boy dispatched. It had therefore come as rather a surprise to have the doctor arrive at his doorstep even before the patient had.

Thankfully for all parties, they arrived before the disgruntled doctor had remounted to take his leave. The excitement of the event was enough to assuage his wrath, however, and soon he was holding court in one of the large bedchambers on the first floor. The young man, while still uttering periodically a theatrical groan, had not yet regained consciousness, a circumstance that allowed the doctor to relocate the shoulder and splint the arm without any resistance from his patient.

The doctor historically might have been able to rile Mrs Leighterton but in Mr Smithson he had met his match. Mr Smithson was learning to have no time for condescension and was soon demanding the facts without preamble. The doctor, a mite overawed by the magnificence of the Reach, capitulated and responded to Mr Smithson's questions in an unusually helpful manner.

'As you see, Sir, the left shoulder was dislocated and the arm broken. I can find no other breaks except possibly a couple of ribs. There has been no penetration of the lungs, his breathing is normal enough under the circumstances and his pulse gives me no cause for anxiety. My one fear is that he had a bad knock on the head and then a cold night in the open. He is very cold. He must be made warm.' He indicated the fire, which was already being stoked by one of the servants. 'I would have someone stay with him at all times.'

'I will be here,' Jessamy piped up from the corner where he had settled the dog on a pile of rugs. During the time they waited for help, the bitch had given birth to three wriggling black puppies, which she was now nursing. Jessamy had already provided her with a little food and water, having been prevented by his ever-cautious father from offering her all the food she would eat. 'Never give a ravenous animal too much too soon, young man,' Mr Smithson had found time to say. 'You will leave them in pain and discomfort and will not have served them well.'

Dr Osborne did not think Jessamy was adequate for the task of sickroom nurse and on his way down the magnificent staircase was discussing with Mr Smithson whether he should arrange for the local midwife to come and act in that regard.

'I can look after him.' Polly came hurrying up to the bottom of the wide staircase, her face eager. She, Elena and Edmund had been waiting in some impatience in the hallway to gain the latest news of the patient.

The doctor threw an enquiring look at Mr Smithson, who did not take long to consider. 'My cousin is used to nursing sick children, I am sure she is the very one who would be most suitable for the task,' he said, delighting Polly.

'Thank you, thank you,' she cried breathlessly, lifting her skirts slightly so that she could hurry past them up the stairs to take up her duties immediately.

Mr Smithson saw the doctor out and then turned back to Edmund and Elena, who were waiting as keenly for news as Polly, only with more restraint in their demonstration of it.

'Thank you for coming to their rescue,' said Mr Smithson, taking Edmund's hand and shaking it vigorously.

'You are most welcome, Sir, I was pleased to be of service,' replied Edmund courteously, guessing correctly what the man had said.

Elena had found a slate from somewhere and presented it to her father.

'Tell us how he fares, Papa,' she begged.

Taking the two young people into his study, Mr Smithson wrote out the list of the man's injuries and the doctor's fears.

'We have no way of knowing who he is until he wakes,' observed Edmund. 'Has he no papers on him?'

'I will have to look again,' wrote Mr Smithson. 'A search through his pockets has revealed nothing so far and he has no baggage, it must all have been stolen when he was attacked.'

'So he was attacked?' Edmund was not sure that this information was something that could be assumed from what he had seen.

'That or a very serious fall,' Mr Smithson scribed quickly. 'If so it begs the question what he was doing and where now is the horse?'

Elena remained silent during this exchange. She did not want to speak without a slate and complicate the exchange of information so she waited and watched and listened. Now Edmund turned to her.

'Do you have an opinion, Miss Smithson?' he asked. 'You came upon the scene as one of the first.'

Elena tried to remember just how the young man had been lying when they had discovered him. She took the slate from her father.

'It could not have been because he was jumping the hedge because it was far too high to contemplate such a thing.' Then she recalled that the slope of the land had been severe down to the hedge and the ditch and that there had been clear marks of a horse skidding towards it.

She wiped the slate and added: 'I think he was riding very fast and was probably being chased.'

The men exchanged glances; this did not bode well in their eyes.

'If I were you, Mr Smithson, I would have a footman on call at the bedchamber door at all times,' recommended Edmund firmly.

Mr Smithson nodded. Elena suspected afterwards that this suggestion coloured her opinion of their unexpected guest from then on for she could not shake the niggling feeling of suspicion about him. She went with Edmund to the front door wishing that she could more accurately express her fears. She shivered and he looked at her in quick concern.

'Of course you will be cold,' he said solicitously. 'To have been without your pelisse for so long, you should have retired immediately we reached here to put on warmer raiment.'

'No, no it is not that.' Elena shook her head in denial. 'I think a goose has just walked over my grave,' she said.

Edmund withdrew his own smaller slate from his breast pocket and gestured to Elena to write what she had just said as he could not make sense of it but she could not find the courage to share her fears with him, so she shook her head again and put her hands out to push the slate back to him.

Edmund saw the gesture as a rejection of him, another manifestation of his shortcomings irritating her, for otherwise he could not adequately or immediately explain to himself why she would not make him party to what she had said. He wheeled around on his heel and quitted the house without another word to her. Elena was left forlorn and alone in the middle of the great hall, knowing that she had wounded him but not knowing what she could have done to prevent him responding so when she wanted to keep what she felt were ill-founded fears to herself.

Edmund's horse took the brunt of his anger and humiliation, being urged to career up the drive from the Reach at a speed he should have known could be injurious to its legs. Fortunately he recollected himself before any harm could be done. He had come far enough along the road to recovery not to want to destroy what he had achieved but what he could not reconcile was why Miss Smithson, who had instigated his salvation, now seemed to be shunning him. He conveniently forgot that she had just agreed to help him with his studies of speech. His longing to be able to have a full and frank discussion with her about her feelings for him and his for her clouded his judgement and made him believe it could never be.

Edmund returned to the Manor and leaving his horse with Golding entered the house with dragging feet and a heavy heart. As he made for the stairs to change out of his riding clothes he was confronted by his stepmother wanting to know what had happened. He was forced to put a brave front on his emotions and promise to enlighten her as soon as he was more suitably attired.

Back at the Reach, Elena did not know how long she would have stood irresolute in the hallway if Mr Timery had not recalled her to a sense of the ordinary by closing the front door with a snap.

'Miss Elena, can I be of assistance?' he asked, alarmed by her obvious agitation. She gave him a bleak smile and waved him away with her hand. Mr Timery took his dismissal in good part but was concerned enough for her well-being to track down her father and suggest that she might need his support. Poor Mr Smithson already had enough to tax him. The young man was coming erratically to his senses and Polly needed assistance in keeping him on the bed for his thrashing around was in danger of depositing him on the wooden floorboards, Jessamy was inclined to be petulant because his father had refused to allow him to sleep the night in the chair next to the puppies and now Elena, who rarely needed attention, was apparently wanting it. A few moments' reflection brought him to the conclusion that Elena's need was the greatest by the very virtue of its rarity. He summoned Johnson and commanded him to assist Polly with their unknown guest. Jessamy he left to sulk.

Elena was discovered wandering along one of the great galleries that formed part of the length of the house. Few of the ancestors who looked down from the panelled walls at her displayed more than a supercilious interest in the unhappy girl dawdling along beneath.

'My dear Elena,' cried Mr Smithson as he strode up the gallery in pursuit of her. 'Tell me what ails you, child; tell me at once.'

Elena turned to greet him and found herself enfolded in his strong arms.

'Oh Papa, Papa, forgive me but I feel so foolish,' she confessed.

'In what way, my sweet, tell your Papa.'

Elena extracted herself gently and went to look out of one of the long windows, whose view was over the park.

'I fear that I have allowed the mystery surrounding our new friend's accident to unsettle me. If it is revealed that he was set upon by marauders, then our safety when we meander along the lanes too is in jeopardy.' Here she paused before saying heavily: 'but if it was because he was somewhere he was not meant to be, then what was he doing and have we invited someone malevolent into our midst?'

Mr Smithson moved from his position in the centre of the walkway along the gallery to come up beside her.

'Are you not being a little melodramatic?' he asked.

'Ha, now that is my point.' Elena pounced on his words. 'That is what I fear almost as much: that I am overreacting. That is why I could not divulge my fears to Mr Leighterton for I am ashamed of them. Polly clearly has no such concerns.' Her voice was reaching a higher pitch now as she looked to express the ambivalence of her feelings. She turned abruptly to confront her father. 'I pushed him away, Papa. I refused his request for an explanation. How could I be so selfish, so cruel? Knowing as I do what isolation he is enduring.' She was lashing herself into a state verging on hysteria. Mr Smithson put a hand on each of her upper arms and held her strongly.

'Elena, Elena, I have never seen you thus. Calm yourself, please. I am sure that Mr Leighterton will not view it as you think.'

'But he did, Papa, he did. He left in high dudgeon and I did not go after him as I should have. What am I going to do? If I have set him back on that ruinous path, I shall never forgive myself.' Then all of a sudden she burst into tears. 'Never,' she sobbed thickly. 'Never.'

Mr Smithson released her but only so that he could draw her to him. 'I think that there is no fear of that, my sweet,' he said, caressing her hair. 'I believe Mr Leighterton has seen the error of his ways and has no plan to tread that path again. Come, dry your eyes and go and write him a note to thank him for once again coming to your aid.'

Elena fumbled for her handkerchief and blew her nose indelicately. 'I will do that,' she said. 'Although I am not ready to admit my frailty, he has thought me equal to all situations and I find that I am not. It is very lowering.'

Pleased to see her recovering, Mr Smithson chuckled. 'I think we all like to think we are capable of more than we are,' he said. 'It is therefore fortunate that there are people able to accept us with our weakness as well as our strengths.'

He had meant just to provide reassurance to her but Elena was too quick for him. 'So Mrs Leighterton will have you, will she?' she demanded, wide-eyed.

William Smithson was thunderstruck that she had made such a leap, and read so much into what he had said. Yet he could not lie to her. 'Wish me happiness, Elena,' he said proudly. 'I am to be wed again at last.'

'Oh, Papa, how wonderful.' Her fears forgotten, Elena threw her arms around her father's neck and kissed him hard on the cheek. 'I am so delighted for you. What does Mr Leighterton think?'

There was just enough of a pause for Elena to realise that they had not told him.

'Oh Papa,' she gasped. 'You must inform him as soon as may be. Can you not see it will only add fuel to his isolation if he finds out that others knew before him?'

At the Manor, Edward would have learned gladly that his mother-in-law was to remarry for he had used up all his fledgling reserve of patience conversing with her on the subject of the stranger. She wished to speculate on that man's origins and it all took so much longer because of the need for a slate. Edmund kept his temper on a very tight rein despite drinking freely, determined that he should repay her for some of her constancy over the years. Eventually, to his relief, she tired of the subject and took herself off to bed. Edmund, desperate for some relief from his own feelings made for the parlour. Turning the handle, he found it locked. For a whole minute he stood there, fanning the flames of his anger. The door was locked. How dare he? How dare Purvis lock the door? Because he had told him to. The answer reverberated around his head. He, Edmund Leighterton, had told his valet to use whatever means he could to prevent him from revisiting his old habits.

Brought up short, Edmund took stock for a moment, then, bursting through all the anger and the outrage was a shaft of joy: the man had trusted him enough when drunk to carry out orders given when he was sober. Edmund turned away from the door and climbed the stairs to his couch. He found Purvis already there laying out his nightshirt.

'You locked the door to the parlour,' he said. Purvis looked at him balefully, feeling no need to say anything on the subject. Instead he picked up a slate and wrote:

'I think it would be advisable to put aside the affairs of the heart until we have mastered fully the reading of speech.'

'And when did I start taking orders from you?' asked Edmund evenly, but with a slight edge to his voice. He looked in the young man's face and then waved a weary hand. 'Don't even attempt to answer that,' he said.

20

*P*olly had eventually been persuaded to seek her bed just before midnight. The young man had finally exhausted himself with all the tossing and turning and had settled into a deep sleep. Mr Smithson and the dog took over the vigil. Mr Smithson marvelled at the dog. She had watched the entire goings on around her with large anxious eyes, but she had accepted Jessamy as trustworthy almost immediately. She had shielded her wriggling black puppies with an intensity only a good mother could show and she now sat quietly with them snuggled up to her as she watched her master's chest rise and fall.

William Smithson caressed the silky black head.

'There, there old girl,' he said softly. 'You will see all will be well.'

The bitch cocked her smart triangular ears forward and looked intelligently at him. William Smithson decided at that moment that he would buy one of the puppies for his son if their visitor stayed long enough for it to leave its mother.

He was not now unduly worried about his charge, so he allowed himself to doze in the chair. In fact it was not long before he was soundly asleep and it was not until dawn that the young man made sufficient noise to rouse him.

'Where am I?' The inevitable question brought Mr Smithson out of his chair and the dog up from her rest to nuzzle the clammy hand that hung over the side of the bed.

'You are at Holm Oak Reach, some little way east of Haywards Heath in Sussex.'

The man gave a visible start. 'Holm Oak Reach.' He uttered the mansion's name almost reverentially. 'How can this be? How did I get here?'

'You had a riding accident, we believe, and my cousin found you. We had you brought here in a wagon.'

The young man digested this. Mr Smithson could almost see the man's brain working to assimilate his situation.

'What is your name?' he asked.

The young man dashed a hand across his forehead, pushing aside the strands of damp dark hair.

'George,' he said, and then paused as though calculating how much more to give.

'Well Mr George', said Mr Smithson, accepting it temporarily as the young man's surname. 'You are very welcome here and I wish you a speedy recovery.'

'Thank you.' He began to pull himself up with some difficulty because of the splinted arm but with insufficient pain to give lie to the doctor's suggestion of broken ribs. 'No, no, not George, my name is George Long.'

'Forgive me, Mr Long for the error,' said Mr Smithson promptly, watching his guest keenly, 'but the sentiment remains the same. You are most welcome in my house.' He hoped his words did not sound as hollow as they felt to he who had uttered them. This young man was doing nothing to allay the suspicion planted in his brain by his perspicacious daughter.

In the days that followed, Mr Smithson did his best to shut out the voice in his head that prompted these thoughts for Polly was smitten. Her whole being, which he had come to consider colourless, now radiated a glow. Her mouse-blonde hair shone and her pallid complexion gave way to rosy cheeks and sparkling eyes. George Long appeared to reciprocate her feelings, expressing fulsome gratitude for every errand she ran for him while he was laid up and then when he was allowed to progress to a chair. Elena and Mr Smithson could only look on helplessly, not knowing what best to do for their cousin.

Two days after Mr Long's return to consciousness, his horse was discovered wandering the lanes, leather saddlebags still attached. Returning his belongings to him Mr Smithson ventured to ask how he thought the accident happened.

'I do not recall precisely,' was Mr Long's evasive reply. 'I fear we took the steep hill too quickly, which is why I came a cropper.'

Mr Smithson was still dubious, for everyone could see that the man cared for his dog, and who in their right mind would have made the dog run at such speed in the very latest stage of her pregnancy? Mr Smithson used this to probe a little further. 'You have a very fine dog, Mr Long,' he said.

'Is she not beautiful?' he agreed. 'Ma Belle, I called her but here in England I find she has often to answer to the name of Mabel.'

'What breed is she? I have never seen her like.'

'No, indeed,' agreed George Long. 'She is a St John's water dog. I came across her on my travels up the coast of America. Such dogs are much favoured by the fishermen of Newfoundland; they work to haul in the nets. I believe a few have crossed the Atlantic over the last decade; indeed I was lucky enough to secure a mate for her in Dorset on my way here as you can see.'

'So you have spent time in the Americas?' Mr Smithson pounced on the nugget of information.

'I have,' acknowledged George Long on a hesitant note; Mr Smithson thought him slightly reluctantly to admit it.

'Most people have been doing the crossing the other way, Sir. Was it not to your liking?' Mr Smithson now wondered how such a handsome man with such regular features and open face should make him feel that all was not being revealed. Mr Long was clearly uncomfortable with this line of questioning but he felt he must respond more fully.

'My father, as a young man, was a soldier fighting for his king and country, but after the end of hostilities in '79 he returned to England for some years, entered into a marriage with my mother but could not settle. The vast landscapes of the Americas called him always and, when my mother died, he decided to return there, taking me with him.'

George Long looked pained. 'My father was ever restless and we travelled much. We lived on his winnings at poker, which made for some lean times. When he died three years ago, I rode north looking for work but the climate was too harsh for me and I decided my best course was to return to England. I picked up Ma Belle on a crossing on my way from Charlottetown to Newfoundland. She has been a source of great companionship for me ever since.'

'Quite an adventure for so young a man,' observed Mr Smithson dryly.

'I am not as young as you believe, Sir! I am six and twenty.'

Looking at Long's face with greater scrutiny, Mr Smithson decided he believed him. At least in that aspect he had become more suited in age to Polly. Previously Mr Smithson had believed him to be not long out of his teens.

'Well, I look forward to hearing some of the tales of your adventures,' he said politely. 'And I would like one of your puppies for my son, Jessamy. I believe he deserves the treat for all the care he has taken of them.' Mr Smithson had every intention of paying for the dog but he was eager to see Long's reaction. He first saw consternation before it was masked by politeness.

'Of course, if I am still here when they can be weaned I would be delighted to leave your son in possession of one, but I cannot trespass on your hospitality for many more days and they are far too young to be parted from their mother at this time.'

Mr Smithson made a noncommittal reply. For all that Long paid lip service to leaving, Mr Smithson sensed that he was not eager to do so. He thought there was a real possibility that the young man had nowhere to go.

Elena thought it too. Short of company again because of Polly's attentions to George Long and Jessamy's to the dog, she wrote at length to the Delrymple girls describing the mystery surrounding his presence. She expected to receive letters of excited speculation but instead their letters were full of news of Mr Ingram Deacon who had stolen all their hearts.

'How can I express to you our delight in having him here,' wrote Lady Caroline. *'Even Maria blooms when he is in the room. We are all captivated and hang on his every word. He is universally charming but Father and I detect an added warmth in his manner when he converses with Dorothea. My father has invited him to extend his stay but he is determined to meet his obligations to his parents. I do believe however that he plans to return to us as soon as he has ascertained that his father is to make a full recovery.'*

Elena could have wept with frustration; she longed to unburden herself to someone and her thoughts kept returning to Edmund Leighterton. She knew he would give her rational counsel if only she could overcome her embarrassment to apply to him.

The weeks were drifting by and still Mrs Leighterton had not divulged the news of her engagement to Edmund. They had settled into a comfortable way of being together at mealtimes and she feared her revelation might jeopardise the harmony in their existence. It was not that she wished to delay her union with Mr Smithson but her resilience had suffered over the long months of Edmund's illness and she could not easily contemplate the possibility of upsetting him and thus returning to the adversarial existence they had led before. She had convinced herself that he would take it badly on the strength of very little evidence.

Edmund though was increasingly finding that he could follow the nuances of others' behaviour. Gradually his understanding of people's speech when they were directly in front of him grew, promoted by the amount of practice he was getting. Purvis never now wrote out what he was saying, always catching Edmund's attention by touching him on the shoulder. He had also instructed Cleverley to do this and, although this had horrified the elderly stickler, he was learning to overcome his reluctance, especially as it made it so much easier to hold a conversation with his master. So the only member of Edmund's close personal retinue who continued to use slate and chalk other than Mrs Leighterton, who also remained in ignorance of his increasing skill, was his head groom. Edmund could not bring himself to tell Golding that his lettering was no longer necessary. He had wounded the man once and did not plan to do it again, even though Purvis urged Edmund to make a clean breast of it.

It was only when Golding arrived in the stables one evening with his face beaming that Edmund was able to tackle the problem. Edmund had been out late having ridden further afield than usual. He had lost track of time because Golding was not with him, it being his afternoon off. Edmund was now seeing to his horse himself as darkness fell, as he was unwilling to call out one of the stable boys and have to struggle through communication with him.

'Well,' he marvelled as he discovered his groom's face transformed by glee and looking almost goblin like in the lamp light. 'What have you been about that affords you so much satisfaction?'

Golding whipped out of his bulging pocket a racing form book and waved it with much gusto.

'I'm a winner,' he announced as he stepped closer. 'I've bin studying form since I learned m'letters and today I've won.' The bulge in his pocket was revealed to be a pouch full of coins. 'Twelve guineas, three shillings and six pennies. 'Tis a fortune to me, Sir, a real fortune.'

'Many congratulations, Golding,' responded Edmund, delightedly slapping him on the back. 'You deserve it. I am so pleased for you.'

Golding was riffling through his own pockets as Edmund was saying this and brought out the slate. He was just going to write what he had said when he realised that Edmund had responded without recourse to the slate. He stopped short, his eyes full of wonder.

'As your 'earing returned, Sir. Praise be, let it be so.'

'No, no.' Edmund held up his hands to ward off such a thought. 'No such miracle has occurred, my friend, but I have learned to watch the movement of a person's lips and it tells me what they are saying.'

'Well I'll be damned,' said Golding. 'Who'd 'ave thought it possible?' He looked at the slate. 'No need for this then.' He cast it down on the straw-covered floor of the stable.

'Don't dispense with it yet awhile, Golding,' Edmund was quick to request. 'There are always going to be words that I cannot decipher. The slate and the written word are a tool with which I cannot completely dispense.'

Golding gave him an impish grin, his joy in the day returning. 'Very well,' he said, stooping down to pick the slate up, forgetting Edmund would not be able to see him speak. 'But 'tis very likely that the word you can't read is a word I can't write.'

21

*G*olding's ready acceptance of Edmund's new-found skill emboldened Edmund to tackle his mother. Coincidentally it was the same evening that Mrs Leighterton decided that she must make her son a party to her future plans. She knew that Mr Smithson intended to tell Jessamy and Polly that he was pushing for a summer wedding. Edmund was the greatest obstacle to his hoped-for outcome being brought to fruition.

Supper had been held back because of Edmund's late arrival and it spoke volumes for the greater ease with which Mrs Leighterton viewed her stepson's behaviour that she had not become too agitated by his absence. She certainly wished that she had not been kept waiting as she was keen now that she had reached the decision to unburden herself, but she accepted that Edmund was entitled to arrive late for dinner if he so chose.

Once he was changed and they were settled in their usual seats at the dining table, Mrs Leighterton drew out her slate from her reticule and began to write. Edmund, steeling himself to make good both his confession and his apology placed a firm hand over hers.

'There is no need for that, Mama,' he said gently. 'If you look into my face and articulate clearly, I believe I can understand you.'

Naturally she too mistook the matter and thought that perhaps his hearing was returning but he quickly disabused her of the notion and explained the lengths he had gone to in order to overcome the restrictions of his impairment. At first she could not imagine how it might be done and made exaggerated movements with her mouth, which were of little use to him, but gradually he gained her trust and she relaxed into it.

'Now tell me what you had planned to write,' he said once she had mastered the task.

Almost Mrs Leighterton lost her nerve, but the patience and expectancy in his face reconciled her to attempting her confession. She placed a hand on his arm and looking directly at him, spoke the words she had never expected to be able to say.

'Mr Smithson has requested my hand in marriage,' she said plainly.

Edmund was silenced firstly by the surprise and then by the enormity of what this meant.

'And you have accepted?' he asked eventually, knowing that the only reason why she might not have done was in consideration of him and that he would not be able to bear.

Mrs Leighterton nodded. 'I have been so long alone,' she mumbled, making it difficult for him to follow.

'As has he,' agreed Edmund when he had worked it out. He sprang to his feet and took a turn around the still-laden table. Cleverley came in to clear away the dishes but he waved him away. Mrs Leighterton's eyes followed her stepson anxiously. Eventually Edmund came back to his seat and drew himself up with a straight back. 'I think, Mama, it is only what you deserve,' he said gallantly. 'You have sacrificed your young life for me without demur. I who have enjoyed a life unfettered by financial concerns or filial responsibilities have let you bear the responsibility far beyond what could reasonably be expected.' Here he took hold of both her hands again and drew them to his lips to kiss them; he took in that there were tears sparkling on her lashes. 'You should have long ago abandoned me to my fate, but instead you answered the call of duty and cherished me in the very best way you were able.' He sighed deeply. 'And

I let you. And do you know, Mama, I cannot reconcile my conscience with the fact that I let you squander all those years on me? And to what end? Have I ever thanked you? Have I ever shown you reasonable affection for all the trials you have borne for me? No!' He released her hands and raked his through his hair. 'No, not once, not until ten weeks and four days ago when I was plucked from the abyss and shown the error of my ways.'

The tears were now running down her cheeks, reaching her chin and falling on to the table. She tried to contain a sob.

'How can I apologise to you, Mama?' he asked. 'What can I do or say that will repay you for all those wasted years. You should have been in London enjoying the season, or Brighton or anywhere but buried here. Forgive me, Mama. Forgive me, please, for all my misdemeanours. I cannot list them for there are too many but if you would give me absolution, I would welcome it although I know I do not deserve it.'

She tried to speak but was too choked with tears to do so. Edmund pulled out a great white handkerchief and handed it to her. She put it to her quivering mouth, forgetting for only a moment that he would not be able to see her words. She removed it to say 'I forgive you,' stuttering on a sob, 'and I love you.'

'As well as any mother,' agreed Edmund. 'And now it is time for you to throw off this burden you have been carrying for me and make yourself a happy life with Mr Smithson, for he is surely a worthy husband for you.'

'But what of you?' she asked. Then, getting no response, realised it was because she had absent-mindedly covered her mouth with the hanky again. She wiped her eyes and touched his arm to indicate she wanted to speak.

'What of you, Edmund? How will you fare if I remove to the Reach? I cannot suffer to leave you alone and lonely. I know Mr Smithson desires an August wedding but I am sure he will accept a delay if I request it.'

'No, Mama, no more sacrifices for my sake. I must plough my own furrow. Come let us retire now.' He felt spent by the release of so much tension. 'You to contemplate your nuptials and me to savour your forgiveness.'

They quitted the table and then the room. The full candlelight in the hallway exposed the emotions that had ravaged Mrs Leighterton during the past half-hour.

Cleverley, seeing his mistress with the aftermath of tears visible on her face, grabbed Edmund by the arm.

'What have you done?' he demanded, his anger crossing the line between master and servant. 'What have you said to upset her thus?'

'Only my apology, Cleverley,' said Edmund, lifting the man's hand from his arm. 'I have finally said that I am sorry for what I have done.'

He then ran up the stairs two at a time, leaving the butler gaping after him.

For Mrs Leighterton there was now one last final hurdle. She wished to ascertain that Jessamy did not resent her new role in his life. So, despite Mr Smithson's assurances that Jessamy and Polly would be as delighted as Elena, she could not persuade herself to believe it until she had discussed the matter with the young man himself.

To this end, Mr Smithson arranged for her to take a light lunch with the family some two days after the announcement had been made to them.

Sitting around the table with the young people and her fiancé, Mrs Leighterton felt no tangible evidence that they were engulfed by an aura of resentment but she still had to pursue the matter.

'So Jessamy,' she said, striking out on her task. 'How would you like to address me once I am your father's wife?'

The boy, who had been chewing enthusiastically on some cold roast beef, looked up at her in some surprise.

'Call you?' he enquired once his mouth was empty. 'I thought you were to become my Mama.' He looked for affirmation at his father. 'Is that not the case, Papa?'

Mr Smithson made an 'I told you so,' face at his beloved. 'Without doubt,' he said reassuringly to his son.

'Well, that's a relief,' replied the boy matter-of-factly. 'For I am to start at school in September and it will be so much easier to have a Mama and a Papa. Fellows ask much fewer questions.' His eyes travelled between his father and future stepmother. 'You are getting married in August, are you not? I would have you wed before I start school.'

Elena, who had been aware of Mrs Leighterton's fears, could not help spluttering with laughter. 'So much for your concerns, Ma'am,' she said. 'If only all matters could be so comfortably resolved!'

Elena felt this even more acutely when Jessamy came to her several days later with a problem that was exercising his mind. He had tracked her down to a parlour that she used for sewing as it had windows on two sides and the light was perfect for stitchery. The day was a typically squally late spring day and Jessamy had chosen to seek his sister out before braving the elements for a rendezvous with his friends the farmer's sons.

He arrived dressed for the outdoors with thick trousers and gaiters protecting his legs and a serviceable canvas jacket to keep out the wet, but his face displayed anxiety and Elena was quick to put her work aside and beg him to unburden himself to her.

'If you had heard ill of someone, whom you like,' he began without preamble, 'what would you do?'

Elena took a moment to answer; she suspected that the rumours of Edmund's behaviour after the party had finally come to his ears and she was prepared at once to defend him.

'The first action is to establish whether what you have heard is indeed true,' she said carefully.

'I cannot do that,' said Jessamy emphatically, 'as it has passed through many people before it came to me.'

Elena felt guilt assail her. She knew she should have over-come her embarrassment at her own behaviour and told

Jessamy at the time so that he did not get a garbled view.

'Is this about Mr Leighterton?' she braved.

Jessamy gave a derisory snort. 'Of course not! Papa has explained everything to me about Mr Leighterton and if this were said about him, I would disregard it as I know it could only be untrue.'

Elena was startled by his vehemence. 'You respect Mr Leighterton, then?' she ventured.

'Indeed I do,' he declared. 'He has told his staff to treat us like family even before we are. Mr Leighterton is a very generous man but he would not need to poach either way.'

'Poach!'

'Yes, is it not extraordinary? The gamekeeper, Mr Tolputt, has heard from Colonel Campden's man, who heard from the gamekeeper at Willow Grange, to which the land where we found Mr Long belongs, that they suspect that it was Mr Long poaching at dusk the night before we found him, and that the labour force gave chase but lost him in the gloom. Do you think it is true, Elena? Do you think Mr Long is a common poacher and do you think I should tell Papa? I don't want to because Polly would be so upset with me.' He ended on almost a wail.

To Elena the rumour, such as it was, fitted neatly with the facts as she recalled them. If Mr Long had been making his escape in haste, he might indeed have galloped down the hill, the half-light making the gradient of the slope deceptive. If she could but make sense of why he should have been doing it, it would not take much to convince her it was true.

Jessamy waited impatiently for her to speak. 'What should I do, Elena?' he demanded. 'He seems so gentlemanly; why should he stoop to poach?'

An explanation presented itself almost too conveniently to Elena, but she decided to use it, as it would justify him to Jessamy without exonerating him.

'When Papa searched through Mr Long's pockets looking to find who he was,' she said carefully, 'he found nothing but a few coins. And I do believe that his saddlebags when they were subsequently found contained nothing but a change of clothes, a set of hairbrushes and a small cooking pot. I think you will find that for all his gentlemanly ways, Mr Long has no money. If that is the case, he will have been hungry and cold with no place to stay. You know well that at this time of year there are many pheasants. Perhaps the temptation to feed himself and the dog was just too much.'

'So you don't think I should expose him to Polly or to Papa.'

'No, my dearest boy, I don't,' said Elena with a heavy heart. 'No-one will dare accuse him to his face while he is our guest, nor do I think they will say anything to Papa. Unless we have knowledge that he has done anything worse, we will keep it to ourselves.' She paused, a thought suddenly occurring to her. 'What is Mr Tolputt's view on this?'

'He says if he comes anywhere near his covets, he'll shoot him,' said Jessamy.

22

*E*lena's decision not to expose Mr Long to her father's censure did not sit comfortably with her conscience. She could not even explain her silence to herself for the rumours only endorsed her suspicion of him. While he was unfailingly polite and apparently grateful, Elena sensed that it was a façade. Only with Polly did he appear genuine, returning all her affectionate overtures with grace and an increasing devotion. He had talked from the outset of remaining only a few days but the uselessness of his broken arm had been excuse enough to keep him with them. As the days drifted by the puppies grew and were soon tumbling around his bedroom, enchanting everyone. Elena wrote to the Delrymple girls describing them in exquisite detail and was surprised to get a fuller response to all her previous letters. This was quickly explained by Lady Caroline whose letter arrived first.

My dearest Elena,
What must you think of us? What friends are we to have neg-
lected you so. On Mr Deacon's departure we all sank into
lethargy; boredom drove us to reread previous letters and
imagine our mortification when we realised that we had
ignored all your requests for advice about your unexpected
visitor. Our thoughts had been so totally taken up with Mr
Deacon. The only item discussed with him was the existence of
the dog. *Mr Deacon recalled seeing one such as her in the past*

on his arrival from the West Indies. He recommends that Mr
Leighterton purchase one of the puppies for he says he heard
of an old night fisherman who enjoyed a spree at lunchtime.
He had trained his dog to rouse him from his stupor as the sun
went down. Mr Deacon thinks Mr Leighterton could train
the dog to recognise the clanging of the doorbell or when
someone has come into the room without his realising and
indicate to Mr Leighterton what has occurred....

Here Elena stopped to consider the idea; she had seen many
different forms of working dogs and she could imagine that the
gentle, joyful animals upstairs could be persuaded to undertake
this role. She could not help but wonder how she should
broach the subject with Edmund Leighterton. When she read
on she realised she did not have to as Lady Caroline continued:

...When Mr Deacon has settled into his parental home, I
believe he intends to write to Mr Leighterton in that regard.
    Now Elena. (Her ladyship's pen stuck deeply into the paper
as though she was emphasising a point.) *The matter of Mr Long*
is in truth very vexing. I enquired of Papa if he had heard of
him but he could not recall ever meeting someone of that
name which in itself is disquieting as Papa is acquainted with
many military men and might have been expected to have
heard of Mr Long's father. I did not tell Papa the reason for my
interest but it alarms me that you have such reservations
about him, you who are normally so uncritical of others.
Write at once and tell me how he goes on.
    Ever your affectionate Caroline.

Elena could have wished that the Delrymples had not had
leisure to reread her letters for the letters that arrived from
Lady Maria and Lady Louisa the next day were riddled with lurid
speculation of what the young man might be plotting in the
Smithsons' house. Elena put the letters aside more afeared than

she had been since Mr George Long's accident had brought him to their attention.

How much more of this unsettling correspondence Elena would have stood before going to her father was not tested for the next letter from the Delrymples, penned by Lady Dorothea but endorsed by them all, appertained to another matter. Lord Delrymple had broken the news to them of Mr Smithson's approaching nuptials just a day before it was due to be announced in the society journals. The girls were torn between delight at his happiness and concern that Elena should not like her new mama. Elena spent much of the remainder of the day drafting a letter worded sufficiently comprehensively to rid them of any such anxiety. Her only comfort was that they were no longer dwelling on linking her name romantically with Mr Edmund Leighterton although they had not quit giving her nuggets of news about Mr Sawyer, who it seemed, had been unsuccessful in securing the hand of his latest amour. Elena grimaced at the postscript; she did not know whether to be glad or sorry that she had been proved right about his inconstancy. It gave her little consolation because it enhanced the possibility that she might also be right about Mr George Long.

George Long would have been rather alarmed if he had been aware of the workings of Miss Elena Smithson's mind. Because she had been reserved from the moment he had met her, he thought that was her natural demeanour. So whilst common sense should have dictated that he made up to the lady of the house in preference to the cousin companion, Polly's open admiration had captivated he who had struggled throughout his life to secure a comfortable existence. Also Polly's history resonated with his and he found himself much in tune with her hopes and fears and priorities.

The days drifted past for him in a blissful luxury he had never before experienced and, if he could have maintained it, he would have been satisfied with that, but the reasons for sustaining this extended interlude were rapidly diminishing. His arm was mending and the puppies would soon be eight weeks old and able to leave their mother, who clearly thought it was time for them to make their own way as they now had very sharp little teeth.

Each puppy already had a home to go to, Jessamy Smithson and Edmund each having one and Colonel Campden succumbing to the third. George had been delighted to find that each purchaser had agreed the extortionate sum of one hundred guineas because of the rarity of the dog. To George this was wealth indeed but it was not the wealth that he had travelled to England to secure. He could still not believe his good fortune in finding succour at Holm Oak Reach for it had been his destination from the outset of his long journey. Stitched inside the tails of his coat were the papers that proved he had a claim on this estate and he was determined to realise that claim.

On the day he found he had strength enough in his arm to control his horse, he knew he would have to make his move. His first consideration was to make his intentions known to Polly, for he did not want her to suffer any insecurity. He tracked her down one fine morning in late May and asked her to take a turn with him in the newly laid-out wilderness.

Much gratified, Polly hurried to collect a light shawl and accompanied him out into the sunshine. They talked for some minutes on the progress of the various shrubs and the glorious scent of the full-blown lilac until they were out of sight of any of the hundreds of windows of the house. Then George turned to confront his lady love.

'Dearest Polly,' he said, taking both her thin hands in his, 'would you do me the honour of accepting my hand in marriage?'

Polly's eyes went wide with wonder and she could not immediately articulate a reply. 'Your wife?' she managed eventually in a hoarse whisper. 'You want me to be your wife?'

'Yes, yes,' he said, laughing at her amazed response. 'Yes,' he repeated, shaking her hands up and down to emphasise his enthusiasm for the prospect. 'Yes, you must know how I have revelled in your company and enjoyed your ministrations to my care and comfort. I can think of no-one with whom I would rather share my life and good fortune.'

Blissfully unaware of where this declaration was leading, Polly could only stutter and dissemble and ultimately accede to his request. The happiness of a dream coming true percolated through her body and an image of the dark days in the attic at Mrs Yardley's when her only comfort had been to dream of being rescued by a tall, dark and handsome stranger were cast aside for the even more charming reality. She perceived in that moment that George Long was everything she had aspired to find in a husband: good-looking and kind and in her eyes gallant to be taking on a penniless girl.

She tilted up her face as a mute invitation to be kissed and he did not reject her. The new sensation set the seal on her bliss. She released her body into his arms and he held her there, giving her the perception of protection.

'I love you so, George Long,' she said at last. 'And I cannot wait to share my happiness with my kind family.'

Here then was the moment when the bubble had to burst.

'We must hold off with our declaration for a while, Polly,' he said, still cradling her in his arms, 'until my claim is settled.'

She looked surprised. 'What claim is this? I know nothing of it and, if it is a valid one, I am sure Mr Smithson would be only too glad to help you pursue it.'

It took a moment's resolution to make a clean breast of it but George Long knew it had to be done. 'The claim is against him, Polly. I have papers here' – he let her go and shook the tails of his coat – 'in here, that could make me the rightful owner of this estate. This would all be ours. Yours and mine. We would no longer be the guests but the hosts. Can you not imagine how wonderful that will be after all the trials we have separately endured.'

Polly, as the realisation dawned, felt the shock like a physical blow; she stepped back away from him, her hands at her mouth taking the force of the breath that rushed from her lungs. She bent forward, not knowing how to protect herself from the surge of alarm and disappointment. If she had been capable of anticipating the future at the blissful moment of his declaration, she would have assumed that she and George would have remained comfortably accommodated with the Smithsons, repaying their generosity with acts of loyalty and service. She had never envisaged that George could support her; she had not been blind to his lack of worldly goods, but this revelation was beyond anything she had ever considered. William and Elena Smithson had rescued her from drudgery and obscurity and whatever came after that, she knew her first duty was to them. This was unequivocal and no desperate calling of her heart was going to subordinate it to more selfish concerns. The sorrow and bitterness she felt at suddenly having to make that stark choice left her incoherent.

Misreading her shock, George thought she must see how marvellous it made the future for them. He attempted to take her in his arms again but she would not have it.

'Polly, Polly.' Elena's voice was heard calling out to her. 'Polly, where are you? We must away to the Leightertons'.'

George gave an exclamation of annoyance. 'Can we not be private even here?' he demanded. 'Now, Polly, not a word of this for now. I have yet to decide how best to pursue it. It is our secret for the present.'

Polly could do nothing but nod. Drawing her inadequate shawl around her, as the world seemed suddenly a much colder place, she made haste to be away from him. Then, struggling to collect herself, she hurried to locate Elena on the terrace.

23

*T*he next week was a species of nightmare for Polly. Each day she would steel herself for the moment when George would reveal himself to the Smithsons. Each night she would lie in bed tossing and turning as she agonised over her best course of action. There had never been a moment when she did not know that she was committed to the Smithsons whatever the outcome, but a small forlorn part of her hoped that, if she pretended there was no such outstanding claim, then it would miraculously disappear overnight. But each fresh morning brought the realisation that it was still to be confronted. Rarely did she fall asleep before dawn, so she awoke little refreshed. Her eyes once again became dark pools in a pale face. She found she had little appetite either for food or for improving her own appearance. She could only marvel that George made no comment about the loss of her looks but, now free of the confines of the sickroom, he was enjoying his new-found status as a guest of the Smithsons. The advance William Smithson had given him on the puppy meant he had money to enjoy a spree and he had been out in the evenings to cock fights and gambling sessions.

Polly felt no less love for him, but she shivered at the thought of George in charge of the huge estate that Mr Smithson ran with such calm efficiency as though he had been born to it. Even Colonel Campden, in the short months he had known him, had come to rely on Mr Smithson's wise counsel on every subject from crop rotation to animal husbandry. It was this thought that finally pushed Polly into acting on her choice.

Of course it was to Elena she went, for she was always everyone's first port of call. They used the maxim that, if Elena had the matter in hand, then their own part was played. No-one who unburdened themselves to her ever considered what this meant for her: that they loaded on her a weight that might almost be too much to bear. So it was a pale and drawn Polly who put Elena in possession of the facts and left her to deal with them as she might. At least for Elena there was no shock, no disillusionment, just a pained acceptance that she had been right and that George Long had always had a hidden agenda. He had trespassed on their goodwill and he had taken them for fools; but if the mansion and the estate were indeed his, then, morally, she supposed she had no right to feel aggrieved. For more than an hour after Polly had left her, she strove to find the best course of action, all the while acknowledging her hope that George Long could have it wrong and that he had no entitlement.

Elena, through firm principles and lengthy scrutiny of the possible effects of each of the actions she considered, decided at length that her father must be protected for as long as was possible. She did not doubt Mrs Leighterton's regard for him but, such was his own strict code, Elena convinced herself that her father would offer her release from their engagement if he was no longer able to offer her a grand home. Mr Banbury was her next thought. He had been adamant that the Reach was theirs. It had to be to him that the papers were taken. Only he would know their value and their veracity. How to get George Long to Bristol or Mr Banbury to the Reach without divulging what was afoot to her father seemed nigh-on impossible. She was still trying to solve this riddle the next day when she was persuaded by her father to visit the Leightertons. Polly had cried off this time, whether to shut herself away in her room to lament or to keep an assignation with George, Elena did not know but she felt no desire to find out. She could not find enough energy or heart to console Polly.

Once at the Leightertons' Elena struggled to maintain her spirits in the face of the lively conversation of her neighbours; she wasted no time in seating herself in an alcove away from the general throng. Mrs Leighterton had once again found herself deluged by morning callers as, with the wedding approaching, they were all hoping for an invitation. Elena's heart was too heavy to discuss haute couture or alternative toilettes. For her there was the real possibility that the marriage would not take place.

Edmund Leighterton entered the room some little while after the guests had arrived. Now that he could hold a conversation with an individual, visitations from the neighbours ceased to be quite the ordeal they used to be. He cast his eyes around the company looking for someone with whom he might converse. At first glance he did not see Elena and was disappointed. His heart still swelled when he saw her and he could not refrain from the hope that one day they might reach an understanding. He was just about to embark on a conversation with young Campden when the group in front of him opened up and he saw past them to the alcove. He caught sight of Elena's lilac dress with which he was familiar and he walked past the animated visitors to seek her out.

She was sitting, head bent, her fingers fiddling with a loose thread on the skirt of her dress.

'Miss Smithson.'

She looked up and he saw the depth of misery in her eyes and could not help recalling the times when her face had lit up when she had spied him. 'My dear Miss Smithson, what is the matter?' He moved to sit beside her on the window seat, his concern palpable.

Elena shook her head and then, remembering to look him full in the face said, 'I wish I could tell you,' she sighed. 'But it cannot be, certainly not here, not now.' She indicated with a look at the others in the room the need to be private.

Edmund considered for a moment and then crossed the room to pick up a slate from a pile that was generally redundant now that he could read people's speech.

'Come,' he said on his return, 'let us use this to our advantage. No-one will think anything of the matter if you write it down for me. And once it is done it can be brushed away, never to be revealed again.'

Elena took the slate with a bleak smile. There was a moment while she formulated what to say and then suddenly it came gushing out and she scribbled with such intensity that the chalk squeaked against the slate. One or two people turned around at the noise but made nothing of it.

Seeing that she was in full flow, Edmund gathered up two further slates so that she could continue to write while he read the completed slate. His eyes widened as he discovered the form of the dilemma in which she found herself. She finished with a flourish and, handing him the final tablet, she gave him a look of mute enquiry.

'You know,' said Edmund after barely a moment's thought. 'I can help you with this.'

'How? In what way?' she demanded eagerly.

'I think you should leave that to me,' he said, conscious that she might not approve of his methods.

'I will not have him harmed, nor his claim if it is a rightful one overlooked,' she said deliberately.

Edmund smiled affectionately into her upturned face.

'I would expect nothing less from you, Miss Smithson, and I give you my word of honour as a gentleman that I will respect your feelings on the matter.'

With that she had to be satisfied for he would say no more and indeed it was impossible to say more as the gathering was breaking up and her father had come to find her. Elena could speculate endlessly on what Edmund planned but, in not knowing its detail, she could give no indication to either Polly or George as to what might be going to happen and for that she was deeply grateful. It allowed her to comfort Polly with more sincerity and to maintain her reserve with George Long. All she could do was watch and wait to see what would happen.

The following evening, George Long once again went out to the local hostelry to try his hand at cards. Thus far he had lost quite some fifty per cent of the money Mr Smithson had given him and he felt it was time to recoup it. His luck he felt was about to change.

As the night wore on, he found this was not to be and it was close on midnight when his money ran out and he had to retire from the gaming table. Food had been laid out in one of the small parlours and he went there to help himself to some sustenance, as the relentless excitement of the game meant he had not partaken earlier in the evening. He was not unduly worried by his losses because he knew he had more money to come from the puppies and there was still the security of his claim against the Smithsons.

There was a rattle at the door and he looked up to see Edmund Leighterton enter accompanied by two henchmen, one of whom was carrying his saddlebags.

'What's this?' he demanded, springing to his feet, suddenly seeing that there was threat lurking there. The bitch who accompanied him everywhere now she could leave her pups growled at the intruders, aware like her master that there was malicious intent. One of the men closed the parlour door and forced home the bolts.

'We have come to have a little talk with you, Mr Long,' said Edmund, watching his face intently. 'You see I don't like people who take liberties with my friends. You have enjoyed some extraordinary hospitality, generous to a fault. Further, you have inveigled your way into the affections of a defenceless and tender-hearted young lady. And how do you repay her and them?'

George Long's face was a study of horror and near terror. For there was nothing conciliatory in Edmund's tone, just a throbbing anger indicative of his disgust at what the other man had done. George had heard the stories of Edmund's temper before and knew that others had been hurt. He thought he stood in fear of his life and little realised that one of the henchmen who stood behind Leighterton was in fact the groom he was supposed to have beaten within an inch of his life. George Long knew not what to say in his own defence. It had not occurred to him previously that he had done anything particularly wrong. He believed he had a rightful claim and that the Smithsons were living off what was his. He had not understood that while they and the world perceived it to be theirs, he had no right to use it as his own. He opened his mouth but no words would come out. In the pause, Edmund reached past the laden table and grasped George's coat, which had been hanging on the back of a chair.

'I believe this is what I have come for,' he said and grabbed at the tails of the coat, ripping it along the false seam. The papers tumbled to the ground and were snatched up by Edmund before George could even make his move, slowed as he was by a quantity of alcohol and the stiffness from his previous injury.

'Those are mine,' he blustered at last, making a step towards Edmund. 'You have no right to those.'

Even as he moved Golding and Purvis blocked his way and view of Edmund.

'And you,' said Edmund rolling the papers up and with a deft movement of the hand slipping them into a long pocket of his greatcoat and withdrawing another roll which he cast on the valiant little fire that still warmed the rooms in the evening, 'have no right to Holm Oak Reach.'

'No.' George's cry was full of anguish as Golding and Purvis moved aside in time for him to see the last of the paper turn black and then catch light in a flurry of flames. 'No, no.' He sank on his knees down to the fire and tried to drag out the embers frantically. 'That was my birthright; you had no cause to destroy it.'

Edmund pulled out a heavy pouch full of coins.

'You are no longer welcome here,' he said as he tossed the heavy moneybag on to the table. 'Your few possessions are here,' he indicated the saddlebags, 'and this contains the balance that is owed to you for the dogs. I recommend that it is in your best interests to leave this county and forget that you ever had any designs on Holm Oak Reach.'

Then Edmund turned back to the door, withdrew the bolts and he and his two escorts left the inn, satisfied that they had prevented Long's pursuance of his claim for the time being. Edmund patted his coat before swinging up on to his horse.

'You do realise,' he said to the others, 'that this means a journey to Bristol and, come what may, the discovery of whether he is indeed the owner of the Reach.'

Both men nodded for neither would have agreed to take part in the recent pantomime if they had not known that the truth would out in the end. The man's anguish at the loss of his papers had rocked them, as it was clear that he believed he was now bereft of something very valuable and quite irreplaceable. Purvis in that moment envied Edmund the fact that he had not heard that desperation.

There was a rushing noise from the back of the hostelry and George Long appeared before them, distraught and angry. He pulled Edmund from his horse and grabbed him by the collar, ignoring the protest of his weakened muscles.

'You have no right to destroy what is mine,' he yelled. 'You, who have everything: a comfortable life; a beautiful home. You are the very devil to take what little I have from me.'

Purvis and Golding dismounted to go to Edmund's aid but he did not appear to want it. He remained calm and had clearly seen what the man was saying by the light of the lanterns that hung around the end of the building.

'Do you honestly think that I would not change places with you without a moment's hesitation,' he said deliberately. 'You have your health and your hearing and how have you used it?

To leech off the worthiest family in the district. No, Sir, you could have my home and my comfortable life if you could restore to me what I have lost.'

George Long let him go and, turning away, stumbled, vanquished, back into the building.

24

*A*t breakfast the next morning there was considerable consternation when George Long did not appear. He normally partook of a hearty repast with the ladies some ninety minutes after Mr Smithson had breakfasted. Polly and Elena looked at each other in alarm when the gong elicited no appearance from him.

Timery was summoned to request that someone went to rouse the sleepyhead. Mr Timery, who had had a very illuminating conversation with Mr Smithson's valet, Johnson, lately of the Manor, when he had caught him the night before trying to slip unobtrusively down the back stairs carrying George Long's packed saddlebags, felt it was incumbent on him to make an announcement.

'Mr Long did not return yesterday evening, Miss. His bed has not been slept in.'

'Tis true.' Jessamy burst into the room full of the news. 'His horse is still gone from the stables and Mabel is nowhere to be seen.'

'I think you should inform my father, Timery,' said Elena, a great dread upon her. Polly's face crumpled.

'He has left me,' she whispered. 'I have driven him away.'

'No, no.' Elena leaped up from her chair and went to comfort her cousin. 'I am sure it cannot be the case. He will return, I am sure he will.'

Mr Smithson, when put in possession of the facts, was not so sanguine. He ordered a full inventory to be taken of all the silverware and valuable, yet portable, items in the house. He had had a suspicion that George Long had been girding himself up for something like this, as he had seemed tense and jumpy over the last few days. Mr Smithson was saddened but not much surprised. It was only when he looked into the sorrowful face of his young cousin that he could feel anger at the young man who could so carelessly cast aside her finer feelings.

The inventory took all morning to complete and resulted in finding nothing missing. Mr Smithson was astounded, for, as far as he knew there was still money owing on the puppies. Unbeknownst to the young ladies, he made enquiries at the inn he knew Long had visited that night to be told that yes, Mr Long had been there; that he had received an anonymous visit from some persons unknown but that he had stayed the night after they had gone, had paid his shot and had left very early the next morning.

William Smithson was none the wiser.

Two days after these stirring events, Edmund had what his stepmother thought later was rather a curious conversation with her.

'Mama,' he had said abruptly when he came upon her in the rose garden. 'If Mr Smithson was not in possession of such wealth, would you be allying yourself with him?'

Mrs Leighterton was momentarily bereft of speech, such was her surprise.

'What can you be about?' she asked when she had mastered her voice again. 'Surely you are not accusing me of marrying him for his money?'

'No, no, you misunderstand me.' Her stepson was quick to refute such a charge. 'I am just concerned whether you have considered the consequences if some other person was discovered to have a greater claim on the estate than he has.'

It was her turn to surprise him. 'We have discussed the

possibility, Mr Smithson and I. Mr Smithson has been very frank with me but I have a generous competence left to me by your father, and Mr Smithson has an allowance that will be made over to him if just such an eventuality should occur. I have no fear that we would be left destitute.' She stopped and looked Edmund squarely in the eye, checking that he had got the gist of what she had been saying. 'But were it so, I would rather live out the rest of my life with him in straitened circumstances than submit to a life without him.'

'I am glad,' said Edmund and left her as abruptly as he had arrived.

The following evening he once again demanded her attention.

'Mama, I have decided it is time to face the world. I plan a trip to Bristol in a few days hence and trust that you will go on comfortably without me.'

'Bristol,' she cried, astonished. 'Why would you wish to visit Bristol?'

He had the answer ready. 'You may recall that when I was unwell' (it seemed the best way to describe the time when he had shunned everyone and everything and indeed it was the way most people referred to it, if they referred to it at all), 'I had a visit from some friends from the regiment.'

Mrs Leighterton nodded.

'You will agree that I was less than civil!'

Again Mrs Leighterton nodded.

'Well, I have heard from our mutual acquaintance, Mr Ingram Deacon, that Laurence Aldwyn has had a fencing accident and has had to abandon the season and retire to his paternal house near Bristol to recuperate. I thought I should visit him and make amends.'

'Must you?' she asked, her brow furrowing as she thought of all the pitfalls such a journey might include for a deaf man.

'I think I must,' he said quietly. 'It is time for me to take my place in the world again and this makes a start.'

'But what protection will you have from people who want to exploit your impairment?' she asked. 'People will not know to look you in the face. They will not understand that you do not follow every word. It is too dangerous, Edmund, please reconsider,' she beseeched him.

'I can't remain cocooned here forever, Mama. What chances have I of a fulfilled life if I do not attempt such things? You are soon to remove to the Reach. I will no longer be your first consideration. Indeed, I have been that for too long. I must attempt to reacquaint myself with my former life whatever the perils. Come, have no fear; Golding and Purvis will accompany me. They will protect me as well as any armed guard.'

'I know they will,' she conceded, 'for they are very loyal, but what if there is a fire in the night at some roadside hostelry. You would not hear the rousing call. While you are away I will be for ever afraid that you will be burned in your bed!'

Edmund gave a chuckle. 'Purvis has already thought of such a situation and, where we cannot obtain adjacent rooms, he will take on the role of master and I will share a room with Golding. How's that for a solution?'

'Oh, you think you are very droll,' remarked Mrs Leighterton. 'I wash my hands of you. Go, take your chances on the high road but do not be surprised if, when you return, I am white-haired with the strain of it all.'

'I'll sure you will look charmingly,' he said and kissed her cheek, before quitting the room.

Preparations began the very next day for the journey to Bristol. Edmund had not lied to his stepmother. He did plan to visit Laurence Aldwyn but only briefly to offer him an apology, before presenting George Long's papers to Mr Banbury. He had not had an opportunity to visit Elena and inform her that his plans were progressing well although he had learned (courtesy of Purvis) of the fracas at the Reach after Long's disappearance. After due consideration, he thought perhaps it would be best if Elena remained in ignorance of the exact details of that night at the inn as she might not have approved of his methods.

So, in the teeth of his stepmother's opposition, Edmund and his devoted retinue set out westward at the beginning of June. Edmund would have liked to take his puppy with him for she was already becoming a boon companion, despite her propensity to chew anything, but he knew it to be unfair; so reluctantly he had sent her back to the Reach to be reunited with her brother and be cared for by young Jessamy. Jessamy was deeply delighted and sent back assurances via Golding who had made the delivery that he would continue her training.

Elena, who had hoped that Edmund might visit, had been deeply disappointed by his absence and was quick rightly to suspect that he was avoiding having to explain to her what he had been about. The news that he was on his way to Bristol was in some measure a relief as it concurred with her expressed wishes at the outset. Repeatedly she wondered if she should hint to Polly that all might yet be well, for Polly was most clearly in decline. Her porcelain pallor was almost alabaster and her appetite had not improved. She was unable to settle to anything and her face, when in repose, was tragic. However, whenever Elena tried to devise an outcome that would be happy for all, she could not find one and knew that any words of commiseration would end with both of them in tears. It was better, she concluded, to keep all excessive emotions pinioned until the full extent of their difficulties was revealed. She must just trust to Edmund Leighterton to resolve the matter with Mr Banbury.

Edmund would have been heartened if he had known Elena retained so much faith in him. The first day's journey, for which he had elected to travel in the chaise, had allowed him much time for reflection. It was not lost on him that this was the first expedition he had undertaken since his illness that took him beyond the sphere of his closest neighbours. Whether it was the vestiges of his stepmother's anxiety still clinging to him or the uncertainty of the unknown that gave him pause, but Edmund discovered himself to be rather nervous of the immediate future. He cast a look at his valet, who was sitting forward and currently watching the countryside, waiting to speak only when spoken to. Taking covert stock of him, Edmund marvelled at his own willingness to rely so heavily on a man younger than himself and less experienced, but Purvis had an innate wisdom and had proved his determination to aid Edmund whenever he might. Edmund could only be grateful that he had enjoyed the good fortune to secure his services. This led his thoughts on to Golding, who was currently being buffeted by a strong west wind, sitting next to the coachman as they bowled along the post road. Again Edmund had to acknowledge how lucky he was. As he made an assessment of his own life, he saw it more clearly from George Long's perspective and it begged the question: would he really trade the loyalty of his servants and the unfailing devotion of his stepmother, not to mention the friendship of Miss Elena Smithson, for his hearing if in their place he was offered only loneliness and destitution? A conundrum indeed; he was glad he did not have to make the choice. As this sentiment rattled around inside his head, Edmund gave an audible gasp of sheer astonishment that the man he had been, who six months ago had railed so forcefully against his lot, should have come so far as to acknowledge that he would find it so difficult to give up what he had previously derided. Purvis turned his head at the noise to enquire if Edmund had need of anything but Edmund just shook his head.

The first night's stop on the journey west did not tax Purvis much when it came to the protection of his master. The inn they chose was some ten miles short of Winchester and was small so that none of the rooms were far apart. The room Purvis was to have as his bedchamber was just across the landing from the only two good rooms. Purvis would have had to walk past Edmund's door to get to the stairs, so in a fire he would be well placed to rouse Edmund.

The next day Edmund decided to ride alongside the coach and left Purvis to seek his own entertainment within the vehicle. The gorse was just going over but the flowers along the verges were just beginning to reach their fullest glory. Edmund wished he had Miss Smithson with him to identify all the flora and fauna.

That night they rested at Devizes because Edmund preferred the smaller town to Bath where he might meet some acquaintances. Devizes may have been smaller than Bath but the coaching house was vast. Edmund deplored the appalling distance between guests' rooms and those of their servants and feared they might have to use the ruse suggested to his stepmother that Purvis became master and he servant. However he reckoned without Purvis, who in puffing up his master's consequence through a bit of judicial boasting, managed to acquire a suite of rooms which allowed him to be put up in the dressing room. Golding, however, was relegated to the spartan room above the stables with the coachman, something he was philosophical but not enthusiastic about.

The next morning saw them arriving at the home of Laurence Aldwyn only four miles to the north-west of Devizes. It was so close to their route that it most certainly would have been discourteous not to have called in.

Alighting from the coach, Edmund stared up at the grey-stoned façade. None of the beautiful pale gold stone that elevated Bath was exhibited here. The house was Jacobean with steep eaves and small windows and it looked no less haunted than Edmund had fancied it was during his only previous stay during a holiday from school.

A gloomy butler, who was clearly mirroring his demeanour from the aura of the house, took his card before ushering him and Purvis into the open hallway. The butler seemed neither interested nor to care that his valet accompanied Edmund.

There was a short delay and then a flurry of activity as suddenly a lady could be seen hurrying towards them from the back of the house. She was dressed in pea-green silk with lace cuffs and collar and she wore a matching lace cap. The brightness of her clothes was in stark contrast to the leaden tone of her surroundings. She stretched out her hands to Edmund even before she had reached him.

'My dear Mr Leighterton, what a charming surprise!' she cried enthusiastically. 'Laurence will be so delighted that you are here.'

25

*L*eading the way upstairs to her son's sickroom, Mrs Aldwyn bustled along chattering nineteen to the dozen, blissfully unaware that Edmund did not even know she was speaking. It was only at the turn of a narrow corridor that Purvis was able to catch up with her.

'Ma'am, Mrs Aldwyn, please,' he pleaded. 'Mr Leighterton cannot hear you at all. If you wish to converse with him, you must indicate that you are about to speak and then allow him to see your face.'

Mrs Aldwyn whirled round to face the earnest young man who had demanded her attention.

'Cannot hear! Still?' she said incredulously. 'I had heard from my son and his friends that he had been taken very poorly, but I assumed because he was here that he was fully restored to health.'

'He is fully restored to health, Ma'am,' Purvis assured her, slightly embarrassed that this conversation was taking place in Edmund's full view, while not allowing him to take part in it. 'But his hearing loss is permanent.'

'Good heavens.' Mrs Aldwyn launched herself on to Edmund's chest. 'You poor boy,' she said thickly into his chest. Edmund, startled by such a demonstrative expression of sympathy, at first knew not what to do. He looked at Purvis who mouthed what Mrs Aldwyn was saying. Edmund took a bracing hold of the ample lady's arms and held her away from him.

'My dear Mrs Aldwyn, there is no need to pity me,' he said, once again astonishing himself to find he believed his own words. 'I am well enough as you see and able to fill my time very pleasantly. Now come, take me to Laurence and let me see what he has done to himself.' He let her go and she fumbled for a handkerchief, eventually finding one up her sleeve. She wiped away a tear.

'Forgive me,' she said, remembering to look at him. 'To see Laurence so unwell, so pale and wan and then to discover you glowing with health, even after your ordeal, made me want to believe all at once that Laurence can make a full recovery too. It brought joy to my heart, and it is a bitter blow to find you still suffer,' she said with a rueful smile. 'Come, let us visit Laurence but I beg you do not allow him to talk too much, it taxes him so. It is why we had to leave London to give him quiet. But,' and here she sighed again, not taking full account of the tactless nature of her own words, 'too much quiet can be a very lowering thing.'

Edmund, catching most of what she said, guessed rightly that his friend was finding his injury very irksome. Edmund prepared himself to be rebuffed. Instead he was welcomed with breathless acclaim by the invalid.

'Look…at…you,' wheezed Laurence. 'When…I…saw…you …last…you…were…like…a…circus…bear…growling…and …snarling…at…all…around…you….You…give…me… hope…Leighterton…that…a…little…patience…will…see… me…right.'

Laurence Aldwyn benefited so much from Edmund's visit that it seemed churlish to refuse Mrs Aldwyn's invitation to stay a few days. That young man, in the absence of jovial companions, had fancied himself tied to his bed labouring over his breathing for the rest of his life. He had been in the slough of despond. The arrival of a renewed Edmund, whom he had last seen careless of dress and demeanour and deeply in the doldrums, brought hope to his heart. The doctors had told him that the wound to his lung would eventually mend but he had begun, as the weeks dragged past, to disbelieve them. Now his faith was restored and he begged Edmund to stay and relate the tale of his own road to recovery.

They remained two nights with the Aldwyns and then, conscious that Miss Smithson and his stepmother were waiting anxiously at home for news, Edmund insisted that they must press on to Bristol. He did promise to make a further visit to his invalid friend once the current matter had been resolved. It was only as he was taking his final leave of Laurence Aldwyn that the man lying prone in his bed put up a hand and grabbed Edmund's lapel. In a hoarse whisper he unburdened himself.

'I…owe…you…an…apology, Leighterton,' he rasped. 'I… was…responsible…for…the…ill…reports…of…you…which …reached…the…ears…of…the…ton…I…had…no…idea …no…idea…at…all…of…your…suffering…of…mind. Only …now…' He faltered and, seeing what a struggle it was for him, Edmund prevented him from continuing. He took the other man's hand and placed it back on the coverlet.

'You need wear a hair shirt no longer, my friend,' he said, 'for you can see that you have done me no injury. I am blessed with kind friends and family who have steadfastly refused to allow me to ruin myself. I beseech you to put aside your cares and let others help you on the way to recovery as I have belatedly done. And I am sure I will soon be given good reports of your improved health.'

Once in the carriage Edmund leaned against the squabs with a certain relief. It had been no easy matter to bolster the family's failing spirits and he could now see how it must have affected his stepmother over the extended period of his illness.

'A salutary lesson,' he said aloud.

Purvis turned his head from watching the disappearance of the house behind some trees.

'I beg your pardon, Sir,' he said. 'What do you mean?'

'These last few days, Purvis, have taught me how difficult it must have been for all concerned during my convalescence. I am hugely sorry that I taxed and vexed you all so.'

Purvis grinned. 'I came to it late in the day, Sir,' he said, 'so I hardly feel qualified to speak on others' behalf but I would say even Johnson who was most helpful with the George Long affair is in a fair way to forgiving you.'

No more was said on the matter and the men travelled the remaining leg to Bristol in virtual silence. They had given themselves time to call at Mr Banbury's rooms and make an appointment for the morrow.

When Mr. Banbury read the name in his diary, he could not recall why it was so familiar and yet unexpected. He simply could not place it to his own satisfaction.

On Edmund Leighterton's arrival the clerk showed him up the stairs to Mr Banbury's office. Mr. Banbury was momentarily taken aback to be confronted by a man and his two underlings and, in the seconds it took Edmund to take in the panelled room lined with bookcases and almost filled with a huge leather-topped oak desk, Mr. Banbury was somewhat perturbed. Then Edmund collected himself and stepped forward, reaching across the desk to shake the legal man's hand.

'We have not met, Mr Banbury, but I believe you will have heard the name Leighterton frequently. I live at Holm Oak Manor just short of the Reach, which is currently owned by clients of yours: Mr William Smithson and Miss Elena Smithson.' He stopped, seeing Mr Banbury look past him at Purvis and Golding.

'Please forgive the presence of my servants,' he said quickly. 'I mean no disrespect but you must know that I am profoundly deaf and must rely on them to take account of anything I miss.'

Suddenly Mr Banbury recollected who he was and returned the handshake vigorously.

'My dear Mr Leighterton, so good to make your acquaintance at last.' He indicated the chair. 'Please do sit down.'

Edmund did as he was bid, but, before doing so, he drew out the papers they had removed from George Long.

'I come on an errand for a lady, Sir,' he said by way of explanation. 'She requests that you review these papers. Miss Smithson fears that they may disinherit her father, but she would have their veracity authenticated before her father is troubled by them.' He cast the papers on to the great flat surface in front of him.

Mr Banbury spread the scroll out and began to examine them with a magnifying glass.

'Well, well, Mr Leighterton,' he said, looking up and meeting his eyes, stare for stare. 'I do believe that you have done my work for me.' He looked down at another of the sheets. 'Yes, indeed you have!'

26

Feelings of both anxiety and impatience left Elena struggling to control her emotions.

Edmund Leighterton had been gone for more than a week and it felt like forever to the two ladies who eagerly anticipated his return. While Mrs Leighterton did not know the full extent of his errand, she could still be consumed by worry that he might find the journey injurious to his health and well-being. Elena, on the other hand, knew how much depended on the results of his visit and was desperate for his return.

As with all things eagerly anticipated, when she finally espied his carriage on its route up the main drive, she found that the living in hope was much more comfortable than the racing pulse and dry mouth that preceded immediate revelation.

Elena rushed to the hallway and waited for Timery to open the great black front door. To her horror, Mr Banbury was to be seen descending from the carriage with Edmund following in his wake. This had to mean that George Long was the rightful heir; she could put no other construction on it. Elena backed away and sank down on to the bench on which she had waited less than a year ago. She felt faint and choked.

Edmund ushered Mr Banbury into the hallway and allowed Timery to take their hats and overcoats. Only as he glanced around the great marbled area did he spot the wilting Elena on the bench. He strode forward and, catching up her hands, he drew her to her feet.

'Come, Miss Smithson, do not fail me now. There is a lot to tell but nothing seriously to concern you. Come now with me to see your father and Mr Banbury will explain all.'

Elena looked up into his face with eyes of wonder. 'What can you mean?' she asked, bewildered.

'Come,' he said, 'come now and Mr Banbury will make it plain. Well,' here he caught himself up, 'well as plain as is possible with this matter.'

They were closeted in Mr Smithson's office for nearly an hour before

Edmund Leighterton took his leave. Elena escorted him to the door.

'Thank you,' she breathed with shining eyes. 'Thank you for all you have done and all that you are about to do. There are hardly words to express my gratitude to you.'

Her smiling face, so increasingly dear to him, drove all thoughts but the desire to kiss her from his head. He put a hand to her cheek and moved towards her when she sprang from him. Momentarily, he was smitten by hurt that she was once again rejecting him, when a touch on his arm made him realise that Timery was holding his coat. He guessed that the man had cleared his throat or given some such indication of his presence, which was why Elena had reacted so.

'Good bye, Miss Smithson,' he said smiling ruefully. 'On my return let us hope that the matter will be resolved to take account of everyone's happiness.'

'Yes indeed,' she agreed silently so only he could understand. Edmund gave a formal bow. 'I am yours to command,' he said and quitted the house in a rush so that he could not be tempted to reveal more of his feelings in front of the butler's inhibiting presence.

Edmund Leighterton had more difficulty in leaving his own home for a second time. Mrs Leighterton could not imagine why he should want to go off again when he had only just returned from an exhausting trip. Although it was not his story to tell, he eventually had to divulge his mission to her. It did not really reassure her but it resigned her to it, and in a sop to her feelings he remained two nights at the Manor before leaving again.

For this Purvis was inordinately grateful, for whilst his master had enough clothes to pack without waiting for the travel-stained ones to be cleaned, Purvis himself did not. The house-keeper grumbled at him when he told her how quickly he needed his clothes turned around but she did not refuse to have it done although the poor laundry maid threatened, only to her best friend the parlourmaid, to go in search of other employment.

Whilst all these stirring events were going on in Sussex, George Long had wended his way eastward through Kent. He had spurned London and now found himself near Canterbury. There was no reason for his meanderings; he had just gone where the fates had driven him for a cloud had settled on him. He had started out with wrathful energy, determined that with the gold from the sale of the puppies he would make his fortune and come back eventually to prove himself to the Smithsons. He could think of Edmund Leighterton with nothing but bitter hatred and envy. The man had stolen his future and blighted his life. Yet, as the gold began to dwindle as it inevitably did, he recalled the feelings of security and well-being that had enveloped him at the Reach. His thoughts of betrayal by Polly diminished and he began to have an insight into her dilemma. She who after all had had nothing when the Smithsons had rescued her was irrevocably bound to them. George Long tried to assuage his longing to be back there even as a lowly guest by playing hard and drinking deep. The drink inevitably had a negative influence on his ability to play cards and soon the two hundred and seventy guineas were two hundred and seventy guineas no longer.

It had seemed such an enormous amount of money to someone who had been used to surviving on very little:

George Long had thought it wealth indeed but the toll taken on it by his losses and paying for his lodgings had it reduced by half before three weeks were out. Horrified, he curbed his extravagance, cutting the value of the money he was prepared to stake, but he still kept on losing and the money kept on dwindling. Thus five weeks and four days after his banishment from the Reach, George Long was sitting in a noisy taproom as dusk was falling. He sat, head in hands, knowing that the few coins in his pantaloon pockets would not settle his shot on the morrow. He was faced with the choice of going hungry and owing less when he made his early morning flight or eating now in the knowledge that he was to all intents and purposes stealing the food he was consuming. His dog sat quietly at his feet. George knew she too was hungry and he knew that she was his only valuable asset; the horse was nothing but a break-down and of little value. He had never been tempted to part with Ma Belle and even now knew that only the debtors' prison would force him down that road. He put a careless hand down to fondle her ears. She nuzzled it reassuringly. The roar of the people around him in the tavern made his head pound and George Long moved his hands to cover his ears to muffle the sound. It reminded him again of Edmund Leighterton and he was diverted from his own plight for a few moments to try and decide whether he believed Leighterton when he had said he would rather have his hearing than his wealth. George doubted the man would want to exchange places with him now for his clothes were soiled and threadbare; he had traded the good ones he had bought, those five weeks ago, for money as his purse had become lighter. George could only flail himself with the thoughts that he need never have revealed himself to Polly. Knowing the Smithsons' good nature they could have married and lived at the Reach in style and comfort without ever having to admit his claim. Even George Long was honest enough with himself to acknowledge that he would have floundered if he had tried to take on the running of that big estate. Well, now it was not to be; the absence of his papers made that a certainty. George had to face the fact that those papers had been the mainstay of his life; no matter how bad life had become, the existence of the papers had meant there was always hope.

Hope. It was of hope that he was now bereft. No hope, no home, no Polly. He peered into the bottom of his tankard; no drink. He had not ordered more to drink because it would only have run up his tab even more. He saw it as a bitter irony that he could not even afford to drown his sorrows.

There was a bang of the bar-room door making George look up. Standing in front of him was his nemesis, thoughts of whom had never been far from his mind over the last five weeks. George Long did not even have the fight in him to stand up or to question how the man had followed the tortuous trail he had left in order to find him. He looked out from under the hand on his forehead and the curtain of dark hair.

'What do you want of me now?' he asked dejectedly. 'I have nothing more for you to take.'

Edmund Leighterton found in himself a lurking sympathy for George Long, for there had been a detrimental change in his appearance since their last meeting. Edmund flung down the papers on the grubby wooden table.

'I came to return these to you.' The room suddenly went silent around them for people sensed strife in the air.

George's eyes, with a startled flash in Edmund's direction, devoured the crumpled parchment. There were the ragged edges from rubbing against the seam, the singe from an occasion when a candle had set light briefly to his coat tails, the fold where he had had to reduce the size. These were most definitely his original papers.

'But you burned them,' he said incredulously as he scanned the legal writing. Edmund made no reply. Remembering, George looked up at him.

'But you burned them,' he said again less emotionally.

Conversation around them began to swell again as drinkers realised there was to be no altercation.

'I only made it appear that I had burned them, for I did not want you chasing after me trying to recover them.'

'But why, having taken them, have you now returned them to me?'

'I was instructed by a lady to ascertain their authenticity.'

'Polly? Miss McNeath?' he asked eagerly.

'No, Miss Smithson.'

'Miss Smithson!' George almost yelled his disbelief.

The room flinched and eyes were turned in their direction but because Edmund's response was calm the noise, which had subsided, rose again.

'Miss Smithson has been vigorous in championing your rights. You have nothing to fear from her.'

'But you have returned my papers.'

'I have returned your papers for two reasons: one is they are yours and I did not steal them – I borrowed them. Two, they do not entitle you to the ownership of Holm Oak Reach; that remains firmly and rightly in the capable hands of Mr William Smithson. However, these papers prove you to be Sir George Herbert-Longfield. The baronetcy comes with no seat or property but it does come with an allowance of two thousand pounds per annum payable from the receipts of the estate and the tenancy of the Dower House at the Reach if it is unoccupied.' Edmund halted in his narrative briefly to let the news sink in. 'Mr Smithson has agreed to honour the allowance and to backdate it but he requests that should you wish to declare your engagement to Miss McNeath at an end, you find some alternative accommodation as it would be too distressing for his cousin to have you residing so close.'

Fixing on the only bit of this discourse that he really understood and had taken in, despite Edmund's efforts on his behalf, George said:

'It is up to Miss McNeath to cry off. I cannot.'

His words gave Edmund pause. Suddenly it looked as though perhaps after all George Long was gentleman enough to be associated with the Smithsons.

'I believe Mr Smithson feels that Miss McNeath's actions, subsequent to your disclosure to her, absolve you from being in honour bound to her. I also believe that Miss McNeath now has no expectations of your wishing to marry her.'

'Yet you say my presence would discomfort her?' George was getting a crick in his neck looking up at Edmund. 'Oh, sit down, man,' he said impatiently and indicated to the tapster to bring them some ale. He had assimilated enough to know that he could now afford a drink.

'I did not say that Miss McNeath wants the engagement declared at an end. Indeed, I know it to be quite the contrary. What I am saying is that she readily accepts that you might.'

'But I don't!' burst out George in a shout of joy. Once again heads turned. 'But I don't, I don't. I want to marry Polly and live with her in the Dower House.'

Whilst this interchange was continuing, Purvis had slipped away and negotiated the use of a private parlour with the landlord. Mine host, looking askance at Sir George's appearance, was inclined to demur but a judicially placed guinea in his hand convinced him of Edmund Leighterton's worthiness to occupy the smartest room in the house and it was up to him with whom he associated.

Tapping Edmund on the shoulder, Purvis persuaded the two men to remove from the taproom. He then indicated that he would retire to ready Edmund's bedchamber. He felt that both he and Golding could withdraw, as Sir George was familiar enough as a result of his prolonged stay at the Reach with Edmund's needs not to require them to act as Edmund's ears. He also appeared to have lost any vestiges of animosity he might reasonably have been expected to feel previously.

Almost without the two men's noticing, supper was served by a morose servant, his unfriendly attitude completely lost on the protagonists as they continued to explore the change in Sir George's circumstances.

'So,' he said as he broke into the huge country loaf that had been placed between them on the table. 'I am afraid you will have to explain to me again the nature of my inheritance. I knew of course that my name was really Longfield. I have been used to use it but when I awoke unexpectedly at the Reach I foolishly chose to conceal my true identity. I had seen journals brought over from England to America calling for any descendants of George Terrance Herbert-Longfield to make themselves known to the Trustees and I presumed I was a rival to Mr Smithson's claim. Tell me, tell me, please, again how matters stand.'

Edmund drew out a scroll from his jacket pocket and moving the various dishes from the centre of the table made space to unroll it. Revealed upon it was a vast family tree.

'You will see that your great-grandfather had six children of which your grandfather George was the sixth.'

George, following Edmund's pointing finger intently, nodded vigorously.

'Older than him were three brothers and two sisters. While the first two sons married and had children their lines came to an end, which meant that the descendants of the third son became entitled to the inheritance in precedence to his two older sisters.' Here Edmund indicated Jeremiah Tobias Herbert-Longfield on the drawing. 'Jeremiah had only daughters, which did not preclude them from inheriting the estate but did not entitle them to the baronetcy. William Smithson is the son of the eldest daughter Willamina. The title had to go back two generations to find the next living male heir which, because of the demise of your father and grandfather, is you.'

'Sir George Herbert-Longfield, it sounds very well, does it not?'

'I'm sure it does,' answered Edmund, fighting hard not to give the words any edge to them but Sir George picked up on his own mistake immediately.

'Good God, man. I'm sorry, tactless of me!'

Edmund shook his head, rebuffing the suggestion. 'Forget it,' he said. 'I after all have done worse to you.' The two men's eyes met and held and in that moment a bond formed between them and instinctively they reached across the table in unison and shook hands.

Not long after that Edmund put away the scroll and the two men ate a hearty supper. Conversation was desultory because of the need for Sir George to stop eating and to look up whenever he wished to address Edmund but the atmosphere was companionable, even cordial, with both men conscious that they had undervalued and underestimated the other.

27

*E*dmund was determined that they would not commence the journey back to the Reach without first acquiring Sir George a new set of clothes. When he had devised a plan to appropriate the papers, it had not occurred to him that the other man would be reduced to such straits in such a short space of time. The money he had given him was equivalent to many top servants' salaries for a year. Sir George should have been well set up for considerably longer than the five weeks that had separated him from his inheritance. Despite this, Edmund acknowledged that it did not reflect well on him that the man was now dishevelled and evidently penniless. While the financial situation was easily remedied as William Smithson had sent him an advance on Sir George's allowance of some two hundred guineas, nothing but a tailor could rectify his appearance. Luckily for all parties Sir George was amenable to guidance and soon found himself the centre of attention at the tailor's in Canterbury. Had Edmund been able to hear, he would have laughed at the discreet rivalry between the pompous tailor and Purvis, both of whom thought they knew best what would suit Sir George.

Back at the Reach, Elena was anticipating Edmund's return with some trepidation. She very much hoped for Polly's sake that Sir George would wish to continue his engagement, for poor lovelorn Polly had suffered much over the last few weeks. Yet, beset by feelings of guilt, she was fading away before

Elena's eyes. There had been no question of telling her the conclusion of Edmund's travels, even that they were taking place, because no-one wished to give her false hope.

The arrival of Mr Banbury had to be explained, but she knew so little about the family affairs that she accepted he was simply at the Reach for a periodic visit. Each fresh day had Elena hoping the matter would be resolved happily but each morning brought no news. It was apparent that Edmund was struggling to find Sir George. However Elena never ceased to jolly Polly along, insisting she dress prettily, keeping to herself her desire for Polly to look her best should Sir George decide to forgive her for her duplicity and return to the fold.

At last the day dawned when two horsemen were seen trotting up the drive followed by an eager black dog and a travelling chaise.

'Polly, Polly,' cried Elena as soon as she perceived the arrivals. 'Come, come at once, George is returned.'

She need have said no more. Polly let out a screech of alarm and delight and raced down the stairs to greet him, almost falling over her gown in her haste. Elena followed more slowly and was halfway down the grand stairway when Timery admitted the men.

Polly, after her initial burst of energy, stood stock still, almost as white in the face as the majestically disinterested statues around her. Her breath was coming in light gasps as she tried to contain her joy and her dread.

Edmund stood back and let Sir George enter first. He looked very fine in his new dark-green coat and well-fitted gold-leaved waistcoat. His dark hair, now unrecognisable from the lank hanks it had been reduced to days before, glowed like burnished mahogany.

He stretched out his hands to the girl.

'Polly, Polly,' he said, taking her trembling ones. 'Will you have me still after the hollow promises I made you?'

Polly accepted his words at face value. 'If you will have me,' she managed, fairly choking with emotion.

Sir George laughed and drew her closer. 'Of course I will, for you have made me the happiest man alive.'

At that moment William Smithson put in an appearance.

'My dear Sir George,' he said heartily. 'How marvellous to have you back with us and to know that we are so nearly related, second cousins I believe.'

Sir George released Polly and turned to Mr Smithson to take his hand and shake it vigorously. 'You are too generous.' He inhaled a deep breath to master his emotions. 'So generous to take me back after my reprehensible conduct. I am so grateful that you are determined to give me a second chance. I shall not disappoint you.'

'What is this? What is this?' Polly's eyes were wide with wonder. 'Tell me, tell me.'

Sir George turned back to her. 'Come out with me to the terrace and I will tell you how you are about to become my Lady Herbert-Longfield.'

Descending the rest of the stairs Elena watched them go with tears sparkling in her brown eyes, so moved was she that her cousins were reunited. She stepped forward to Edmund who had been standing quietly by the door during the exchange between Polly and Sir George, which he was not in a position to follow.

'It seems I am in your debt once again, Mr Leighterton,' she said, a hint of the smile he so adored dimpling the edge of her mouth.

Edmund captured her hand and carried it to his lips. 'I am as ever yours to command,' he said. 'I am only glad that the resolution is such a happy outcome.'

Here William Smithson came up and touched his arm.

'You have done us a great service, Leighterton; I am most grateful.'

'You are very welcome, Sir,' said Edmund, exhibiting a formal bow but conscious of a degree of irritation that his tête-à-tête with Elena had been interrupted. 'I am sure Sir George will soon become an asset to the family.'

'Indeed he will,' agreed Mr Smithson, who then pressed Edmund to stay and lunch with them, but Purvis had already taken down Sir George's one small bag and Ma Belle, with the unerring skill of a tracker, had sought out Jessamy and the two puppies, so Edmund now had all he needed to return home. Knowing there was unlikely to be an opportunity to be private with Elena, he once again used his stepmother as an excuse and beat a hasty retreat.

Elena watched him go with eyes full of longing and had he but seen it he would have retraced his steps immediately.

For Polly the following days were full of wonder. Nothing had prepared her for the joy and happiness she felt at the prospect of becoming Sir George's wife and for someone who had been rescued from destitution, to become Lady Herbert-Longfield was the stuff of beatific dreams. That they were also entitled to a home at the Dower House at first enchanted her. In much eagerness she pressed Sir George to come with her to examine their prospective new abode.

The Dower House was a charming multi-gabled building, predominantly seventeenth century, with panelled walls and lower ceilings than Polly had become used to at the Reach. It nestled below the Reach, protected from the gaze of its myriad windows by a belt of trees. Polly began her tour of the many ground floor rooms in eagerness and excitement, dragging Sir George from room to room, exclaiming and pointing out every fascinating detail, but as their tour continued she became steadily quieter and more subdued. It was not lost on her either that Sir George's enthusiasm had waned too. At one point he had been studying a particularly ornate doorway virtually hidden in the panelling as if his life depended on it, such was his determination not to think about the greater nightmare of their setting up home in this house.

'I think this must be even older than we were told,' he said. Then, as this remark elicited no response, he turned to find the room behind him empty. Following the trail of open doors, he found Polly sitting on a window seat in a large room, the only one they had so far found furnished. A number of chairs were under yellowing Holland covers.

'What is amiss, my love,' he asked, looking at her troubled face.

'Do you think we must live here?' she asked forlornly.

Sir George came up to her. 'Do you not like it?' he asked.

'Oh, I am so very delighted with the house,' she said unconvincingly. Then she took a deep breath and looked him straight in the eye. 'But humour me in this, Sir George, and do not be affronted. We, you and I, have no notion how to run a home like this. You have your two thousand a year and I have my allowance, which Mr Smithson is kind enough to give me.'

'I also have the money that has been put aside since the death of my predecessor. It accounts to a tidy sum, Mr Banbury assures me,' said Sir George, interrupting her.

'My darling, it is not enough,' said Polly with determined candour. 'You and I need lengthy tutoring on the subject of keeping a household. This home deserves at least eight servants and between them they would cost as much as six hundred pounds a year, not to mention the cost of setting up stables. You tell me you spent three hundred guineas in little more than a month. We would soon be in debt.' She paused, fearful that she had been too frank; Sir George was staring at her, perplexed.

'What would you have us do then?' he asked. 'I would relish a settled future; I have spent too long with nowhere to call my own to want to abandon this opportunity.'

Polly sighed. 'Could we not request of cousin William a suite of rooms at the Reach?' she asked plaintively.

'I would not wish to make further demand on him, Polly,' replied Sir George sternly. 'I have only just come to know how generous he has been. How would it be perceived if we asked to remain at the Reach?'

Polly held back a sob and dashed a hand across her eyes. 'I

know, I know,' she wept, 'but I am frightened, Sir George, frightened that we will let our current good fortune slip through our fingers through ignorance.'

Unable to deny her anything, Sir George went over to her and drew her to her feet. 'Very well,' he said, 'we will go now and ask him but we must pay him a rent, Polly. I cannot be any further beholden to him.'

She nodded submissively and allowed him to lead her back to the Reach. The band of trees protected them from the sunshine, allowing only a dappled effect. Insects were humming on the ivy flowers and parent birds were calling to their fledglings. Both Polly and Sir George savoured their surroundings each in their own way, transported to a world so different from what they had known before. Both were now conscious of what they owed William Smithson and neither wanted to jeopardise his patronage so it was with some trepidation that they pursued the course they had just agreed upon.

At Mr Smithson's study door, Sir George knocked and on being asked to enter opened the door to let Polly go through before him.

'Well, well, my dears,' said Mr Smithson, rubbing his hands and coming out from behind his desk. 'How did you fare at the Dower House? Is your mind full of samples and colour plates?' His enthusiastic encouragement almost made Polly change her mind about saying anything but he must have seen the residue of fears on her face.

'So what is this?' he demanded sharply. 'My dear Polly, what can be wrong?'

Polly looked into the kindly face and found herself blurting out her anxieties. 'I cannot live there, cousin William, I cannot. I have no command of servants, no experience of keeping house.'

Mr Smithson's eyes travelled from her face to that of Sir George. 'And this is a decision of you both?' he asked.

Sir George nodded. 'Sir, forgive us,' he said, attempting to explain. 'This wealth is so new to us, so unfamiliar, we would so much prefer to remain as your guests, paying of course.'

Mr Smithson was silent for what seemed to the young couple to be an age. Then he turned on his heel.

'What do you think to this suggestion, Elena?' he asked. Both Polly and Sir George were startled at the question for they had not been aware that she was there. Elena, who had interrupted her father's peace some twenty minutes before, was sitting on one of several beech-wood chairs with a cross-shaped splat placed against the wall and she had been shielded from their view on entry by the open door. Once in the room they had had their backs to her. She had not meant to be party to any private conversation but once they were in the room and talking with her father she felt it would have been rude to interrupt. She stood up and came towards them.

'I think it would be a very prudent arrangement,' she said. 'For this house is so vast that it needs a large family to inhabit it. I am sure your affianced wife would have no objection.'

Polly's face lightened. 'We would wish to pay our way, cousin,' she said diffidently.

'Oh, no need for that,' said Mr Smithson, cheerfully brushing aside such a suggestion. 'The rent I can get for letting the Dower House will easily cover any additional costs I might incur housing you.'

'Then it is settled?' asked Sir George, wanting affirmation immediately.

Mr Smithson opened his mouth to agree when Elena spoke again. 'There is one outstanding matter, Papa,' she said, her face set as though steeling herself to broach the subject.

'And what can that be?' asked Mr Smithson, wrong-footed with surprise.

'The matter of the allegations of poaching, which are circulating with regard to when Sir George arrived in this area.'

There was a shocked silence. Polly wide-eyed turned and clung to Sir George's arm. 'No,' she cried, 'that cannot be. Tell her such accusations are unfounded, Sir George, please,' she wailed.

Mr Smithson looked out from under his thick brows at his daughter. He guessed she must have good reason for raising the matter now but he did not immediately see what it was.

Sir George too did not make the mistake of thinking Elena was his enemy. He had already on several occasions tried to thank her for her kind offices on his behalf and to apologise for causing her so much unnecessary anxiety but she had not let him. She had merely assured him that she had done what she felt to be right and that she was sorry if he had been discommoded while the enquiries had been taking place. Now he looked at her and although his heart pounded and his throat was dry, he knew he had to make a confession and beg for their help to establish his character.

28

*M*r Smithson went to the side of the room and carried to his desk three of the set of eight beech-wood chairs. He persuaded the ladies to sit and then he sat himself. Unable at this stage, because of his inward agitation, to take his place on the remaining chair, Sir George stood behind it, gripping its back. He cleared his throat.

'You will recall no doubt that I told you that my previous circumstances had been straitened, particularly after the death of my father,' he began.

William Smithson nodded but once again Elena made her voice heard.

'Can you tell me, Sir George, how it was that you sported the character and manner of a gentleman while professing to be so destitute?'

'My father, Miss Smithson, was born a gentleman. He knew how to conduct himself and, though he was a spendthrift, he knew the value of manners and breeding. He never let me forget it. He drummed it into me from almost before I could walk or talk. I might have had no possessions but I could be proud of my lineage, a lineage that he demonstrated to me time and time again in the lines of papers he gave to my safekeeping on his death bed.'

'I see, thank you, pray continue.'

Feeling that he was up in front of the magistrate, Sir George released the chair and loosened his cravat. 'The passage from

America to England cost me dear and by the time I reached these shores I had but a few coins to my name. Nevertheless I was determined to travel into Sussex to view the property to which I believed myself entitled.' He cast an apologetic glance in Elena's direction. 'I know now that I would have been better advised to make my way straight to Mr Banbury's office. So much unnecessary upset would have been prevented.' He sighed and at last sat down but within seconds he was back on his feet.

'I wanted to be assured that the prize was worth having or alternatively that I knew the extent of it so that no-one could swindle me of what was mine.' Here he looked again at Miss Smithson. 'I had not previously experienced such moral clarity and rectitude as I have subsequently discovered in you, Miss Smithson. I presumed everyone would want to take what should be mine.'

Elena bowed her head and looked at her hands clasped tightly in her lap. In truth there had been moments when her resolve had been tested but she did not think she need confess it, as it had only been momentary. Sir George's voice drew her away from her thoughts.

'You will guess, I think, that it is not easy to travel penniless through the unfamiliar land of a country almost foreign to me. I was soon, to use your word, destitute, Miss Smithson, my only things of value the dog and my papers. Hunger was never far away; the breeding birds so many and so tame were just too much of a temptation for me. I planned only to take enough to sate the bitch's and my immediate needs but I was seen and chased. We lost our pursuers but in the half-light I mistook the lie of the land. The rest you know. You found me the next day. It was a complete shock to awake and find myself in the house I thought my own.'

There was silence as there was no need for him to relate further his misdeeds. All now knew the details of the subsequent events.

'Did you take any of the birds?' William Smithson broke the silence with his question.

Sir George shook his head.

'Could we not pass it off as a misunderstanding?' asked Polly eagerly. 'That he had no such intentions but was startled by the unexpected outcry his visit provoked.'

Sir George first looked at Elena and then at Mr Smithson and realised that, though they might not be thinking it now, this was a test of his integrity he could not fail.

'I am of the belief that I should admit my guilt and pay for any reparations necessary,' he said quickly, not quite able to meet Elena's eye.

'No!' Polly sprang to her feet, almost knocking her chair over in her agitation. 'No, they might call the magistrate and have you committed for trial. No, please, no.'

'Polly, Polly.' William Smithson went to her and put a strong arm around her. 'I am sure that the Miss Wainwrights will do no such thing, especially if I accompany Sir George and vouch for him.'

'Would you do that?' asked Sir George, much moved. 'I do not deserve that you should do so. Thank you; how can I ever thank you?'

William Smithson smiled his broad good-humoured smile. 'By making and keeping my dear cousin here happy,' he said succinctly.

So without further ado it was agreed that William Smithson and Sir George would ride out the very next day to Willow Grange and make peace with the Miss Wainwrights. It turned out not to be so very difficult, as the kindly ladies who were guarded by an extremely loyal staff had been looking for an opportunity to make Mr Smithson's acquaintance. When the reason for the visit was explained, they were quick to accept the apologies of the very handsome young man and would not have accepted his proffered payment if Mr Smithson had not insisted that reparation should be made for the upset caused. The ladies dithered and quavered until their steward was summoned and the cause was explained to him. He had no trouble in accepting the generous compensation, which he knew would ease the slight shortfall his good ladies were currently experiencing. It then dawned on him that he could do worse than ask Mr Smithson's advice on some agricultural matters. He therefore seized the opportunity and ushered him away to his office, leaving Sir George to entertain the ladies with stories of his travels. A less affable young man might have found this more of a penance than parting with some money he was not yet used to having.

There was now no impediment to the early marriage of Sir George Herbert-Longfield and Miss Polly McNeath, so, in consultation with the rector, Reverend Ezekiel Lansdale, the first banns were called the following Sunday and preparations were made for the ceremony three weeks hence. There was no question of spoiling the occasion of Mr William Smithson and Mrs Clarissa Leighterton's marriage set for a further month later, because Sir George and Polly's was to be a quiet affair. Neither felt they had enough friends and acquaintances to warrant a party but, even so, the church was well attended. Edmund Leighterton acted as groomsman for Sir George, Mr Smithson supported Polly in loco parentis and the congregation included the rector's sister and nieces, senior downstairs staff and Colonel Campden who had already removed his family from London to make preparation for an engagement party in September for his second daughter. The Campden girls had had a good season.

After their union there was no intention on the part of Sir George and Lady Herbert-Longfield to have a honeymoon; both felt they had travelled far enough both metaphorically and in actuality in their lives thus far to want to do anything other than to settle themselves into the magnificent suite of rooms Mr Smithson had provided for them to call their own. There had been some ribald suggestions that Sir George should accompany his wife to her previous employer and flaunt her now elevated position but the idea distressed Polly and was soon dropped.

Mrs Leighterton, preparing happily for her own change of circumstances, could only marvel at the difference the year had made since she had received from his rescuers the body of her stepson awash with fever. She was not however so taken up with her own affairs not to notice that the two people who most deserved happiness had yet to find it. In the few remaining weeks she had still living at the Manor she tried to find opportunities amongst all the preparation to talk to her stepson, to urge him to make his feelings known to Miss Smithson, but he was resolute in refusing, sure that he had said and done enough for her to know. Also the instances when she had been irritated or impatient with him could not fail to rankle and he was increasingly too afraid of rejection to put it to the test. In addition he convinced himself that although all the uncertainty over the inheritance had been removed, Elena, not having had this season as her come-out, still needed time to adjust to her new position. In all honour, he believed she should have the opportunity to have her pick of the desirable parties of the upper ten thousand. He espoused the hope that if she found no-one then he would be free to offer himself as a poor alternative. His stepmother's encouragement fell on stony ground. So all through the run-up to the wedding he maintained his reserve and Elena, who longed to feel his arms around her and experience the same happiness as she saw daily in others, was bewildered and hurt. There were no opportunities to be private with him to iron out any misunderstanding about her feelings for him, so behind the bright face she presented to her father she cried bitter tears of dejection.

The wedding came and went, a great success made more memorable for Mr Smithson as Lord Delrymple had agreed to be his groomsman and half his estate workforce had made the tortuous journey to attend the ceremony.

The Reverend Ezekiel Lansdale gave an uplifting address about the rewards for hard work, integrity and loyalty and the weather was kind enough to allow the two hundred guests to be entertained on the lawn at the Manor. Watching her father give his speech of thanks with happy tears in her eyes, Elena too had to marvel at the change in their circumstances. Despite the vicissitudes they had experienced over the last year, she knew that the radical changes in their lives brought about by the inheritance had been made easier by her father's long experience of management of others' land. She shuddered to think what might have happened if Sir George had in fact been the heir.

'Cold, Miss Smithson? Can I get you a wrap?'

Elena smiled. 'No, thank you, Mr Deacon, I am well enough.' She looked at the pleasant man who had so quickly become part of their world, even if only from afar. 'I was delighted when I learned that you would be accompanying Lord Delrymple. I don't believe I have thanked you enough for encouraging Mr Leighterton to have one of the puppies. It has been a great success I understand.'

Mr Deacon smiled a broad smile. 'You may not have, Miss Smithson, but he most surely has. Despite being still little more than a puppy it is devoted to him and I gather from Purvis that it is no longer possible for him to sneak up on Mr Leighterton without the dog's giving him away.'

Elena chuckled. 'That will certainly curtail Purvis's activities. Perhaps he does not thank you then.'

'I do not think he minds that much; he can see the advantages for Mr Leighterton.' Here Mr Deacon brought this particular line of conversation to a close. He put his hand into his breast pocket and drew out a wad of letters. 'I come as messenger, Miss Smithson. Your friends regret that they too could not make the journey for they long to see you. I am charged to hand these to you directly.'

Elena looked at the letters in delight. 'Thank you,' she

breathed. 'Replying to these will give me much to do while Papa and my new Mama are away on their travels.'

'Are they away long?' Mr Deacon asked politely.

'Oh no, not long, merely a trip to visit the town house. Papa wishes to know how Mama would like it decorated. They have promised the Colonel to return for Beatrice's betrothal party.'

Across the lawn from them Edmund watched the pair, his face a mask. His love for Elena and his respect for Ingram Deacon could not prevent the jealousy he felt that they could converse so freely, but he was determined to suppress it, if they were to find happiness together.

Noting that they were being watched, Mr Deacon positioned himself so that his back was to Edmund, obscuring any response Elena might make to him.

'And when will I hear happy news of you and Mr Leighterton?' he asked boldly.

Elena's expressive eyes flew to his face.

'What can you mean?' she asked. 'I'm sure Mr Leighterton has no thoughts of wedding me.'

'Do you indeed? I, on the other hand, would say it is something he thinks about a great deal.'

A deep blush infused Elena's cheeks. 'Please, Mr Deacon, do not speak so. I am sure you are mistaken.'

Having satisfied himself that he would not be doing his friend Leighterton a disservice if he added his encouragement to others, Mr Deacon took pity on Miss Smithson and let the matter drop. He was not unhopeful, though, that there would be a happy outcome.

29

*H*ardly had Elena allowed the ink to dry on her final letter in response to each of the Delrymple girls' letters than her father and his new wife returned from London, such had been the girls' clamour for every detail of the marriage event.

Elena had done her best to satisfy them, dividing her time between recalling all that went on and preparing her little brother for school. She could not fail to feel the warmth rise in her cheeks each time she remembered Mr Deacon's words. She hoped she had not given herself away but was conscious that she probably had. A small part of her hoped that Mr Deacon would have persuaded Edmund to make a declaration and that she might therefore expect a visit from him while the newly-weds were from home. There was after all no need to fear the gossips if he did, with Polly a married woman and therefore an acceptable chaperone.

Elena had waited in vain. Had she but known it, it was with considerable difficulty that Edmund kept himself away from the Reach. Mr Ingram Deacon had urged him to put the matter of a possible union with Elena to the test but Edmund had not been able to master the fear of rejection and had kept away.

When Mrs Smithson returned, her first duty was to visit her stepson to see how he had fared in her absence. She was pleased and relieved to hear from Cleverley that he had not regressed to his earlier ways, but a secret meeting with Purvis had made her appreciate that her stepson was struggling to maintain a cheerful front.

'Can you not do something, Madam?' Purvis begged. 'Can you not get Miss Smithson to indicate her willingness in some way? I believe Mr Edmund has determined that he will be rebuffed.'

All the lady could do was promise to do her best. To this end she sought Elena out when she returned to her new home and, deciding frankness was the only route to follow, laid the matter before her.

Once more covered with embarrassment, Elena knew not what to say. 'It would look as though I am setting my cap at him,' she wailed. 'Have I not already risked my reputation by indicating my strong partiality?'

'Not to him, my dear,' Mrs Smithson responded gently. 'Not to him. He knew little of the degree to which you exposed yourself for his sake. You must remember that he knows nothing of gossip.'

Elena, her face almost as pink as her rosebud-coloured dress, stood up from the chair in the parlour where her stepmother had found her and stared out of the window. 'What are you advising me to do?' she asked tightly.

'Give him clear indication that you would welcome a declaration on his part. Tell him to his face.'

Elena was shocked. 'I cannot do that. It would be most unbecoming in me. Can you not say something to him? Surely it would be better coming from you?'

Mrs Smithson shook her newly coiffed hair. One treat she had allowed herself as a result of marrying into such wealth was to employ a smart lady's dresser. She now started each day turned out to perfection. All she had to do now, she had ruefully explained to her husband, was learn how to comport herself so that she looked as elegant by the time she returned herself to the hands of this alarming individual to change for dinner as she had when she had left her in the morning.

'He will not take it from me, my dear; I am afraid that it must come from you.'

Baulked on this front, Elena tried a different argument. 'There is no opportunity for me to talk to him,' she pointed out. 'He did not visit me once this last fortnight and there was no impediment to him doing so as both Sir George and Lady Polly were here all the time.'

Mrs Smithson sighed. 'Then you must visit him.'

'Mama! How can you suggest such a thing!'

'But of course I would accompany you,' Mrs Smithson assured her hastily. 'There would be no question of your visiting him alone.'

Their eyes met and there was no need to express the impossibility of the situation. Edmund would most surely think the visit had been orchestrated and therefore not believe Elena's sincerity.

The ladies remained in silence for a few minutes, each searching for a ruse that was both plausible and feasible, Elena finally acknowledging that to secure her own happiness she needed to give Edmund the confidence that he would not be rejected if he made a declaration.

'I have it.' Suddenly Mrs Smithson jerked forward in her seat and grasped the arms of her chair. 'He will have to put in an appearance at the Campdens' party, it would be deemed very off if he did not. One cannot expect him to dance for he cannot hear the rhythm of the music. No-one would think it irregular if you were to sit out a couple of dances with him. You must find the right way to express your sentiments to him.'

Elena pursed her lips in order to prevent herself from listing the flaws in this plan. She could readily see them if her stepmother could not: a crowded room full of interested parties, constraint between them, no possibility of the written word. This last she could at least ameliorate; she resolved to put a slate in her reticule, but mostly she hoped that Edmund would visit them in the intervening ten days and deny her the need to jeopardise her reputation once more in full view of the local gentry.

Edmund did visit Holm Oak Reach more than once but he took care to arrive at the busiest time for morning callers and foiled any attempt by his stepmother to manoeuvre him and Elena into a private conversation. In doing this he was only acting in self-preservation. He knew all too well what his stepmother was trying to achieve.

At last the day of the party dawned and in some trepidation Elena started her preparations early, wanting to look her very best for her first grand party. The Campdens, who not so long ago had seemed almost foreign to her in their ways and thoughts, had mellowed in her mind. Colonel Campden's willingness to be advised by Mr Smithson pointed to an open and liberal mind. His son, though clearly having no great intellect, was amenable and always willing to take pains to make Edmund feel included. Even Beatrice's predilection for tittle-tattle could be forgiven as it was clear she never meant any harm. The successful season for both Campden girls – Amelia too had become engaged but had not yet been given leave to announce it formally and so steal her sister's thunder – had resulted in the momentous event of Mrs Campden's quitting her day bed and reappearing in society to arrange their nuptials. All these circumstances had meant that their party could be looked forward to as a great event. Elena had a new dress of a delicate salmon-pink silk. Her dancing slippers were beaded with pearls as were her hairpiece and jewellery set. Mrs Smithson, as keen as Elena to have her look her best, had sent her dresser to fashion the girl's hair. A soft shimmering shawl completed her toilette. Mr and Mrs Smithson let out a joint sigh of appreciation as Elena descended the main stairway in all her finery.

Lady Polly and Sir George too had made every effort to turn themselves out well for the event and Mr Smithson beamed his pleasure as he saw the young couple approach along the corridor. Their happiness outshone any shortcomings in Polly's waif-like figure and the slight hint of dissipation that had not quite cleared itself from Sir George's countenance.

Two carriages set out for the Campdens' home, the Smithsons in one and Sir George and Lady Longfield-Herbert in the other. All the occupants felt very grand as the horses swept them up the curved drive lined with flaming torches to the front door.

Before she descended from the carriage Mrs Smithson gave Elena's hand a reassuring pat of encouragement. Elena cast her a smile but said nothing.

The Smithsons joined the throng that was entering the house and were soon through the hall and into the first reception room, which was not so fully occupied. Elena's eyes, even before she had taken stock, alighted on a tall, dark man. She made her way to him immediately, surprisingly glad to find an acquaintance so readily.

'Mr Sawyer. How do you do?' she cried as she extended her gloved hand.

'My dear Miss Smithson, how delighted I am to see you. I was hoping that I might.'

'Indeed, but I had no expectation of seeing you, Mr Sawyer. It is a most pleasant surprise. What is your connection with the Campdens?'

'Oh, none, none at all,' the curate was quick to say, 'but as you know, since his illness Lord Delrymple prefers to travel accompanied and Mr Deacon was unable to attend on this occasion, so his Lordship invited me in his stead.'

'How delightful for you,' exclaimed Elena, conscious all of a sudden that in her determination not to allow the legacy of their previous parting to result in any awkwardness between them, she was displaying rather too much pleasure in their re-acquaintance, 'but I do hope there is nothing amiss with Mr Deacon?'

'None whatsoever, I can assure you,' said the curate. 'In fact I have been charged with the most exceptional errand. Indeed, although I carry the news to you in letter form, I have been granted permission to convey it to you in person.'

Elena's eyes widened. 'What are you about to tell me? Pray, please make haste. I am consumed by curiosity by what you say.'

'It gives me great pleasure to inform you that Mr Ingram Deacon and Lady Dorothea have become engaged.'

Elena's face lit up, radiating joy. She clasped at Mr Sawyer's hand as he withdrew the letter from her friend detailing the turn of events. 'What wonderful, wonderful news!' she cried. 'More marvellous because it was believed that not one of the sisters would ever be in good enough health to enter the happy state of matrimony. Mr Sawyer, tell me that she is well.'

'Yes, Miss Smithson, she is most well. You have nothing to fear and Mr Deacon plans to remove her to the coast for their honeymoon, where it is believed she will enjoy even better health. They will then return to Leicestershire to take up residence at the Delrymple seat.'

Elena nodded, too overcome to speak, for though her joy had been immense at the news, it had quickly been followed by the thought of the other sisters being left forlorn without their sister. She might have guessed that Mr Deacon, so sympathetic to the needs of others, would know that he could not part the sisters. The smile returned to her lips and she mastered her emotions enough to enquire after Mr Sawyer's own interests.

From the doorway to the hallway, Edmund Leighterton had seen that brilliant smile transform Elena's face as she gazed in what seemed to him like rapture into the visitor's face. It pierced him like a knife for he had always claimed that smile as his own. It mortified him to see it used on someone else. He had planned to stay at the party, proving to all that he was once more one of their number. He had not expected to dance, but young Mr Campden had promised him a game of cribbage in the card room. His resolve not to put his case to Elena had been weakening and, had the opportunity arisen, he might have been tempted to test the water. In fact even Purvis, who so often had preached patience and caution, hinted that the time was ripe. Now seeing Elena's pleasure in another man's company, he knew he had lost the battle before he had even begun to fight. He turned sharply on his heel and made to leave. He was almost at the front door when young Jolyon Campden touched his arm. Edmund wheeled round.

'Yes,' he said abruptly.

'Leaving so soon, Leighterton? What of our game?'

Taking time to collect himself, Edmund responded as best he could. 'Another time, Campden. I am afraid I feel rather unwell and must return home.'

'My dear chap, what a frightful shame!' he exclaimed. 'Let me call your carriage.'

Edmund shook his head. 'No, no, please do not trouble yourself. I am well enough to do that.' He turned back to the door but a thought occurred to him and he turned again. 'The tall man dressed in black in the saloon. He has the appearance of a man of the cloth. Do you know his name?'

'Oh yes.' Campden was eager to exhibit his knowledge. 'He is the curate from the Delrymple Estate in Leicestershire. There was some talk of an attachment to Miss Smithson before the Smithsons removed here but it came to nought. Mr Smithson saw to that.'

Edmund needed to be told no more. He knew of Mr Sawyer, should have guessed it was him from his attire. Miss Smithson had told him of her reservations about the sincerity of the man's regard for her but from what he had seen, Edmund was convinced that Miss Smithson's feelings had been reanimated towards him.

30

Journeying home that night was for Edmund a form of purgatory he had not endured for many months; the twin feelings of desperation and bitterness had been banished some time ago only to return with a vengeance. Elena was his; the notion reverberated around his head. Whoever he might have imagined he would relinquish her to in previous, more altruistic, moments of reflection, it had not been to a penniless preacher who did not even have good looks to recommend him. The jolting progress of the carriage seemed interminable even though it was but two and a half miles to his home. His anger and disappointment festered, blackening his brow. When he quitted his carriage he strode into the house, ignoring the footman who had opened the door and marched into the parlour before slamming the door.

The nights had been drawing in for some time now and it had been dark for two hours or more but it was not yet ten o'clock. Purvis might have been expected to be up but, prior to his departure for the party, Edmund had given him the evening off. Purvis had used the opportunity to catch up on his sleep and was now slumbering deeply two floors above him. All previous precautions to prevent Edmund overindulging were no longer in place. To all, his predilection for drowning his sorrows was a distant memory. The sideboard once again supported an array of decanters. Edmund grabbed a glass, clinking it against one of its fellows and filled it to the brim with brandy.

He knocked it back in one great gulp, the fiery liquid catching in the back of his throat. He coughed and poured himself another more moderate one but the effect had given him pause. He surveyed the room, which for so long had been witness to his misery, its leaf-green walls reflecting back his brooding air. Edmund went to the candleholder on the wall and extinguished the flames that had been burning when he entered the room. He moved an occasional table close to his favourite chair and then placed a single candleholder and the decanter on it. He sat down and swilled the liquid around in the glass, watching the candle flame through it. He shivered and for a moment contemplated lighting the fire that had been laid in the fireplace but a great lethargy had assailed him and he made no move to do it. The effects of the alcohol, drunk so quickly and on a stomach that had not had food since lunchtime, were taking hold and his limbs felt limp and uncontrolled. He put the glass down with exaggerated care on the little table and sat back deep into the chair. He knew he was facing the final test, an irrevocable decision and the choice was his alone. There was no denying the temptation that beckoned to him from the contents of the beautiful crystal glass. He could sup and sup again and drink himself into oblivion, trying to escape the disappointment that he would never hold Elena Smithson in his arms as a lover. Or he could resist the siren call, count his blessings and play the hand fate had dealt him. Had he not shown himself capable of serving others? He brushed aside the fact that he needed Purvis and Golding to assist him because he knew too that they could not have accomplished the various tasks they had undertaken together without the part he played.

The clock on the mantelpiece, barely visible through the gloom of the remaining candles, ticked determinedly and time carried him further away from his last drink. Try as he might to chase it with another, his conscience resisted and although twice he clutched the short stem of his glass and carried it to his lips, he could not make himself drink. In frustration he raised his arm to cast the glass at the wall and then he remembered that the set had been a wedding gift to his father and mother and could not do it. Midnight passed with a flurry of activity from the clock and then one o'clock. Edmund was becoming stiff and cold but he had not taken another drink. At last his eyes began to close and despite his dejection he fell asleep.

Purvis found him there the next morning, snoring gently in the chair, the glass still with a measure in it and the decanter nearly full. It took the valet some minutes to assimilate that Edmund was not the worse for wear from drink and the jarring sensation that this suspicion had caused in his body eased. He took away the glassware and moved the little table back to its habitual place before shaking Edmund awake. Edmund's eyes opened, then closed again.

'I don't want to know,' he said with a groan, keeping his eyes closed. 'I won't let you tell me that I have transgressed. Ah!' He stretched out his legs and tried to ease the stiffness in them.

Purvis shook him again more vigorously.

'All right, all right.' Edmund put his hands up in mock surrender after opening his eyes and sitting forward in the chair. 'Tell me the worst,' he commanded, looking at Purvis directly.

'There is no worst, Sir,' Purvis was quick to assure him. 'You appear to have fallen asleep in the chair.'

'So I do,' Edmund replied, surprised. He stood up and as he did so, the recollection of the night before flooded back to him. 'She is lost to me, Purvis,' he said, so quietly that Purvis had to strain to catch his words.

'How can that be?' the valet cried once he had understood him. 'I do not believe it!'

'It is so; I saw with my own eyes her delight in being reunited with her previous suitor. You know how she smiles...' He halted mid-sentence, aware that he should not be burdening Purvis with his unhappiness. Purvis shook his head in disbelief.

'I am so sorry, Sir', he said inadequately. 'So very sorry.'

'Well, so am I,' said Edmund brusquely. 'But nothing can now be done. Fill me a tub, Purvis. Let us see whether we can chase away the aches and pains in my body even if we can make no impression on those of my heart.'

Not far away at the Reach, Elena was stirring. She had not spent much longer talking to Mr Sawyer for she saw that he was alive with the possibility that he might yet secure her. He became all at once oppressively solicitous and, catching her father's eye, Elena made good her escape as Mr Smithson moved in to draw Mr Sawyer away from her. For the rest of the evening, Elena did her best not to appear fretful but she could not prevent herself from watching the door avidly in case Edmund Leighterton should arrive. Although she enjoyed dancing, in part thanks to the numerous young men who appreciated her twofold charms of wealth and beauty, and she reacquainted herself with many of their near neighbours, there was one glaring omission: Edmund Leighterton was not present. Three times she exchanged looks of mute enquiry in the direction of her stepmother and each time all Mrs Smithson could do was shake her head.

As the evening drew to a close, Elena found herself some quiet corner to sit in, protected from the glare of curiosity by a huge potted palm tree. She eased off her pretty shoes and thought how she had suffered them for no good reason. Mrs Smithson, on the watch for some reaction from Elena to Edmund's baffling absence, discovered her there some minutes later.

'Do not say any words of comfort or optimism, Mama, please,' Elena begged before the poor lady could open her mouth. 'If you say anything sympathetic, I know I shall weep.'

'Very well, I will say nothing till the morning but I urge you not to despair, there will be some reasonable explanation. Mark my words.'

Not long after this exchange, Mr Smithson indicated that it

was time to leave and they sought out their hosts. Jolyon Campden was much in evidence saying the necessary goodbyes and adjuring people to have a safe journey. Knowing from his remarks when they first arrived that he had intended to spend part of the evening with Edmund, Mrs Smithson felt it behoved her to make an apology for him.

'Oh, but he did put in an appearance, Ma'am,' Jolyon was quick to tell. 'But he declared he wasn't feeling too well and had to leave.' Jolyon touched his rather bulbous nose with his finger and he lowered his voice. 'But my guess was that he could not abide seeing Mr Sawyer making up to Miss Smithson.' The young man chuckled, the Campden love of gossip giving Mrs Smithson instant insight into Edmund's defection. She too had seen Elena smile on Mr Sawyer and had been thankful, erroneously now it appeared, that Edmund had not seen it too. She was tempted to put Elena in possession of the facts on the way home but in the gloom of the carriage Elena's face shone pale and wan. Tonight was not the time to burden her with details she could not act upon until the morning.

So, no sooner had Elena quitted her bedchamber and arrived at the breakfast parlour to pick forlornly at her breakfast than Mrs Smithson, who too had suffered a disturbed night, began to unfold the circumstances surrounding Edmund's hasty departure the night before.

Elena was aghast. 'He thought I had taken up with Mr Sawyer again?' she demanded. 'That cannot be! He knows my sentiments on that score; surely one smile, one gesture should not have negated all that I have said to him before on that head?'

'Elena, Elena.' Mrs Smithson shook her head sagely. 'You forget that in order to understand the world around him he has to try and interpret what he sees. And he saw you delighted, nay, ecstatic at seeing Mr Sawyer again.'

'It was not seeing Mr Sawyer, Mama, truly it was not. It was the news he brought.'

'Then I think it is time that you and I made a visit to the Manor to set the record straight, do you not?'

Elena could only nod in submissive agreement.

31

The many pitchers of hot water that had been carried aloft to Edmund's bedchamber to fill the tin bathtub had done their work. His bodily aches had gone and he was now dressed but with no sense of purpose. He drifted out of doors and wandered down to the paddock to watch the foal which he and Golding had saved those months ago canter exuberantly around the field. Every so often it would venture to the gate and let him fondle its ears before dashing away. Edmund had to acknowledge that he had achieved something in helping save this filly's life. He looked down at the devoted puppy that sat at his feet, and marvelled again at her intuition. It had not taken her long to understand that he could not hear. Edmund leaned on the gate and tried to draw comfort from the unexpected warmth of the autumn sun and the hint of the beauty yet to come in the trees around him, which were just beginning to turn.

From some little way away Elena saw the hunch of his back as he allowed his body to express the cares of his mind. She knew he could not hear her approach but she could not help treading carefully on the gravel. She wanted to surprise him. As she came closer the puppy turned dark soulful eyes on her and made to move to indicate someone was there but Elena quelled her with her eyes and the dog remained where she was, her expression watchful. As Elena took the final steps to the gate, she had no idea what she was going to do or say. She knew only that despite her qualms it was imperative that she be bold. Once beside him there and with his dear face turned towards her in silent wonder, she drew his right hand across his body and with her finger wrote on his palm.

'I adore you.'

Although he watched and felt the words and thought he got their meaning, his diffidence was such that when she had finished he pushed his hand forward and said but one word. 'Again.'

'I adore you.' Elena wrote the phrase slowly and deliberately so that there could be no misunderstanding. Then she wrote it again with more urgency and then again at speed.

'You adore me.' Edmund said the words at last.

'Yes, yes, yes, I adore you,' she shouted, careless of who might be listening and forgetting that Mrs Smithson and Purvis were watching from some upper window.

'And I adore you.' Edmund did not say it but he wrote it on her palm. 'I adore you.'

For a moment it seemed they could not get beyond that point until Edmund, waking from this beautiful dream, shook his head. 'But last night you were staring adoringly into the eyes of Mr Sawyer. How can I believe you?'

'He was telling me that Lady Dorothea is to wed Mr Ingram Deacon. I defy you to forbid me from receiving such momentous news with joy and acclaim. You know my fondness for the sisters.'

'So are you not to wed him?'

Elena shook her head. 'No, because I am hoping to wed someone other,' she said playfully, but Edmund did not respond in kind. His eyes were pools of sadness.

'Don't jest on such a subject as this,' he said harshly. 'For I know that my impediment irritates you. I have seen it on the day George Longfield fell and, subsequent to that, you would not repeat something you had said so that I could understand it. I know you to be good and kind but I try your patience and in the end it might destroy our union.'

Mortified, Elena had to resist turning her head away from him.

'You must allow me my moments of agitation in extremis,' she said carefully. 'And you must accept that there are times when I cannot express my thoughts, as on the second occasion to which you allude. I was ashamed of my own suspicions about Sir George. If you had been able to hear, I would still have kept silent.'

He digested this slowly, still perversely clinging to his grievances. Then suddenly he cast them aside. What greater demonstration of her regard could she have given than by coming here this morning and risking all by making her sentiments known to him in such an unequivocal fashion?

'So you are saying that if we were to wed there might still be occasions when we could be at odds?'

Elena grinned mischievously. 'Yes,' she said, and then she too became serious. 'I cannot give you back what you have lost,' she said, 'but that should not stand in the way of us having a happy life together.'

'No,' agreed Edmund. 'I may have lost my hearing but,' and here he took her face gently in her hands and brushed her lips with his, 'in you I have found a lifetime's solace.'

From their vantage point of the landing window, the two people who had given so much of themselves to achieve this happy outcome exchanged looks of deep satisfaction and in unison turned away leaving the young couple to enjoy their much deserved happiness.

ॐ ॐ ॐ

Also published by **Bosworth Books Ltd**

J A N E Y   W A T S O N

*'Charlie, what can you be thinking of? You cannot
marry the Stanley girl.'*

Ernestine Greenaway's and Charlie Winstanleigh's plans
to wed are blighted by the debts of his family.
The only way to stall the creditors is for Charlie to
become betrothed to Ernestine's friend, Davina Stanley,
a considerable heiress.

Bullied into the false engagement, Davina finds herself
adrift in Polite Society unable to distinguish between
friend or foe.

978 O 9553289 0 9

Also published by **Bosworth Books Ltd**

JANEY WATSON

The Apparent Heir

Giles Thornton, good-looking and diligent, is apparently everything
any man could ask for in his heir. It is surprising then, that his uncle
requires him to prove his worth, and not so surprising that his
dastardly cousins are determinedto discredit him. Only Miss Felicia
Makepeace of Castle Leck is prepared to accept him as he is.

*'Almost I am decided to run away with Giles and live
in some hovel with him.'*

*'What, and foreswear your castle? Miss Makepeace without
her castle would not do. I see you clearly as Rapunzel in her turret,
her golden tresses cascading down the walls of the castle!'*

*'You mistake, I am more like the sleepng beauty
awaiting her prince for a hundred years.'*

978 0 9553289 2 3

Also published by **BOSWORTH Books LTD**

JANEY WATSON

A
Marriage of
Mixed Motives

Driven from her elderly uncle's home by his scheming second wife,
Lady Harriet Tarlton finds rushing head-long into marriage with
the Duke of Wyverne fraught with difficulties.

Beset by misunderstandings, Harriet finds it easier to solve the
problems of others than her own.

'Can you honestly tell me, Uncle, that she loves this man?'

*'If I had not believed it, do you think I would have
let her proceed?'*

'And subsequent events have not altered your opinion?'

*The Earl shook his head sadly. 'I can no longer be sure of
anything where Harriet is concerned. I always thought of her
as in some way promised to you.'*

978 O 9553289 3 0